"Julia..." She heard herself speak again, in a voice she barely recognized as her own. As the dark head bent toward her, Eliot reached up, her mouth hungry for the sensation of Julia's lips, starving and yearning for their full, sweet-tinged softness. Even as her mouth opened to Julia's tongue, she knew herself to be frantic for more. There was no way to go but forward into Julia's ardent embrace and as Eliot clasped the broad shoulders beneath her hands she was rocked to the core by the raw wanting and need to touch that crashed ferociously through her veins. As Julia's mouth explored hers, Eliot absorbed the aching familiarity of Julia's physique with feverishly moving hands and with every nerve in a body that somehow now seemed entirely connected to her searching fingers.

She shivered convulsively as Julia's fingers traced down the line of her neck and spine beneath her sweatshirt. Obeying the honeyed pain of her own craving, she pushed herself higher into Julia's embrace, but there was no relief for her burning breasts in the contact; in the blur and flurry of sensations, all she knew was that she wanted and needed more. Then Julia's strong hands grasped Eliot's hips and instinctively, Eliot's legs parted as their bodies came together in an undulating and electrifying caress. Eliot shuddered at the power of the inner convulsions that had begun readying her body to receive what it hungered for.

"Julia," she murmured, as her body obeyed its own commands, "Julia, please..."

FORTY LOVE

Diana Simmonds

THE NAIAD PRESS, INC.
1997

Printed in the United States of America on acid-free paper
First Edition

Editor: Christine Cassidy
Cover designer: Bonnie Liss (Phoenix Graphics)
Typesetter: Sandi Stancil

Library of Congress Cataloging-in-Publication Data

Simmonds, Diana, 1949 –
    Forty love / by Diana Simmonds
        p.   cm.
    ISBN 1-56280-171-6 (pbk.)
    I. Title.
PS3569.I4728F67   1997
813′.54—dc21

97-10806
CIP

For Suzi Q and Judy C

Acknowledgments

Deepest gratitude, as ever, for years of unflagging and generous support to my agent and mentor, Margaret Connolly; to my gorgeously old-fashioned editor, Christi Cassidy; and to my very dear Suzi Whitehead for the peace and quiet of Wirringulla in the Hunter Valley, New South Wales.

CHAPTER ONE

"It's time, Ms. Ross, Ms. Andreadis."

Julia inhaled with great deliberation, slowly, quietly, calmly; and exhaled even more slowly and quietly, her nostrils flaring, her eyes closed to glittering dark-lashed slits, until her immersion in calmness had deepened perceptibly. It was an infuriating and unnerving characteristic that had been known to psych an opponent to defeat before either player had actually stepped on court.

But her mind-game was only the opening shot in the Julia Ross arsenal. Even her less psychologically susceptible challengers were wary of her physical presence and prowess. Knowing that although she was less than a mahogany-colored curl under six feet in her superstitiously brand-new white socks, she had none of the gangling awkwardness of the overly tall but rather, the deceptively lazy grace and quicksilver agility of a big cat. Not for nothing was a cheetah at full 90-miles-an-hour-stretch embroidered across the back of her black silk quilted warm-up jacket and hand-painted on her off-court heavy black leather motorcycle jacket. Her uncanny speed and mercuric reflexes and apparent ability to mind-read herself into winning positions had often caused some of her more demoralized adversaries to mutter sarcastically about the appropriateness of the cheetah as the Ross trademark.

And, if that were not enough to contend with, as much as her lesser challengers feared her and the more pretentious of them affected to disdain her occasional brattish behavior and deliberately unladylike, un-tennislike rock'n'roll affectations, the sponsors loved her and her unlikely rough-edged charm.

As the marketing hotshot assigned to the Ross account observed impatiently to the still-dubious ex-player turned marketing director of a leisure wear manufacturer: "Look, you lot are desperate to capture a slice of the non-pastel sports-spunk market, right?" The marketing director had blanched at the description but nodded. "Okay. What more could you ask for? Julia Ross looks like Sabatini but she wins everything and the kids treat her like a rock star. Who else could get Lisa Marie Presley *and* Princess Di squeaking their tits off courtside?" And the

2

marketing director had been unable to suppress a shiver that was part excitement, part dread and part horror at the young man's crude if truthful pitch.

"You're right, of course. And I'm very glad I retired before she came along." This was her unusually honest response before she placed her signature on the "We promise to pay" line of a multi-year, multi-million-dollar contract and tried to ignore her own shaking hand.

Today Julia's challenger was not so easily rattled. For one thing, they had known each other too long and too intimately. Despite her every effort, however, Angie Andreadis found herself glancing across the dressing room toward her one-time lover. Immediately she wished she had not. Julia's impenetrably dark eyes were fixed on a point midway between nowhere and infinity. Angie knew there was now almost no possibility of breaking through the concentration that had settled about the champion like cloud cover on a mountaintop. From this point on, she — Angie Andreadis, number eight in the world and, as the tennis press liked to put it, capable of beating anyone on the day — had ceased to exist as anything other than an obstacle to overcome. She turned away, irritated at herself, feeling her heart begin to pump furiously and the adrenaline surge through her veins. Automatically, she went through her final ritual, knowing only too well that across the room behind her, Julia would be methodically checking her shoe laces, her jacket zipper and the state of the half- dozen racquets in their cheetah-emblazoned black bag before finally choosing the day's color for wrist and head bands.

"I like to make 'em worry about the significance,"

Julia once told Angie. "Let 'em sweat on how I'm feeling or what it means if I choose pink or black."

But even back then, as they lay side by side in a vast hotel bed, still blurry-eyed and drained from lovemaking, Julia refused to tell Angie her secret — or even admit whether or not there was one. At the time it had been a tiny frustration, but one that slotted in, with a thousand others, to form a wall between them that eventually neither had been willing or able to breach.

Now, as she had on so many previous occasions, Angie followed Julia from the dressing room and down the brightly lit corridors. Ahead, the neat mid-height heels of their accompanying tournament officials clicked tattoos of self-importance and the senior functionary tossed back over a smartly blazered shoulder snippets of more or less useful information designed to relieve the tension of the moment.

". . . very hot now . . ." Angie heard in the twangy but cultivated Australian accent. "Hotter than yesterday, I believe . . . prime minister and his wife are here . . . Jerry Hall too, I believe . . . CEO of the sponsors . . . very honored . . . great match I'm sure . . . we're sold out . . . not a seat to be had . . ."

As she emerged from fluoro to dazzling sunlight, the roar of the crowd struck Julia's ears a fraction of a second before the now-familiar but still astonishing Melbourne-in-January heat. The stifling thick air assailed her nostrils and she momentarily paused to take it all in. A step behind and eager to be in the arena, Angie thudded into the tall figure and was shaken into instant, overwrought retaliation.

4

"Damn you, Julia! Watch where you're fucking going!"

"Ms. Andreadis! Please! Language!"

"Ah shaddup, assface!" Angie snarled and angrily pushed past Julia into the brilliant sunlight of the towering amphitheater.

Julia smiled wryly and shrugged at the startled official and sauntered after Angie, acknowledging with an uplifted arm the roar as her name and a much abbreviated list of her career highlights echoed around the arena. There was always an extra tremor of expectation and mutual admiration between this crowd and their defending champion whose truculent lack of respect for the authorities she'd long ago dubbed "the old farts" had earned her the Australian praise of being dubbed "a larrikin spirit." Julia loved it and thrived on it and today was no different. By the time she reached her courtside chair her legs were tingling with anticipation. But larrikin or not, she was no fey, free spirit. With every fiber of her being she willed herself not to look around, not to seek out her coach and his wife nor the box seat where her eager bedmate of the past fortnight was sitting, as she systematically maintained her bubble of detachment, so that the murmuring rumble of the thousands of spectators was no more than surf on a distant beach.

Automatically, she went through the formalities: watched the racquet spin, saw it fall, heard Angie pick her end and elect to receive. Head down, she watched her own sparkling white shoes as she walked back toward her chair and saw her gold-bronze knees bend as she sat down; then she watched her fingers automatically readjust shoe lacings, slip frivolous

5

rose-pink toweling bands over each wrist and then she felt her fingers catch back her exuberant curling waves of almost-black hair with a matching pink sweatband. She carefully chose a racquet, tested its taut strings on the heel of her hand, then finally stood and acknowledged the rising tide of cheers and whistles from the rows of pin-dot faces rising around her into the heights of Melbourne Park's main stadium.

"Come on, Jools. Get out here and stop being such a damn drama queen."

Angie's sharply nasal tone momentarily penetrated the cocoon in which Julia was traveling. She didn't look at Angie, knowing only too well how complete her pretty pouting scowl would be at that moment. She took a deep slow breath, focused on the baseline at her end of the court and walked steadily toward it, even as the noise of the crowd and the extraordinary heat buffeted her once again.

The two players began the rite of the hit-up. Julia enjoyed Melbourne and its comfortable facilities. As well as reigning champion, she was also a five-time winner. It gave her a relationship with the crowd that was worth crucial points on a bad day when muscles and feet weren't obeying instructions. Today was not one of those. The perfect "ping" of ball on sweet spot was an intimate presence and Julia was already enjoying herself. Angie, she quickly realized, was in a different frame of mind. It was the first time they had met on court since Julia had moved her few belongings out of Angie's Santa Monica apartment, and although that was five months in the past, it seemed Angie was intent on extracting some kind of acknowledgment or retribution, here on center court. At the far end her familiar, small, spring-loaded body was quite obviously cranked into a higher state of readiness and furious urgency than Julia had seen in years. For a second she wondered whether it was a cocaine tension or steroid-enhanced aggression, but then the umpire spoke and she resumed her concentration.

"One minute, ladies."

Eschewing further effort — and irritating Angie even more — Julia returned to her chair and the fleeting respite of its shady umbrella. Coming from the Northern Hemisphere winter into Australia's roasting January required special preparation. A virtual warm-up win in the New South Wales Open had been the first part of her plan. Conserving her energy was next. She slowly sipped tepid glucose water, ignoring Angie's intense show of high-kicking practice serves. In a deliberately leisurely fashion she wiped her racquet grip and face with a fluffy, sweet-smelling chilled towel, then walked serenely back to the baseline.

"Ms. Ross to serve. Quiet please, ladies and gentlemen."

Julia noted Angie's position, a meter inside the baseline. It was an unusually reckless or coercive move for such a notoriously slow starter, Julia thought, inhaling the super-heated air that rose in a tangible shimmer from the court surface. She bounced the ball three times, fixed in her mind the spot where it would hit the court surface, rolled back into her whipping, ripping service action and, a split second later, watched the center lineswoman duck as the ball narrowly missed her hat.

"Fifteen love." The umpire's voice was almost

drowned by the roar of the crowd and Julia turned away from the thundercloud scowl on the face of her opponent and prepared to serve again. This time, after lining herself up, she took an almost imperceptible half-step sideways; it was a move that few in the crowd would have picked up, but Angie did. Her anticipatory dancing shuffle instantly took her just slightly wider, and this time she was a meter behind the baseline and moving the wrong way as Julia's serve again drilled a straight line down the center line and into the blue canvas wall.

"Thirty love."

Julia did not look at Angie. She knew the fiery Greek would be a blaze of embarrassed bad temper and she was aware of a fleeting sense of relief that she no longer had to deal with its aftermath off-court.

"You like to humiliate me! You try to make me look an idiot! You're a bitch!" Angie's shrieks of rage on that long ago occasion had seemed to Julia to echo through the hotel with paint-peeling ferocity. But nothing Julia could say would placate or quiet Angie; and Julia had finally fled the hotel and her own dismay and embarrassment at the all-too-public spectacle. As brash and extrovert as was her public image, in those moments Julia discovered she hated such displays of flagrant emotion. It had been the first of a dozen such confrontations and never had Angie experienced the satisfaction of beating her lover — on court, at any rate. What passed for their private life had been another matter.

* * * * *

Deliberately, Julia pulled her mind back to the present and her third serve. So far, she had barely moved from the small area between the baseline and three running steps toward the net. She glanced at Angie and saw the indecision and rage in her agitated and uncertain movements. She knew that her adversary could not believe Julia would once more serve to the center line, but it was obvious from her frenzied movements that neither could she trust herself to leave the center zone unprotected.

Julia wiped her wristband across her streaming face, bounced the ball three times, tossed it high and corkscrewed her long body into a slicing stroke that sent the small yellow missile curling away to the tram lines, where it hit the line perfectly and spun out of court, leaving Angie lunging desperately, yards away and protesting halfheartedly that it was out. This time the noise of the crowd was deafening and the umpire waited before making her call.

"Forty love."

Julia's relief was expressed in a lungful of the thick humid air. It soothed her pumping heart and helped keep her actions at the deliberate pace she knew would be necessary to survive such a furnace of a day. She prepared to serve for the game, unmoved by the perpetually dancing figure at the periphery of her vision.

Her favorite service was from the left-hand court, whipping her racquet head down and across the ball to send it spinning out wide to the right. It gave her all the time in the world to get to the net and offered righthanders almost no option but a frantic chase and lunge — and little chance of accurately placing a return shot. Julia knew Angie would be expecting it, but still she decided to go for it, reasoning that her serve was working with such precision that today was not the day to doubt it.

She bounced the ball three times, paused, wiped her wristband over her upper lip, bounced the ball again, rolled lazily into her service action and saw, as if in slow motion, her arm swing skyward and the ball spin upward from her fingers, high and straight, a black dot against the bleached blue sky. Her eyes stayed unflinchingly on it as she sprang high, the air whistling through the strings of her racquet as it zipped up and over to put maximum spin on the falling ball. Then she was off and loping her three long strides to the net as Angie sprinted frantically, racquet outstretched; somehow she connected with her target. The off-key sound of the edge of the racquet catching the ball told Julia that it would not come back in play, but her well-drilled instinct to be sure rather than sorry brought her to a skidding halt as she pivoted sharply to the right to be ready with a killing cross-court backhand return.

Later she would tell the plainly smitten, horrified and glamorous *60 Minutes* reporter, "It was a funny thing, I heard it go crack before I felt it."

And it seemed that the entire stadium heard it too. Lying in the middle of the court, stupidly aware of the sting of abrasion burns on her elbows, palms and chin where she'd hit the court surface at full speed, Julia also heard the dismayed gasps and squeals of thousands of people before she realized the unearthly scream echoing out above them all was her own. Even as she grabbed despairingly at her left knee, the pure red agony of the destruction exploding within it crashed through her defenses and in the instant before she fainted she heard her own voice, howling like an animal in a trap, screaming, "No-o-o-o-o-o."

CHAPTER TWO

For a thirty-ninth birthday, it could have been worse. The early morning sun streamed between the slatted shutters and lay in soft-edged stripes across the subtly buffed red cedar floor. Eliot Bancroft Barron lay on her back, watching specks gently twirling and glittering in the shafts of light. The silence of the room was bordered by the muffled and distant boom and sigh of the Pacific breakers rolling up the beach and the close-at-hand twittering chatter of lorikeets in the trees outside. She stretched her legs and arms out wide. Her husband's side of the bed was as unrumpled as only unslept-in sheets can be.

It had been empty when she awoke the previous morning too. Neatly empty — Jack was never messy. Whatever he set out to do, he did neatly and thoroughly. Jack the Lad, Jack the finger-snapping handsome man. Jack the irresistible charmer. Whether he was being a husband, a successful lawyer with political ambition or a lying philanderer whose current girlfriend was almost young enough to be his wife's daughter, Jack Barron was always orderly. Eliot was still smiling sourly at that thought when the bathroom door opened. Jack was obviously about to leave. In place of his favored leisure image of neatly pressed Ralph Lauren polo shirt and tailored khaki shorts he'd resumed his even more favored image of immaculate white shirt and perfectly tailored dark gray suit. He looked, as always, eye-catchingly attractive, a wide white smile on his healthy face.

"Awake already, darling," he said, smiling as he hitched the knee of his pants before perching on the edge of the bed. "Did I disturb you?"

Eliot's grin widened. "No, you don't disturb me at all." It was a curious slip of the tongue, she recalled. And she also remembered that if he'd noticed her choice of words he'd elected to ignore them, instead, patting her hand rather — she thought in the moment — as if she were a faithful old dog.

"I forgot I have to prepare some extra material for the Indonesian gas exploration case. It's scheduled for Monday and I need a few extra days on it. I'll try to come up on the weekend." His voice had the warm and firmly convincing successful lawyer-massaging-the-jury tone. Eliot nodded as she watched his wide blue eyes, which crinkled at the corners and were framed by discreetly tinted lashes, and her own smile gave not the slightest hint that her heart was long ago broken and now almost painlessly cold, nor that she disbelieved what he was saying.

Now, on this morning of her solitude and thirty-ninth birthday Eliot reveled in the smooth creaminess of the clean sheets and the entire width of the bed and she considered her disbelief.

"When did you ever forget to prepare for a big case, Jack?" she asked out loud, pleased to note that her tone was healthily sardonic rather than aggrieved. She rolled over and checked the bedside clock. It was a minute after 7:30. "Happy birthday, Eliot Bancroft," she said with self-conscious drama, and then realized that for the first time in more than a decade, she had left off her husband's name

It sounded a lot better; sounded like herself — her old self, the one she'd owned long ago. She sat up and swung her legs out of bed, examining them as she stretched her toes into points. Not bad, she decided. Firm flesh, good shape, light natural tan, no sags, no bags, no wrinkled knees, good muscle tone, no out-of-place dimples. Not bad — for almost forty.

But at that last thought an unbidden and unexpected lurch of fear punched her in the stomach. "Forty," she whispered, staring into space. "I am almost forty years old. My husband is going to leave me for a twenty-three-year-old. Happy birthday? Who am I kidding?"

She collapsed back onto the bed and squeezed her eyes shut — then quickly relaxed again, remembering the crow's feet at the corners of her eyes and the faint crease that had recently appeared between her eyebrows. Oh god, she thought. What a mess. What am I going to do? For once, the tranquility of the wood-scented room offered no comfort and certainly no reply. Tears pricked her eyelids and, despite the threat of wrinkles, she screwed her eyes shut against them.

"Mummy, are you okay?" The bedroom door had silently opened and, framed in sunlight, looking even more like a Botticelli angel than usual, stood Morgan Bancroft Barron, seven years old and heiress to Eliot Bancroft's heart and Jack Barron's ambition.

Eliot sat up and despair was instantly dissipated by her daughter's presence. "Hello, sweetheart." She said softly, "I'm fine. Just thinking too hard — and you know how painful that can be."

Morgan grinned, willing to be reassured, and stepped lightly across the floor, seeming hardly to touch its surface. She wound her thin golden-brown arms around her mother's neck and kissed her hard. "Happy birthday, Mummy. Could we go shopping so I can get your present? I have it all planned, but Daddy was going to take me. Is that okay?"

Eliot hugged the vulnerable but tough little body and buried her nose in the sweet-smelling velvet neck. "As it's *my* birthday I think we can do any-thing I please. And I please to please you. How about that?"

Morgan's answer was a stranglehold grip on her mother's neck and another kiss. It made Eliot im-mediately aware of how unused she was to physical contact — beyond the perfunctory peck on the cheek of a marriage turned passionless and dutiful. In shocking contrast, Morgan's touch was rich in love and feeling. It served also to remind her of a deeper

15

loneliness that seemed only to be assuaged these days by retreating to this shack — her precious hideaway on the southern edge of the metro area. The eight seafront acres — a rare extravagance of space within Sydney's multi-million-dollar and escalating city limits — had belonged to her grandmother and, ten years after her death, still were imbued with that tough old woman's ability to protect Eliot from the world. But it was an indulgent retreat for an artist who was lucky to sell six pictures a year, as Jack kept telling her. The acreage would be worth millions to a developer. But Eliot wouldn't budge.

"What're you thinking about, Mummy? Are you having more hard thoughts?" Morgan's face was full of concern and Eliot grinned and hugged her.

"I'm sorry, my chick. No more thoughts today, promise. But I was wondering whether you're having a good time. You're not too bored?" she asked guiltily. "You sure you wouldn't like to be back in the city with your friends and near Daddy?"

As was her characteristic older-than-seven habit, Morgan considered the question for a frowning moment before shaking her head. "No mummy, I love it here. And I only wanted to go to the tennis and we did that, so why do we have to go to the city?"

Eliot shook her head. "We don't. I just thought you might be missing your friends."

Morgan screwed up her nose. "The only one I miss is Sandra and she's gone camping with Candy and Rob and I think they're best friends now." For a moment she looked bleak, then her eyes sparkled with excitement. "But anyway, now we know Julia Ross is staying at Greg and Ray's, so I don't think we should go anywhere. I mean, we might see her today. She might come out on the beach!"

Eliot shook her head and grinned at the sudden bubbling happiness in Morgan's face. "You mustn't be too hopeful, sweetheart. Don't forget, she's here to get better and she said in the papers she wants to be quiet and left alone."

Morgan nodded vigorously. "I know. I understand. But I may just *see* her, don't you think? I won't be a nuisance or anything. Not like those camera people."

"Reporters, sweetheart, they were reporters."

"But what were they reporting? Why did they come and ask you about her? And they asked me all about Greg and Ray." Morgan frowned. "Should I have told them to piss off, like you did?"

Eliot rolled her eyes and tried not to giggle. "No, sweetheart. You were absolutely right to be polite. And the boys won't mind. You said very nice things about them."

Morgan still looked worried. "Was I wrong to show them Julia's autograph? Daddy was mad as hell."

"Morgan!" This time Eliot failed to contain her amusement, so the stern tone of her voice was canceled out. "Just because Daddy says he's mad as hell, that's no reason for you to talk like that."

Morgan looked quizzical. "But you say much worser things sometimes. Last week you called Aunt Daphne —"

"Morgan! That's enough. I say 'worse' things, not 'worser.' And . . . oh, good grief! What am I saying. Come on, let's get going."

They were both giggling as Eliot grabbed her

daughter and stood up, feeling in her protesting thigh muscles that Morgan was no longer a baby, despite her skinny frame. But the girl wound her legs around her mother's waist and expertly transferred her weight to the hip and so, without too much effort, they reached the bathroom where Eliot plopped her down on the old pine table that served as counter and dressing table. She straightened up with a theatrical groan.

"You are so grown up, little chick, you'll be carrying me before you know it."

Morgan wriggled with delight and busied herself squeezing too much toothpaste onto her mother's brush while Eliot stripped off her nightshirt, stepped into the shower stall and turned on the cold jets to maximum.

"How old are you, Mummy?" Morgan yelled above the hissing water. "Jane-Anne Levy says you're older than her mother and I said you're not."

Eliot considered this as the water stung her sleep-warm skin into full consciousness. Veronica Levy probably was younger, Eliot estimated, but had surely been born matronly and now that she was — in her own view at least — doyenne of the summer beach set, she had become almost regal in her manner. It was an inbuilt sense of gravity and extreme self-worth Eliot knew she would never possess. And never would she be able to attain the blank-eyed serenity of some of the other mothers — the Stepford Wives, as she privately nicknamed them.

"I think she's probably younger, sweetheart." She blew her nose vigorously on the thought, rinsed her

18

fingers and slicked back her fine, dead straight, red gold hair. As she slid open the shower door a balled up bath towel struck her chest and she caught it.

"Good reflexes," Morgan commented, her bare brown feet swinging rhythmically. Eliot wrapped herself in the thick towel and considered her reflection in the peeling pub mirror behind Morgan who peered back at her. "Could we play tennis today — as well as get your present and maybe get something to barbecue for dinner?"

Eliot grinned and reached for a smaller towel to dry her hair. "Why not. Let's get videos as well — and you could invite Jane-Anne over if you like."

Morgan's nose wrinkled and her mouth curved downward. "I don't think it would be much of a birthday if Jane-Anne came over," she observed somberly.

"I thought you liked her?" As Eliot toweled her hair she watched her daughter's expression run through a series of mixed emotions and uncharitable thoughts.

"You'll say this is mean and I suppose it is; thing is, she's okay if there's nobody else around but if there is, then she gets really weird and big headed. And the truth is, most of the time I don't like her one bit." Morgan managed to look ashamed and enchanting at the same time.

Eliot laughed and kissed her forehead. "That is a very, very mean thought, Missy Morgan, but I do understand what you're getting at. I feel like that about Veronica, only worse. I wouldn't mind if I never saw her again, but I still go to her awful lunch parties." She sighed and reached for a wide-toothed comb. "I think that's called being a hypocrite," she added, tugging grimly at a knot.

"But Daddy says it's polite to be sociable," Morgan observed, frowning. "I thought you have to be nice to people even if you don't like them."

Eliot attempted to shake and nod her head at the same time. "It's complicated. Sometimes you do things because it would be unkind not to — like having coffee with Mrs. Cathcart who is dreary as a dead duck and makes terrible coffee but who is very lonely. That's a good thing — at least I think so. But going to Veronica's lunch parties —"

She pursed her lips and wondered whether she was taking her daughter further than a seven-year-old should be taken into the labyrinth of adult behavior. But, she decided, she could not now stop halfway, even if Morgan did one day say something like, "My mother says your mother is more boring than a dead duck, Jane-Anne."

"Going to Veronica's lunch parties is something I do because . . ." She paused again. Why did she go? Because Jack was keen to be on lunch, cocktails, tennis and golf invitation lists with Milton Levy, a political heavyweight and prominent social figure whose good offices he craved. And because it made it easier for Jack to flirt with Veronica when his own wife was on such friendly terms with the social queen. "I go to Veronica's lunch parties because it's something grownups do," she finally said to her daughter. But then, Eliot found herself continuing, "Sometimes, though, grownups finally do grow up — often when they're about my age — and they can decide they are not going to any more lunch parties unless they are —" She counted on her fingers. "One, desperately hungry; two, they like the people who will be at the lunch party; or three, they are so atrociously boring themselves they don't care who they have lunch with."

Morgan's gasp and peal of giggles was reward in itself and the cherry on the cake came with her earnest observation: "I am *sure* Jane-Anne's mother is much much older than you, Mummy. I am *ab*solutely sure." And they laughed like two conspirators.

Eliot dropped her bath towel and reached for the pump pack of body lotion. Under the bright lights she looked dispassionately at her sparely fleshed body. "In some ways you may be right, my chick." She sucked in her tummy and turned sideways. There was nothing much to despair about there, she mused. Time and gravity was being defied with the help of a good, once broken and now slightly broadened aquiline nose and high, wide cheek bones; her small breasts were still more or less where they had been before Morgan's birth and still as round and full; the silvery stretch marks on her hips and belly — another legacy of pregnancy — were as faint as they would ever be and, if she could only persuade herself to do a little more exercise a little more regularly, the slight loss of muscle tone in her thighs, abdomen and arms would be arrested in a couple of weeks.

"You're really beautiful, Mummy." Morgan's solemn voice startled her out of her self-appraisal.

Eliot grinned through a blush. "Thanks," she said, caressing her daughter's peach cheek. "I'm glad you think so."

"Will I look like you when I grow up?"

21

"I think you will be really, really beautiful when you grow up because you will be beautiful in there." She tapped the small chest. "That's where it counts. I want you to concentrate on that, okay?"

Morgan pursed her lips and nodded. "Okay." Her expression was serious. "But how do I do it?"

Eliot kissed her forehead. "By being very nice to me and Mrs. Cathcart."

Morgan looked relieved and hopped down from the table. "I can do that. And now can I go down to the beach for a bit?"

"As long as you don't just stand and stare at Greg and Ray's veranda. Okay?"

Morgan nodded. "I'll just have one look as I pass. But I promise I won't stare."

"Okay. Shall we have bacon? Melon? Eggs?"

"All of it. I'll make juice and do the dishes."

"Deal. Wear your watch and be back in twenty minutes."

"I love you, Mum."

"I know you do, sweetheart. And you know I love you."

"Yup."

Eliot pulled on three-quarter-length black and paint-smeared Lycra bicycle shorts, snugged herself into matching stretchy sports bra and a paint-spattered and anciently faded, once black but still adored tank top. It was a look calculated to raise Veronica Levy's eyebrows — especially if, as she fully intended, Eliot affected it on the impending trip to the deli and supermarket.

Barefoot, she made her way through the old house, stopping at Morgan's room, arrested by the chaos of tennis racquets, balls, shoes and discarded clothing, computer cables, disks and computer games. For a moment she considered the disorder, but decided against any action. The mess was superficial and easily remedied; Morgan was not yet at the age of rebellion and she would happily reorganize the mess into a different disarray when Eliot made the request.

A breeze from the shuttered window caught at the loose corner of one of Morgan's pinup posters and it rattled. Eliot pressed the glossy paper firmly back onto its wad of Blu-tack. She stood back and examined the gallery of stars that occupied almost every inch of wall space and shook her head in wonder. No rock idols — no latter-day equivalent of Elvis, Madonna, Kurt or John Lennon — instead Morgan worshipped tennis players. Eliot knew the pages torn from magazines represented her daughter's deepest aspirations: Andre Agassi, Pete Sampras, Mark Philipoussis, Monica Seles, Steffi Graf, Martina Hingis, Jennifer Capriati. One whole wall was given over to a gallery of action portrait posters of Martina Navratilova, Julia Ross and Evonne Cawley.

"I love the way they play," Morgan once explained to her exasperated father. Jack had got his secretary to search out and buy some large and expensive posters of Steffi Graf and Monica Seles and was annoyed to find they had not replaced the wall gallery. "I like all-court players, Daddy," Morgan said patiently, standing defensively and firmly in front of her precious pictures. "I don't *want* to be a baseliner. I want to be like Martina and Julia and Evonne. I want to serve and volley."

From her position on Morgan's bed where they were cutting out fresh pictures, Eliot could see that Jack's temper was rising and about to burst into something ugly. She interjected quickly and smoothly, "I'm sure Daddy wants you to be the very best player you can be, sweetheart. Daddy likes to serve and volley too. Don't you, Jack?"

Above their child's head their gazes met, locked and wrestled, then Jack clicked back from sneering rage to studied indifference. He ruffled Morgan's hair, a gesture that he refused to acknowledge she hated, even as she shied away.

"Serve and volley is a grand old-fashioned game, darling," he said to his daughter, while maintaining a chilly stare with his wife. "I think your mother might even remember Margaret Court. But you'd do better with some nice modern players. Why don't you put up this great poster of Steffi, eh?"

Morgan obeyed — in her own fashion. The poster had gone on the back of her door and so was most often obscured by her bathrobe and yellow rain jacket, which also hung there, and her beloved serve-and-volleyers remained in pride of place.

Eliot shook herself out of the memory of the ferociously whispered argument with Jack later when he requested, in his chilliest courtroom tone, that she try to influence their daughter's choice of heroines away from "bloody dykes and Abos."

She forced herself back to the present and the poster whose corner she had reattached to the wall. She sighed and wondered what her small girl dreamed of when she read captions such as: "Julia Ross's topspin backhand cross-court volley is one of the most fearsome shots in tennis today." From her bed Morgan could gaze without hindrance at the spectacular picture of the American ace — on the run at full stretch, her unmistakable dark chestnut curls flying, her unusually tall and wide-shouldered frame an anatomy lesson in taut muscle and perfect coordination.

Even in that captured moment of extreme exertion the champion was spectacularly beautiful, Eliot noted. Which was some kind of comfort — if her daughter had to have a crush on a player, at least she had picked the very, very best. Nevertheless, it didn't seem fair that the current Wimbledon champion should make it look so easy and so glamorous.

"You wait till you're forty," Eliot told the pinup grouchily. Only then did she notice the small glass jar of flowers placed on Morgan's bedside table in front of another, smaller picture. Having supplanted the T-shirt autographed by Martina Navratilova, it was her most precious trophy: a smoldering almost James Dean-like portrait of Julia Ross, autographed in silver on the up-turned collar of her black leather jacket and secured at the New South Wales Open. Now it had been turned into an icon with a poignantly makeshift altar.

The contrast between Eliot's happily recalled image of the smiling champion, surrounded by excited children and equally excited tough-looking young women as she signed autographs and posed for snapshots in Sydney, and the TV pictures of her collapse, just days later, in Melbourne, caused Eliot to shudder involuntarily. She clearly remembered Morgan's ecstatic face as she stood, gazing adoringly up at her heroine and eventually shaking her hand, then the shock as they sat and watched the champion's calamitous and dramatic breakdown in vivid detail and close up on television.

The TV commentator had just been burbling that she had *never* seen Julia Ross serving with such authority, when the American had spun and fallen in a rolling sprawl, only to contort in obvious agony. After an age of confusion, as Morgan dissolved into tears and huddled in her mother's arms while the footage of the dramatic crash was played over and over from every available camera angle, they watched the champion being stretchered from the arena. Later that week there was further footage of her, wheelchair-bound and hidden behind heavy dark glasses and protective bodyguards, leaving a Melbourne hospital; and the newsreader announced that she had been flown to Sydney for treatment at Kurrunulla Lodge, the exclusive sports clinic and resort run by Australian ex–Davis Cup stars Greg Bartlett and Ray Freeman. She would not play again for some months.

"If ever," an expert commentator intoned lugubriously. "Julia's twenty-six now. Her coach Brad Denvers tells me they'll take some time out to consider the future while Julia is in rehab after this shocking injury. How must she be feeling and what must she be thinking at this moment, can you tell us, Brad?"

But Eliot had turned off the TV to save Morgan further anguish and herself the inane speculation of the commentator and the grim-faced coach. Now, she removed one small, wilted yellow daisy from the jar and rearranged the rest before leaving them to do whatever they could for the fallen star who, by a curious if not entirely unpredictable stroke of fate, was now holed up less than a quarter of a mile away.

From the white sweep of the beach, Eliot's house was almost invisible, its weathered, silver-gray galvanized iron roof and pale green painted but peeling weatherboard walls blending with the surrounding trees. It was her pride and joy and repository of childhood memories, as she firmly told a bemused Jack when he'd protested that he would prefer to knock it down and build something modern. On its ocean side, French windows reflected the robust yet delicate grace of a stand of tall old-growth rough-barked angophoras and low-growing sheoaks. Two ancient black-barked banksias sheltered the house from southwesterly winds and the gazes of the curious. Behind the house were a couple of dozen lofty smooth-barked angophoras and as many tufty-topped cabbage tree palms scattered across the deliberately wild acres, a remnant of the area's original coastal rain forest whose colors were echoed in the quality of the house's interior. Here the predominant color changed from sun-bleached driftwood to the rich pink-red and golden tones found in the recycled old pine and cedar of the floors and ceilings. White walls reflected their warm tones in the late afternoon sun; in the early morning and at noon it was all cool green as the light filtered through the lacy foliage of the surrounding trees and was further deflected by a deep wisteria-covered veranda.

A wood-burning glass-fronted combustion stove served to warm the whole house on even the wettest and windiest days. It was not as picturesque as an open fireplace, as Jack never tired of pointing out, but its effectiveness as a heat source was undeniable. And, as Eliot also knew but never openly acknowledged for fear of Jack's certain ridicule, it was environmentally better and more efficient and — from the point of view of the person who had to clean the place — it was a lot easier to manage too.

On an early but already hot January summer morning, however, the combustion stove arguments were a memory of last winter and many winters before that. Eliot crossed richly patterned scarlet, dark blue and rusty red expanses of old Persian rugs to the living room's glass doors. Outside, hanging from a tree branch, Morgan's bronze dolphin chimes resonated gently.

The Pacific and the curving sweep of beach south toward the cliffs and the beginning of the vast gray-green wilderness of the Royal National Park were the main aspects visible from Eliot's carefully secluded vantage point. Despite its proximity, metropolitan Sydney was invisible, while across the bay the terrazzo palazzos of the overly comfortable barely impinged at all. Even the closest house — a post-modern weatherboard mansion belonging to a showbiz legend and his young ex-TV game show hostess wife — was only evident at the extremity of Eliot's obsessively private domain.

From her studio, a bare sunlit room that had been converted from an old boat shed in the dunes behind the beach, there was even less to be seen. On most weekdays some matchstick figures, a dog or two and the occasional soaring bright-tailed kite and the lazy glide-by of the area's two resident sea eagles, were often all Eliot would see from dawn to sunset, and that's how she liked it.

From the veranda, Eliot could see Morgan almost at the tideline, in animated conversation with a tall figure swaddled in head-to-toe baggy pale gray sweats. She watched the child's body language carefully, at the same time reminding herself that Morgan knew all about dealing with strangers and was not likely to be foolish or careless.

Nevertheless, Morgan seemed to be agitated, pointing first to the north, then south and finally toward her own home. The stranger turned, awkwardly, to look at the house and Eliot saw sinister wraparound dark shades and the peak of a baseball cap under the gray hood. Morgan caught sight of her mother and waved frantically. Eliot waved back, alarm snatching at her gut. She heard Morgan's voice, high-pitched as a sea bird, the words carried away on the breeze. In that instant, the stranger seemed to reach out and in lurching for Morgan's shoulder, missed and fell heavily on the sand. Eliot's heart leapt into her throat to begin pounding with instant and automatic terror.

"Run!" Eliot screamed instinctively. "Morgan, run!" But she knew Morgan couldn't hear her. And she began to run frantically on leaden feet, across the grass to shallow steps that led down to the beach. For a long minute, her daughter was out of sight. Eliot's breath came in desperate sobs as she cursed the clinging sand. Then, her heart bursting with fear and exertion, she reached the beach and saw Morgan scudding toward her, flying across the white sand as only a naturally athletic seven-year-old could. There was fear in the girl's face and she was yelling at the top of her lungs as she bolted toward her mother. Behind her, the tall figure still lay on the sand, apparently unable to rise. After an eternity that lasted only seconds, Morgan's words became distinct.

"Quickly, Mummy! Quickly! We have to get help. It's Julia. It's Julia. You must get help!" She skidded to a halt in front of her bewildered mother and hopped in a frenzy from one foot to the other, whimpering with fright and frustration, her eyes ablaze with disbelief.

"Sweetheart, what are you talking about? Why were you talking to that stranger?"

Morgan's whimpering rose to a crescendo of frustration as she shook her head hard enough to rattle her whole body.

"No, Mummy," she cried, leaping up and down and gesturing back to the prone figure. "It's not. I wasn't. It's Julia Ross — you know, *Julia Ross*. It's medium crucial. She can't get up. We have to get help." She grabbed Eliot's hand and tried to pull her up the beach toward their house.

"Hold on a minute." Eliot looked again at the prone figure. "I'd better check first," she told her daughter. "Come on." She began to run steadily toward the figure that lay still and waiting as

Morgan scampered beside her, repeating in a horror-filled voice, "She's had a medium crucial accident. Isn't that awful?"

Eliot barely had time to wonder how a tennis player could have any kind of accident on this beach, let alone medium crucial, before she was upon the stranger and easily able to see for herself. The champion's left leg was encased in an ankle-to-thigh brace of metal struts and bright blue webbing, hinged at the knee and, she guessed, impossible to maneuver in the soft sand. Eliot was suddenly at a loss as to what to say and, after a noticeable pause, said the most redundant thing that could possibly have entered her head: "Hello, are you all right?"

Julia Ross propped herself as best she could in a semi-sitting position and regarded her reluctant savior with equal uncertainty. She took off the mirrored wraparounds and slotted them onto the peak of her cap. Without the Klingon disguise, Eliot recognized her immediately — even with the distinctive hair concealed — as the subject of the pinups in Morgan's bedroom. And, she noted, even sprawled and helpless on the beach, she was still the beautiful creature they'd watched at White City and so briefly in Melbourne, and one who was much better looking than even the photogenic star of dozens of televised tournaments and shampoo commercials. But those glimpses could not have made her aware of the deep, dark brown and rather sad and angry eyes that now regarded her.

"Hi," Julia said, trying a smile that didn't quite make it to nonchalant as Eliot stopped in front of her. "I'm kinda stuck. I need some help to stand up and if you wouldn't mind ringing my coach, he can

31

come fetch me and take me back. I'm really sorry to butt in on your birthday."

Eliot frowned. "My birthday?" She looked at Morgan who was staring at the stricken figure as if she were an angel plummeted straight from heaven.

"I was telling Julia what we were going to do today," Morgan said anxiously. "She doesn't have any friends here. I said you don't either because you don't like Mrs. Levy and I thought she might like to come with us but I didn't realize she couldn't walk and that the accident we saw on TV was medium crucial . . ." She had begun to hop again and Eliot held up her hand and laughed.

"Stop, sweetheart. Stop. It's okay. It's not your fault. Now then, Miss Ross . . ."

The tennis player grimaced. "Please, call me Julia. I only get 'Miss Ross' at Wimbledon and if you're going to rescue me from medium crucial circumstances with my busted medial cruciate ligament, you *have* to call me Julia."

Eliot felt a twinge of embarrassment, suddenly aware that there might be more of the stitched-up Stepford Wife in her nature than she cared to admit. "Of course, I'm sorry — Julia." Then she grinned. "You must understand, we don't often find broken Grand Slam champions on our beach. In fact, it's mostly driftwood and an occasional seal, so there's a tendency toward over-excitement."

Julia managed a lopsided half smile. "Well, like I said, I'm sorry for disrupting your birthday, but I bit off more than I can chew for my first solo walk." She poked angrily at the brace with a long, brown index finger.

Before Eliot could speak, Morgan broke in

excitedly, "Julia is going to be at Greg and Ray's for the whole summer, Mummy. We are going to be neighbors. Julia, you can come to lunch if you like and we have a tennis court at our house and —"

Eliot made a grab for her daughter and gagged her with one hand. "Sweetie, we have to get Miss — we have to get Julia up to the house before you wear her out. Now just be quiet for five minutes while we work out how to do this."

Julia, she saw, was almost grinning at Morgan's irrepressible excitement. It was a good grin, full of great teeth and crinkled corners to the dark eyes. Eliot crouched down on one knee beside Julia.

"You must be quite a bit taller than me, but if you put your arm around my shoulders and hang on, I'm sure I can get you to your feet, then be a sort of crutch. Want to try?"

Julia looked both hopeful and doubtful in the same moment, her expression like a cloud passing in front of the sun. "I'm pretty heavy . . . I could wait for my coach . . ."

Eliot looked at her carefully. Around Julia's mouth and eyes were the telltale signs of undeclared pain. Eliot shook her head. "I can't leave you lying here," she said firmly, then grinned. "There are litterbug rules on this beach. Come on." She knelt in the sand and held out her arm.

Julia's sigh of relief was not quite smothered. "Sure. Well, you say go and I'll go with you." Julia adjusted her crippled leg and the grip on Eliot's shoulder was resolute.

"Ready when you are," Eliot said softly, seizing the sweatshirt-clad torso firmly. "And if I hurt you, yell."

33

"I'll be fine, you won't hurt me," Julia said, between gritted teeth. Eliot saw her face change again, its soft hints of humor gone, replaced by steely determination.

"Right, then. One, two, three, let's go. Up." Eliot steadied her legs wide, straightened her back and pressed up from her thighs and calves. Morgan dashed in, placing her thin shoulders beneath Julia's free arm and, with only one stifled gasp as the injured leg jarred in the sand, Julia was standing, a good head taller than Eliot who nevertheless held her with such firmness there was no risk of her falling.

"Omigod!" Julia gasped, half laughing. "Thank you. Thank you. Phew! You're really strong."

"Seven years of carting a growing girl about helps," Eliot said, self-deprecation coming as naturally as competence.

"Well, now you can add another one to your burden. I feel so stupid. I don't really know how I got here." Julia peered down the beach to where the buildings that made up the Kurrunulla Lodge complex were located. In her disabled state they were hardly more accessible than the moon.

"I expect you got carried away with being able to move at all," Eliot observed gently. "And now we'll just get you up to the house and drive you home. Simple."

"You're very kind. I've totally disrupted your morning."

"Not at all. I was just going to make breakfast." Eliot glanced at Morgan. "And before my daughter pops her rivets, you're very welcome to share it."

Julia hesitated, but Morgan clasped her hand and stared up at her in desperate, silent supplication.

After a moment Julia touched Morgan's chin to close her mouth. "Sure I'll stay for breakfast." She turned to Eliot. "If it's no trouble."

Eliot shook her head. "Just the opposite. I'd never hear the end of it if I didn't ask you."

Julia settled her right arm once again across Eliot's shoulders and, as Morgan's adoring eyes gazed up at her, she placed her free hand gently on the girl's slight, bony shoulder and they set off, Eliot intuitively moving with Julia's broken stride, so that she bore the weight as the heavily braced leg took its turn on the sand. It was easier than she expected and Eliot enjoyed the sense of strength and protectiveness that flowed toward her tenacious companion. When she saw Morgan's worshipful demeanor and her small hands gripping Julia's larger brown one, her feeling of well-being was enhanced to something approaching euphoria. The combination of her daughter's evident happiness and the all-too-rare knowledge, for Eliot, of being strong for another obviously strong human being was intoxicating.

They reached the house without mishap and Eliot stood back as Julia maneuvered herself up the shallow stairs to the veranda. There she stood, taking in her surroundings while Eliot felt suddenly and unaccountably shy.

"Would you like to sit out here?" she asked politely.

Julia considered for a moment, then shook her head. "Perhaps I should come in and help Morgan, who I guess is going to help you," she said, her eyebrows simultaneously asking Morgan the question.

"Yes!" The skinny brown child began to bounce in sheer delight and Eliot pointed to the kitchen.

"Oranges out of the cooler, Morgan. You juice, I'll cook." She went into the house ahead of Julia to give her room and time to her make her own way, understanding instinctively that asking for assistance was something Julia would rarely do. When she painfully reached the long-legged chairs at the kitchen counter, Eliot pushed the phone toward her. "Maybe you'd like to tell your people you haven't been washed out to sea. The number is four on the quick-dial."

By the time Julia eased herself out of the back seat of Eliot's elderly Volvo, it was mid-morning and she looked exhausted. Brad and Lauren Denverses' anxious faces loomed as Julia, aided by a solicitous Morgan and flanked unobtrusively by Eliot, hobbled across the pebbled driveway to Kurrunulla Lodge's main building.

The Denverses were gushing in their gratitude to Julia's rescuers. Behind them, his face shaded by a wide-brimmed white cap, stood the tall, enigmatically grinning figure of Greg Bartlett. For reasons she couldn't place, his silent salute to Eliot and the mischievous twinkle in his eye caused her more discomfort than the overwhelming effusion of the Denverses. After having her hand pumped until she knew her bilges were quite dry, Eliot insisted for the fourth time that there was really nothing to be thanked for and began to back away, refusing for the third time their offer of coffee. But before she could haul a reluctant and already visibly pining Morgan back to the car, control was wrested from her grasp.

"Will you come for dinner, Julia?" Morgan asked, gripping Julia's hand hard lest a looser hold might lose her forever.

"Let her go take a rest now, sweetheart," Eliot said quickly, seeing and feeling the bone-weariness in the young woman's face.

Julia patted Morgan's hand. She obviously urgently needed to be off her feet, but at the same time she was clearly reluctant to relinquish the sweetness of the child's happy enthusiasm. She put out her hand to Eliot and tried to smile.

"I really would like to come to dinner, if that's okay by you. I mean, I know it's your birthday and you probably have plans..."

Eliot took Julia's hand in both her own and patted it reassuringly. "As I told Morgan, my plan is to please myself and today that means pleasing Morgan, so if you don't mind a very ordinary evening, you're more than welcome — you too, of course." She turned to the Denverses and Greg who were watching Julia with, respectively, disapproval and bemusement plain on their faces.

"Thank you *so* much," said Lauren Denvers, without smiling. "Perhaps we should wait and see how Julia is feeling later..." She looked to her husband; Brad pursed his lips and nodded. "Sure. Julia may well take a rain check, Mrs...?"

"Bancroft," Eliot offered, carefully avoiding Greg's raised eyebrow.

"Mrs. Bancroft. Perhaps we could call you later?"

Julia stilled Morgan's instant swell of desperate protest. "No rain checks, Morgan, I promise." She looked at Eliot. "Brad can bring me over. Or Greg, if you think you might come too?"

Greg smiled and shook his head. "I'll definitely take the rain check," he said affably, "but we'll catch up with you later in the week." He looked at Eliot. "It's good to see you."

Eliot gratefully accepted his easy warmth and clear display of old and trusted friendship with a wide smile that she hoped conveyed something of her feelings. Somehow, she understood clearly, Julia had made it plain that the Denverses were not included in her evening's arrangements nor were they in charge of them. Eliot turned to her. "We're not exactly all- night ravers, so how about seven o'clock, or there-abouts?"

Apparently satisfied, Julia surrendered her hostess's hand and reclaimed her own from Morgan. As the Bancrofts drove away, she waved to the small girl who hung half out the car window in her eagerness to maintain sight of her heroine. Then, as the car disappeared from view, Julia turned to her coach and said crisply, "I'd appreciate a hand, Brad."

Brad Denvers's face had turned as stony as his wife's. "That was a damn stupid thing to do, Julia." His voice was heavy with rage. "You could've put back your recovery weeks. *Weeks.*" He reached his arm around her waist and roughly helped her up the three shallow steps to where Greg Bartlett stood, his face impassive but his physical bulk pointedly in the way.

"I don't think we need to be too concerned," Greg said to Brad, whose face was instantly suffused with a dull and unhealthy rush of blood. Behind them

Lauren Denvers's intake of breath was as sharp as her thinly clamped lips.

"I think Brad knows best here, Mr. Bartlett," she said, each word clipped off and snapped out.

"Oh bull," Julia muttered between clenched teeth and pushed Brad's arm away. "Don't start on me, Brad. Just don't start." At the open doors she paused and glared at the three who were each, in their different ways and with different motivations, impassively watching her efforts. "Pasta and salad for lunch at one-thirty and I'll do weights and physio with Greg this afternoon. I want you to take me over to the Bancrofts' this evening and I'd like you to pick me up. Any problems?"

"It's your funeral," said her coach, his expression as dark as his heavy eyebrows; Lauren's chilly eyes were equally unforgiving. Julia's spirits sank and she wondered why this sunny morning and pleasant place felt more like a prison than a $2,000-a-week luxury hideaway, and why the Denverses were behaving like prison guards rather than her valued support team. Then Greg Bartlett winked at her wickedly and the cloud passed.

As she lay on her bed willing the pain out of her leg and the exhaustion out of her mind, Julia's mood sank inexorably once again into the dark pit of pessimism that had opened up so overpoweringly after the accident. In desperation, she cast her mind back to the beach and the sunny little girl and her boundless optimism. She had seen the small creature come running and skipping, fairy-light, from the

39

mysterious old house in the trees. Julia watched her with conflicting feelings of exhilaration for the child's conspicuous joy and despair at the thought of ever again being able to move with similar ease and pleasure.

She had stopped to gather herself for the final effort to get back to the beach cottage at Kurrunulla Lodge that she'd left more than an hour — and less than a mile — ago. It was beginning to seem hopeless and foolish, so instead she used the excuse of watching the little girl to stop. Seeing her leap and run along the scribble of weed marking high water, Julia immediately noticed the telltale contrast of child's body and skinny but muscular arms and legs and easy coordination. The girl could have been herself light-years ago. It was an unmistakable look and when the youngster stopped nearby and saucer eyes revealed instant recognition, Julia groaned inwardly, "Uh-oh, a tennis player! A baby Monica!"

Without a hint of self-consciousness, the girl marched right up to Julia and although still goggling, calmly held out her hand. "How do you do," she said in tones of well-trained and well-bred politeness that were nevertheless edged with an unmistakable shudder of excitement. "My name is Morgan Bancroft Barron and I *know* you are Julia Ross. I'm most terribly pleased to meet you."

Julia shook the proffered hand and, despite her dark mood, found herself grinning down at the awestruck face. "How do you do, Morgan," she said. "I'm also pleased to meet you."

Without further encouragement Morgan related her life story, including the seminal moment when she stood next to Julia at the New South Wales Open

40

— which Julia admitted she couldn't exactly recall — to the dreadful moment when she had watched her knee collapse on television, which Julia wished she couldn't recall as exactly as she was able. Then Morgan stared without affectation or pretense at the cumbersome leg brace. "Is it *very* agonizing?" she asked earnestly.

Julia put her weight on the leg without thinking and gasped as white hot pain exploded along the length of the limb.

"Hooo-wee." She breathed. "Well, that wasn't so good." She wiped beads of sweat from her upper lip with the sleeve of her sweatshirt. "But it's mending a bit more every day."

Morgan clasped her hands together in the attitude of supplication she had learned for her role as one of the shepherds in her school nativity play. "Oh, I do most truly hope so," she said sedately.

With difficulty and despite waves of nausea, Julia suppressed a chuckle. "Do you play tennis, Morgan?"

The girl's eyes lit as if from within. "Yes! I'm going to be like you one day."

Julia smiled, going on with deliberate slow deep breaths all the while. "Yeah? And how's that?"

"All-court. I want to be an all-court player. I don't want to be a boring baseliner."

"Is that so? But baseliners tend to win, these days."

"But it's *very* boring. My mother says she'd rather watch paint drying."

"Is that so? Does your mom play tennis?"

"Yes, but I can beat her sometimes and I'm much more aggressive. And she's a painter too, so she actually doesn't mind watching paint dry, I think."

Again Julia suppressed a laugh. "I'll remember that," she promised. "But don't be too much like me, kiddo. I don't recommend trying to make your knee go in two different directions at once."

Morgan's face was a picture of vividly imagined hurt. "Oh," she whispered. "Are you going to be all right? What about Wimbledon? Will you be better by then?"

In an instant, pain spread from Julia's leg to her heart as this new experience — fear of the unknown — opened up before her like an abyss. "I don't know, I really don't know." The rest of the thought was lost as her head spun and fresh stabs of pain shot from her knee. "Oh no." She took another deep breath and tried with every last atom of will power to sound matter-of-fact as she said in a voice she barely recognized, "I wonder if you could help me. I think I'm going to faint."

"I'll get my mother," Morgan said, her face a picture of horror. She began to back away and in panic Julia reached for her, loath to be left alone on the expanse of white sand. "Don't go . . ." she began, but it was too late. Morgan was running and Julia lost her balance and fell, desperately trying to save her leg as the beach came up to meet her.

After a few seconds' pure screaming misery as nausea and tears threatened to overwhelm her crumbled defenses, humiliation and helplessness descended as she watched Morgan and an unmotherly-looking black-clad spunk meet and then run back toward her. She steeled herself against the torrent of gushing concern and curiosity that was already, after a fortnight, driving her to distraction in her dealings with the public. But the woman was not what she expected. There was no emotional reaction to her identity, nor to the dramatic-looking brace. Tangentially, Julia also perceived that this woman did not favor either pastel beachwear or neatly pleated upswept hair, but instead leaned over her in a spunky outfit with body to match that made Julia's eyes pop, despite the unlikely circumstances.

Morgan's mother continued to surprise her as she expertly lifted Julia's six-foot frame and with unspoken insight into what was needed, helped her to their house. And, after she introduced herself, over a glass of sweet fresh orange juice, as Eliot Bancroft ("My mother was a big George Eliot fan; I've always been grateful it wasn't Tolstoy"), Julia found her own wish — expressed in forceful terms to her coach — to keep people away, in particular, Sydney's sporting socialites and their constant stream of offers to cocktails and dinners and yacht trips, being eroded by this nice married lady and her wide-eyed little daughter.

Sitting in the dappled shade of the veranda, Morgan had been, in her undisguised and artless adoration of Julia, a tonic as good as the morning sunshine and Greg Bartlett's low-key humor and effortless competence. Julia enjoyed Eliot too, contrasting her warm and graceful manner with the volatility, filthy moods, occasional violence and unbridled competitiveness which had been the dominant characteristics of her most recent long-term companion. And so, back in the comfortable seclusion of her cottage, as pain slowly released its grip, Julia found solace in the unexpected pleasures of the morning past and the possibility that the coming few weeks of enforced quiet might not be as drearily uneventful as Brad Denvers intended.

CHAPTER THREE

Eliot touched a match to a twist of newspaper stuck, like a fuse, between the chunks of charcoal in the barbecue. While she waited to be sure that the coals ignited and didn't try to die a sulky and untended death, she methodically separated and defined each gradation of color and light to be found in the phenomenon simply known as "sunset." Behind the house, and through the silhouetted trees, the western sky glowed in variations on pink and gold in the wake of the sun. The eastern horizon, where the sky met the ocean, was a tenebrous void of shades of indigo, violet, cobalt and approaching darkness. Immediately overhead, where night and day met, the blue was luminous and fragile and already stars twinkled.

Satisfied that the fire wasn't going to choose this particular evening to attempt delinquency, Eliot turned back to the house. Golden light in each window and the russet reflection of the cedar floors on the creamy white walls within combined in an effect that was pleasingly tranquil and welcoming, and Eliot experienced the familiar sense of deep well-being that made this place so precious to her. It was a feeling she knew had been missing for some time. Probably, she thought, since Jack had begun seriously agitating to sell it to his property developer friend, Clarrie Summers. She shivered and deliberately tried to set aside that train of thought, returning instead to the kitchen to turn the plump lamb chops in their bowl of marinade.

Earlier, as she'd chopped garlic, chili and ginger and mixed them into pungent dark hoisin sauce, it had suddenly occurred to her that their guest might have very particular tastes in food — might even be a vegetarian with some strange extra athlete's requirements — but Morgan had been reassuring and certain in her knowledge that "Julia's favorite food is burgers and pasta and she also likes Mexican food and vanilla milk shakes and . . ."

Eliot grinned at the memory of her daughter's exhaustive knowledge of the minutiae of Julia Ross's life. In the bathroom Morgan was talking to whichever imaginary pal was sharing the tub, while Mozart filled the space in between with his own particular joy. Her day had been unexpectedly full and fun, not least because Morgan was so elated in anticipation of their dinner guest and had been beside herself with excitement after a mysterious phone call from Greg Bartlett which had occupied her for twenty whispered minutes after they'd returned from shopping for dinner and Eliot's birthday present.

Now, as the telephone rang, it instantly crossed her mind that it would be Julia calling to cancel.

"Happy birthday, darling. It's Jack."

Eliot was taken aback. "Thank you, Jack." She could think of nothing else to say or add.

"Having a bit of a party, are you?" His tone was hearty. She wondered where he was.

"No, just a quiet dinner," Eliot said before understanding that she had omitted the whole truth.

"Oh, shame. I thought you'd have a few people over." He sounded both teasing and hopeful. It was a familiar and wearying combination. Usually Eliot played to it by being amused by his teasing and by fulfilling his hopes. Tonight, as she began her fortieth year, she was not feeling the least bit obliging.

"And who would you suggest I have over, Jack?" she asked, her voice sharper than it had been all day.

"Oh, I don't know, friends — the Levys. Maybe Della and Cliff." He still managed to sound hopeful. Eliot glanced at her watch. It was five to seven.

"Actually, I can't stand Della and Cliff," she said in an impassive voice that was at odds with her fast-beating heart. "And if the Levys were the last people left on earth I would *not* invite them over for my birthday."

The silence was so long it was almost comical. Finally Jack cleared his throat and said, tentatively, "Are you feeling okay, darling?"

Eliot grinned. "Absolutely fine, Jack. But you're the first to know my new resolution for the rest of my life. No more Levys."

There was another long silence. Jack cleared his throat once more and this time sounded almost nervous as he tried to laugh. "Well, what's brought this on?"

"Not much. I think I grew up this morning."

The silence stretched between them and Eliot could almost hear the uncertainty bouncing around her husband's mind.

"Right, of course. Well, look, we'll talk about that later, okay? Oh, and darling, I don't think I'll be able to make it for the weekend. I'm terribly sorry . . ." Jack's voice rose a note, whether in anxiety or guilt, Eliot could not tell for sure, but anyway, she experienced something that felt suspiciously like amusement. She smiled into the receiver.

"That's a shame. Poor you, stuck in the city. Still, I expect you'll have a great deal to keep you occupied."

Relief was tangible in his voice. "That's terribly understanding of you, darling. I'll make it up to you, I promise."

"Don't worry," Eliot said in bleak tones. "Just don't do it in our bed. And if you must, please at least buy new sheets before I get back to town."

Whether his shock or hers was the greater she could not afterwards decide. She had never spoken to him in such a manner in their fifteen years of marriage.

After another crackling silence he managed to bluster, "Darling, what *are* you talking about?" Eliot sighed — with exasperation rather than sorrow — and simply said, "Don't be silly, Jack, you know what I mean. New sheets, that's all I ask."

By seven-thirty, the coals in the barbecue were shimmering, powdery white-edged and perfect. Eliot had uncorked a bottle of well-chilled white burgundy and poured herself a glass, but there was no sign of Julia. At eight o'clock Eliot covered the barbecue, and Morgan's wide eyes had begun to seek out her mother's reassurance; then they both heard an engine.

As Eliot reached the porch Morgan was already wrenching open the car door for Julia, while Brad Denvers sat behind the wheel staring straight ahead in an attitude that radiated hostility. Julia swung herself to her feet with the aid of a crutch and defiantly made her way across the grass with Morgan leaping around her like an excited puppy.

In the doorway, Eliot stood aside and smiled. "How lovely to see you again. You obviously don't need any help now." She smiled and Julia grinned back, but her attempted response was drowned by the car's motor as Brad gunned it into reverse. Momentarily Eliot wondered why her guest and her guest's coach were on such bad terms, but then Julia very deliberately pushed shut the front door behind her and the matter of getting her safely across the polished floor and various loose rugs and onto a couch took over and Brad Denvers's ire was forgotten.

* * * * *

Eight fat white candles flickered festively on a wrought iron stand in front of the unlit combustion stove. Propped on cushions fashioned from remnants of worn-out ancient tribal rugs on a raw-canvas-covered couch, with a glass of wine in one hand and Morgan glued to the other, Julia looked startlingly beautiful and very young, the haggard lines and sad eyes of the morning gone as she allowed herself to be entertained. This private person was light-years from the brash, scowling, gum-chewing but often arrogantly witty post-match interviewee Eliot recalled from television.

She listened with affectionate amusement to her daughter's voice, expressing bliss and overwhelming adoration for Julia in assorted unsubtle, childlike ways. For her part, Julia solemnly accepted the tokens of worship and allowed not one flicker of patronage to spoil Morgan's pleasure.

It was unexpectedly kind behavior, Eliot thought, and she watched the play of light and smiles on the young woman's face with a deep sense of enjoyment as Julia carefully examined and admired Morgan's collection of tennis trophies. Quietly, Eliot left them to it and took the bowl of marinated meat out to the barbecue; while the chops sizzled she continued to watch them through the window.

The champion was apparently lost in concentration, reading the inscriptions and minutely considering and remarking upon the different colored ribbons, medals, shields and cups. Then she seemed to sense Eliot's gaze and looked up. Her dark

49

eyebrows and great brown-black eyes formed what Eliot already realized was a characteristically mobile question mark. Eliot grinned and shrugged in response, helplessly embarrassed for reasons she could not quite pinpoint.

When Julia's face lit up in a huge and unmistakably inviting smile, she began to have an inkling. She, Eliot Bancroft, a year off forty, housewife and mother, was being flirted with by a world-famous champion tennis player. She waited for alarm to kick in and save her from the outrageous sensation of delight that was taking its amazing and leisurely course through her veins. But it did not. And she felt pretty sure she should be alarmed, because this glowingly fluid sensation was nothing like her previous experience of sexual encounters with women. Encounter, she corrected herself. There was only one woman with whom she had ever taken the occasional but undeniable sexual frisson beyond long and intense lunches and a few months of uncomfortable if delicious infatuation.

She smiled fondly as she thought of Rachel Taylor, now her best friend of ten years. She was a TV soap star whose great love and frustrated talent was Shakespeare, but whose other gifts included a bottomless well of love for her nearest and dearest, while a sense of pragmatism and wicked humor kept her from frustration as she recited her ridiculous lines all the way to the bank. Most importantly for Eliot — and Eliot acknowledged this — the undemanding but sweet constancy and unabashed sensuality that remained in their friendship had done much to dispel her despair and diminishing self-esteem as her marriage had slowly, but unmistakably, worn itself out. At the same time Eliot had never considered herself to be a lesbian. And, she thought, as she stabbed at a chop to check its state of readiness, she was forced to admit that she hadn't really considered herself to be anything much in these past few years. Now, Eliot wondered whether her own pleasure in what was happening was acting as some kind of anesthetic to her normal wifely sensibilities, or whether this pleasure was simply her normal womanly responses. Whatever its origin, she knew that the inner glow had nothing to do with leaning over the business end of a barbecue; in this brief moment she was reveling in the knowledge that Julia Ross found her attractive.

As she brushed the chops with leftover marinade she tried to remember the last time anybody had voluntarily and honestly flirted with her; finally she managed to recall an occasion at a charity ball the previous winter, when one of Jack's junior partners took on board rather more rum punch than he could handle. He had pressed his suit and an alcoholically flaccid penis upon her under the guise of teaching her the macarena. Neither attempt had been a success.

And she simply did not count the opportunists and social climbers whose guarded slobbering was provoked by the possibility of crawling within the sphere of influence cast by her father, ex-foreign minister and senior party power-broker, Senator Harold Bancroft. Ditto the discreet fumbles and suggestive whispers around the dinner tables of Jack's legal cronies.

She looked up again and this time Julia's gaze was unequivocal and penetrating. A blush started up

Eliot's neck and suffused her cheeks; she was glad of the barbecue's heat, but her breath was short as she returned to the brighter light of the living room and somehow managed to say, "Dinner's ready, you two."

It was after eleven and there were bruises of weariness beneath Morgan's eyes before Eliot managed to separate her from Julia's hand, but not before a promise was extracted from Julia that the backyard tennis facility would be inspected at the earliest opportunity and so be proved "just as good as Greg and Ray's." Then she slipped her hand into her mother's and went to her bed without protest.

Once tucked in, Morgan clasped Eliot around the neck and whispered in her ear, "This has been the best birthday you've ever had, Mummy. Thank you so much."

Eliot chuckled and reciprocated Morgan's hug. "It has been, darling, that's for sure and I love my present." She touched the tiny gold dolphin that hung from her neck on a fine chain and kissed her daughter's forehead.

"Do you like Greg and Ray and Julia's present too?" Morgan's sleepy eyes popped open with sudden anxiety and she fingered the tiny gold dolphins that now hung from Eliot's earlobes.

"I do, my chick, you've all been wonderful, especially you. But you must go to sleep or you won't be fit for anything, especially not to help Julia practice."

Morgan's shudder of delight shook her bony little body from head to toe. "I'm so happy I can hardly bear it, Mummy. Do you think I might die in the night?" Again she was suddenly wide-eyed, this time at the prospect of the overwhelming pleasure and terror that lay ahead. Eliot laid her cheek against the velvet softness of the girl's face to hide her own amusement and kissed her once more. "You'll make it, sweetheart, you'll see. Now sleep well."

Morgan's eyes closed. Eliot snapped off the bedside light and returned to the living room where she found their guest just as she had left her: sprawled full-length on a sofa listening raptly to two English sopranos climbing the sublime heights of Monteverdi. Julia looked up as she heard the chink of glass on glass.

"I don't know what this music is," she said softly, smiling contentedly at her hostess, "but I love it." As Eliot approached she held out her glass and accepted more wine. "And I like this too."

Eliot handed the CD case to Julia. "There's more — wine and Monteverdi." She set down her glass and the bottle on the low table in front of Julia's sofa and went about the room, gathering Morgan's detritus into a weathered wooden chest that perfectly swallowed a child's clutter. She cleared away their plates and the dinner dishes from the long table and within five minutes the room was restored to its previous serenity.

As she finished stacking the dishwasher she once more found Julia regarding her speculatively, this time across the top of her glass. Again she felt herself blushing and was grateful for the soft light. But after a moment Julia grinned and said something that could only deepen the blush.

"You're really beautiful, Eliot."

53

Eliot laughed nervously and struggled to keep her hands from performing give-away small acts of smoothing and checking.

She swallowed on a suddenly dry throat, aware that her mind had gone blank even as her stomach turned a perfect somersault. "I . . . thank you," she finally croaked.

"Does almost being forty bother you?" Julia asked, and her question was as direct and lacking in edge as any of Morgan's guileless interrogations.

This time Eliot couldn't prevent the reaction that made her fingers touch the lines which faintly etched the outer corner of each eye and her mouth. She frowned momentarily and shrugged.

"I'm not sure," she said slowly, feeling her way into her own thoughts. "It's more of a surprise than anything. I didn't expect to wake up and be thirty-nine. Suddenly I'm not young anymore — at least not officially — and I don't know where the years have gone. Nor . . ." She hesitated before going on. "Nor what I've done with them." She smiled ruefully at Julia. "Not like you — grand slams. Wimbledon — how many is it? Seven times? And heaven knows how many titles. And you're so young."

Julia stirred sharply and grimaced. A discernible shadow descended over her face and her eyes darkened and became distant. "You're kidding. I'm not young. Not in tennis. I'm twenty-six, nearly twenty-seven. Before the accident I knew I had at least four more really good years; probably five in the top ten if I really wanted it. I've realized that allowed me to avoid thinking about the future. And now, all I do is think about that future and it's not there." She shrugged and her expression was one of bleak bewilderment. "I don't see a future," she re-iterated flatly. "You have a beautiful daughter. You have a husband and" — she gestured at the painting that dominated the east wall behind her — "if this is what you can do, you obviously have a career that'll last you a lifetime. That's what I call a future. Me? I really don't know. I can't see it at all."

Eliot was silent, shocked at the somberness in the voice and face. Julia stared back at her, the habitual defiance of her chin vying for dominance over anguished eyes. She tried to grin but didn't quite make it.

"I'm feeling kind of sorry for myself," she said dolefully. "It's not a pretty sight. Maybe you ought to call my coach to come take me away."

Eliot was shaken by Julia's clear picture of her own dilemma and shook her head. "Not unless you want to go."

Julia studied her with narrowed eyes and she too slowly shook her head. "No, I don't want to go, yet."

"Fine. Although I have an idea your coach doesn't exactly approve of your new social life."

Julia snorted. "I have an idea I'm going to be looking for a new coach before too long. Tennis is a funny business. It's all in the head, you know? I can see him and Lauren looking at me and right now they don't see a winner anymore. And you know what? If I don't see it in their eyes, then I probably won't win. Crazy isn't it?"

She sighed and stretched back on the couch, but not before Eliot caught the glitter of tears. "That's a really fantastic painting," she said again, not looking at Eliot. "I don't know shit about art but my gut feeling is that it's really something."

Eliot smiled and shrugged. "That's all that matters, I think — if the viewer gets it, then that's all one can ask."

"But do I get it right? Like, I'm not an expert."

"Getting it doesn't necessarily mean that we get the same thing. What *I* mean in that painting and the meaning you take from it can be — and probably are — totally different."

"Shit. No kidding." Julia studied the picture again, her eyes narrowing and widening as she took it in again via this new set of possibilities.

"That's not an original thought, by the way. Jasper Johns said it first and much better."

Julia nodded and pursed her lips, then seemed to change her mind and looked Eliot straight in the eye. "Okay, who's Jasper Johns?"

"American artist, abstract expressionist, to me the greatest master of the late twentieth century."

"Is he expensive?"

Eliot laughed. "Very. But you could probably afford him."

Julia's eyes flashed. "Are you laughing at me?"

Eliot thought for a minute. "I don't think so. It's just not a reaction I've ever heard before."

"So what should I have said?" Julia's glittering eyes were ominous. "I already told you I don't know zip about art. Should I've said some bullshit about abstract expressions, or something?"

Eliot shook her head, alarmed at the mixture of fear, anger and humiliation that flashed across Julia's face. "No," she said gently, "no, no. You shouldn't ever pretend or ..." She grimaced. "... bullshit. You say what you feel. That's what's important."

There was a long silence and Eliot slowly sipped

her wine and let Monteverdi mend the gaps between them while she wondered how on earth she had gotten herself into such an extraordinary situation. But before she could mentally retrace her steps, Julia swung around from staring at her painting and grinned.

"I got a lot to learn. I think you're being kind, Eliot. I mean, please: my first reaction to an artist really shouldn't be 'Can I buy him' — or her. True? I mean, let's face it, I come from a world where, whenever I go to work, like, whenever I step out on court, the first thing they announce is how much fucking money I've made. Like, that's my art — millions and millions of dollars."

Eliot dropped her head in her hands and sighed. "This is a complicated subject, Julia. You *know* that money isn't what counts."

Julia shrugged. "Maybe, maybe not. But do people say to you, 'Hey, your pictures sell for blah blah dollars, that must make you a pretty fantastic artist'?"

Eliot smiled and rolled her eyes. "Actually, yes, that's exactly what can happen — and it does. I sell pictures — not as often as I'd like — but Van Gogh didn't sell one picture in his lifetime. Does that make me a better artist than Van Gogh?" Julia considered the question for a moment then giggled triumphantly as a thought struck her. "I don't know, but you got both your ears."

Eliot snorted. "I think that ball was well out."

Julia looked pleased with herself and lay back on the couch; the Monteverdi ended and Eliot rose to slot in a fresh CD. She chose Mozart and then, as she resumed her seat, surprised herself by asking what was, for her, almost a crudely personal question. "Do you not have anyone to turn to? Or who can be with you at the moment — I mean, aside from your coach?"

Julia looked at her keenly and grinned in a way that could be described as sardonic. "You mean where's my boyfriend?" Eliot shrugged, embarrassed now that the question was out and its underlying meaning obvious. "Don't you read the gossip rags? I don't have *boy*friends. I have *girl*friends. And in this business it is almost impossible to keep one — of either kind. You heard of Angie Andreadis? She used to be my doubles partner?"

Eliot nodded, recalling the fair-haired terrier with the knack of making any ball that came near the net her own — except when she was on court opposite Julia.

"Angie was my partner off-court too for a couple of years and we did real well — three Wimbledons, the U.S., the Australian and four or five other nice ones — but, what she *really* wanted was to beat me in singles. She wanted it so badly she couldn't handle it. And . . ." Julia sighed and her reluctant grin was almost wicked. "I just couldn't let her beat me — not even for love — you know? So no, I don't have anyone right now. I travel all the time and I only ever really meet players or fans, and I don't know which is worse when it comes to relationships."

Eliot struggled to take in this new and startling information. For reasons that were not immediately apparent, she found herself both saddened and disturbed. As she turned it over in her mind it became clearer. Julia's flat delivery of her story only partly concealed the fundamental void that Eliot suspected could prove an even greater enemy to her recovery than the physically injured knee. She could see — now that she understood a little better — the potential terror of the yawning chasm that was inexorably opening up where a certain future had once been. She could understand now how such a gloriously talented athlete could believe herself to be old and near the end at an age when, in truth, her life was barely begun.

Eliot bought time by refilling her glass and then heard herself saying, "And I thought I was on the scrap heap because I'm nearly forty, my husband is having an affair with a woman who is practically half my age, and I know he'd divorce me if I wasn't so useful to him. I've been waiting fourteen months for my gallery to pay me for the six pictures that sold at the last exhibition and I haven't painted a decent canvas in eight months." She began to laugh, but it was close to tearful. "Isn't it pathetic? I mean really. Look at me — I'm healthy, I've got Morgan, I have a very comfortable life — what have I got to be miserable about?"

Julia's gaze was both speculative and unreadable, then she smiled the smallest possible smile and said softly, "I know it beats the hell out of starving in Africa, but it doesn't make it any less painful to be lonely and unloved, does it?"

Eliot shook her head, unable to speak. Fear lurched in her gut and she swallowed half the contents of her glass in one gulp. Julia had instinctively identified the specter which had been lurking in the shadows for months: she *was* unloved.

Jack no longer loved her and, perhaps just as bad, she no longer loved him. The void she saw in Julia's life was so easily recognizable because it mirrored that of her own.

"I know this happens every day of the week," she said quietly. "It's happened to half the women I know. So I don't know why it never occurred to me that I'd wake up one day to find myself middle-aged and divorced. I must be really stupid, or complacent, or something."

"How about trusting? Or an optimist?"

"No, I think the answer is stupid. You don't know my husband, I'm afraid."

"I certainly don't understand your husband." Julia's expression was still serious but also and again unmistakably flirtatious. "If he prefers some ditzy blond bimbo to you he must be out of his mind."

Eliot giggled. Unbidden, her spirits rose a fraction from their rock-bottom level and she squared her shoulders and heard herself say, without a quiver, "Redhead, actually. And she's not a bimbo, she's a junior lawyer in his firm."

"Ah!" Julia nodded. "The old 'no thanks, darling, I gave at the office' routine. Well, I still say he's out of his mind."

"You're very kind."

Julia shook her head. "I've been called a lot of things, but I don't recall *kind* being one of them. And I've had enough of this very good wine to say what I think." She emptied her glass and set it down. "I think you are beautiful. And I think I'd like to get to know you better." Her eyebrows rose in their distinctive questioning mode and her grin widened to the other side of disarming. "Have I gone too far?"

Eliot shook her head even as her heartbeat did an unfamiliar stumble. "No, you haven't. I'd like to know you better too." She swallowed and added hastily, in case Julia should misunderstand her, "I would very much like to be friends. And I know Morgan would too."

Julia nodded and smiled, acknowledging the line Eliot had drawn. "Ah, Morgan. I think we're pals already." She stretched and looked at her watch. "Oh boy. It's *really* late. Brad is going to be one bear with a sore head."

Eliot frowned, "I'm sure Greg would have organized one of the staff to come for you."

Julia's smile was wry. "You have to understand what a guilt-tripping Mother Hen my coach can be," she said, sighing gustily. "He likes to do it because he thinks it makes me feel bad." She grinned wickedly. "But it doesn't."

Eliot laughed as she punched the quick-dial number reserved for Kurrunulla Lodge and, when she was put through, absorbed the hostile crackle at the other end that was Brad Denvers's voice. After their three-sentence exchange she carefully replaced the receiver as if it were hot. "He'll be right over. But I don't think he's very pleased."

"No, I guess he isn't. Ah well, I pay him too much to feel badly. But I'd better be ready or he might just decide to mow me down and do the other leg." She stood up, grimacing at the obvious stiffness that had set in.

Eliot moved to help but hesitated. Resolve

radiated from Julia like a force field as she limped across the room, the muscles in her jaw flexing as she clenched her teeth on the effort of each step.

"Should you be walking on that leg?" Eliot asked anxiously.

Julia's expression was self-mocking. "If I can't, you might as well shoot me now, like an old broken-down horse."

"They can do marvelous things with old horses nowadays," Eliot observed calmly and was rewarded with an unwilling grin as Julia hobbled past her into the cool night air.

CHAPTER FOUR

After an hour of vigorous hit-ups with Morgan,
Julia staggered theatrically off-court and collapsed,
laughing, onto a picnic rug strewn with squashy old
cushions that Morgan had painstakingly arranged
between two tall shady trees. Eliot poured freshly
squeezed orange juice from an insulated jug and it
went down nonstop. Morgan tried valiantly to
emulate her goddess, even to a sigh and scrub of
hand across lips that perfectly mimicked Julia's own
actions. Eliot suppressed a smile.

"That was good, thanks. My god, that's an evil drop shot this kid's got. Did you see it, Eliot?"

Eliot smiled at Morgan's unequivocal pleasure. "I did. But I think in the past two weeks she's learned quite a lot from one of the most evil players in the game."

Julia wrinkled her nose. "Oh but it's such a sweet thing," she protested. "Come on, you *know* how you can drive somebody crazy when you pop 'em over the net . . . like . . . so . . ." She demonstrated, her tongue tucked in the corner of her mouth, her eyes twinkling at Eliot as if she were the adversary about to be left flat-footed and gasping. "See! Doesn't it make you want to just kill me?"

Julia flopped back on her cushions as her audience laughed; but Morgan grasped Julia's hand and said gravely, "My mother would never want to kill you, Julia." She turned round eyes on Eliot. "Would you, Mum?"

Suddenly there were two pairs of equally serious eyes regarding her, waiting for her reply with undoubtedly different motives, and she stopped laughing. "No, I'd never want to kill Julia, darling. But if she ever tries a drop shot on me, I might change my mind."

Julia placed her hand on her heart. "I solemnly swear I will not try a drop shot on you, Ms. Bancroft, unless I give you written warning at least one week in advance. How's that?"

Eliot sniffed. "It might be acceptable. But I reserve my rights."

"I don't think you have the right to kill me. Does she, Morgan?"

Morgan looked perturbed. "I'm not sure. Perhaps

I'd better check my encyclopedia." And she was gone, her scampering feet kicking up whirls of silver-gray leaves.

For a minute the silence was broken only by a gang of rainbow lorikeets whistling and cussing and invisible in the angophoras. Then Julia stretched full length, gingerly flexed her half-braced knee and said, "I don't know about killing me. You and your friends have saved my life."

Eliot's gesture was self-deprecating, but she said nothing.

"I mean it, Eliot. When the Denverses quit I was about ready to throw in the towel and go home — if I could have figured out where home is."

"Don't be silly. You would've come through."

Julia shook her head. "I'm not so sure. And that's the whole point about this game — being sure. The Denverses left because they weren't sure anymore. And I was scared of them because I knew they didn't count on me coming through this. See what I mean?"

Eliot's expression suggested skepticism. "Maybe, but Greg and Ray are fabulously successful with athletic injuries — I mean, that's why you came to them."

Julia shook her head, dismissively. "You don't get it! Good people aren't the problem. There are a dozen good people and good places I could have gone to, but it's more than that." She sighed gustily, her impatience evident. "Let's put it this way. I had a coach a coupla years back, he was brilliant. You'd know his name but I've decided to forget it. But he was also two other things that kinda canceled out how brilliant he was with my backhand; he was a misogynist and he was homophobic. I didn't find out until we'd signed the contracts, but I can tell you, it's pretty hard living in someone's pocket — as you do on tour — and knowing that they'd like you to crawl back under a rock, or maybe die a slow death. So, Greg and Ray's being gay as well as brilliant — *and* really nice guys *and* turning out to be old friends of yours... now d'you see what I mean?"

Eliot did. "Okay, but I worry about you spending so much time practicing with Morgan. I mean, what do we know about rehab?"

Julia laughed. "I'm hurt and need help. I need a bit of fun — and you must admit Morgan is that. I also don't need any hassles right now. You know that yesterday a photographer from one of the gossip rags in the States tried to book into Kurrunulla Lodge as a paying customer? It's just as well Ray is naturally suspicious or there'd be 'tragic Julia's fight to save her leg' pictures in every supermarket in the damn world by next week."

"Okay, that's settled then. I believe you."

"Good! Look, I know I've just dropped out of the sky on you, and if anybody should be worried it's me. I'm the one who's busted in on your holiday with your kid. But there doesn't seem to be any pressure, no expectations, just kindness. And that girl of yours — just feeling her believe I'm the greatest —" Julia broke off, tears in her eyes. "She doesn't *expect* anything of me, she just believes — it's an amazing feeling — and so I believe too. Almost." She flexed her leg and her voice shook as she said, slowly and deliberately, "I can get back on top, you know. I can do it. I know that now."

Eliot nodded and gave Julia's hand an affectionate squeeze. "Then I am sure you can — and will," she said gently. "And if we can do anything to help, we will."

Julia did not release Eliot's hand. "You've been more than help," she said. "It was bad enough with the Denverses, but on my own..." She shrugged. "I mean *me* being on my own — with *me*. Being on my own with the horrors... You guys all feel like family and that's what I need right now." She shuddered.

"And now?"

"And now I guess I have to think about moving on."

Eliot's heart lurched into a cold pit. "Of course," she heard herself say in a voice gone stiff.

Julia's hand tightened. "But not on my own — just yet." Her eyes were wide with apprehension as she scanned Eliot's carefully neutral face. "I have to go to New York and do some stuff and I was wondering if you and Morgan would come — sort of finish your vacation as my guests?"

Before Eliot could open her mouth, Julia leapt in first and rushed on anxiously, "I've got an apartment in a building that's also a hotel and you could stay there — you can do absolutely everything in New York right outside the door. Those big art galleries are close by and I know Morgan's supposed to be back at school but she could have the best time *and* tennis coaching with Phil Maconachie, if you like..."

Eliot was laughing at Julia's sales pitch — at once half joking, half desperate — when Morgan came romping across the grass in a long-legged skip.

"Daddy's on the phone."

Eliot drew her hand away from Julia's and stood up, frowning. Jack's workload had kept him in the city since the day before her birthday — and in the past two weeks, even phone calls had been sporadic. Yet, it occurred to her, she had barely given a thought to his neglect and now, the prospect of talking to him filled her with . . . what? The jagged beat of her heart and the discomfort in the pit of her stomach betrayed a sensation close to dread.

After their ritual pleasantries Jack suddenly changed tack. "And how's your celebrity guest, darling?" he asked jovially.

Eliot was immediately suspicious, remembering his hostility when, ten days before, she had told him about their unexpected new neighbor and friend. "Julia's progressing really well," she said cautiously. "She's working terrifically with Greg and it all seems pretty good."

"Great, great."

Eliot's suspicion deepened as his bonhomie treacled down the phone. "It's nice for you to have company — unusual company too."

"It's been fun," Eliot allowed warily.

"So, I suppose you won't want to come to Hong Kong next week . . . will you? I've got a lot of boring company tax stuff to take care of. You'd be on your own rather a lot . . ."

"This is sudden." Her voice startled her by its chilliness, and Eliot heard herself playing advantage in a way she had never before attempted. Jack's hesitation was momentary, but she heard it.

"Yes, well, Irving Webb was supposed to go but,

the short story is, I have to. It's a real bore, darling, I know, but I thought if you've got a little friend to play with . . ."

Eliot closed her eyes tight and bit her tongue on an instinctively hot response, then she said, in tones of pure reason, "Well, actually it could work out quite nicely. Julia has asked us to go with her to New York."

"New York?" Jack's voice was a kaleidoscope of conflicting emotions; Eliot could sense the different directions in which his mind was racing.

"Phew! Say, is there a chance of getting Morgan some coaching with, what's his name? Phil Maconachie?"

"That's what Julia's suggesting." Eliot hesitated to remind him that Morgan would miss school, but something told her it wouldn't matter.

"Hey, that's pretty amazing." His voice was boyishly enthusiastic and Eliot felt her heart warm toward him. Then he went on, "Well, I think you'd better go on being nice to your dykey pal, eh?" And her moment of fondness turned to stone.

She returned to the garden to find Julia and Morgan side by side on the rug wearing identical expressions of nervous expectation.

"Can we go, Mum?" Morgan asked anxiously, and Eliot could see the same question mirrored in Julia's eyes.

"Sure," she said nonchalantly. "Daddy has to go to Hong Kong. So he won't miss us a bit. Now, I think you better go check what you're going to take, Missy Morgan, and I want your room tidy too."

Morgan scrabbled her way out of the pile of cushions and disappeared. Eliot thrust her hands into her jeans pockets and stood for a moment, nonplussed by the sudden turn of events and the conflicting views of the chasm that was opening up in front of her.

"What are you thinking?" Julia's voice was hushed. She had come to dread Eliot's periodic withdrawal into the role of dutiful and ultra-respectable wife, so accustomed was she to the generous pleasure and solace of her companionship. As if she were awaiting a first serve, Julia watched her friend. Apparently disconcerted, Eliot turned away.

"I'm not sure," Eliot said at last. Then she turned back to Julia's gaze. "Jack is definitely having an affair. Quite a serious one, I think."

Julia nodded, trying to work out how to tread in this new minefield. "It seems so." Awkwardly, she clambered to her feet and moved to stand beside Eliot, longing to sooth the rigidly tense shoulders but paralyzed by an even greater need to maintain the easy affection that had gradually built between them in the days since her impetuous, Merlot-abetted declaration of attraction. Finally she asked, "And what does that feel like?"

Eliot shrugged and began to walk, away from the court and the house, along the bark-strewn path through the old trees that sheltered the rear acres.

Julia fell into step beside her. "Are you sad?"

Eliot shook her head.

"Are you angry?"

Again she shook her head.

"Are you afraid?"

Eliot's pause was momentary, then she stopped

70

and faced Julia, her expression a picture of undisguised pessimism. "Yes, I am."

Without further hesitation Julia slipped her arm about Eliot and hugged her gently. "That makes two of us — for different reasons — but still, two's company. If you see what I mean."

Eliot grinned and for a second rested her forehead on Julia's shoulder. "I do, I think," she said softly, turning into the sanctuary of the embrace. "You're a good friend, Julia."

With an effort that was close to intolerable, Julia held back on her desire to take the moment past the point of friendship. She wondered whether Eliot could feel her pounding heart, or sense the yearning in every fiber of her body, but Eliot simply looked at her with such fondness and trust that Julia could only draw back and smile.

They walked on, arm in arm, in silence. Julia couldn't remember when last she'd experienced such ease and companionable seclusion. Eliot's strong sense of privacy — which meant that Julia had yet to see the inside of her studio — helped, but there was something even more important at work. Being in another country was part of it, as well as the enforcement of a different pace and focus in her life that had as much to do with her new allies as with her injury. They were not, Julia told herself, unpleasant changes, but they were substantial.

"It's the changes," she suddenly said out loud. "Upheaval. Everything in flux. It's frightening. Human beings don't like change."

Eliot nodded, flutters of fear in her eyes confirming Julia's analysis.

"And it's the uncertainty, more than anything,"

Julia went on. "It's the not knowing." Eliot shivered and Julia stroked her back reassuringly, even as her own spine rippled nervously.

They reached the gravel driveway and stopped to watch a flock of plump white cockatoos waddling around in the grass, flashing their lemon-yellow crests, arguing and teasing and seeking out whatever seeds had caught their fancy, and all the while, squawking like ancient gate hinges.

"They're so beautiful and so funny," Julia said softly. "I can't get used to seeing them just sitting around like old park pigeons."

"It's pretty good, isn't it?"

As it did now on a daily basis, Eliot's smile turned her heart over and without thinking, Julia bent her head and lightly kissed her. It was a fleeting touch, almost imaginary, but within her encircling arm Eliot's shoulders tensed and quivered. Julia's internal groan was almost audible and she stiffened and drew back, anticipating Eliot's response.

"I'm sorry," she whispered, exasperation and dismay vying for ascendancy inside her.

A sharp blast of a car horn shattered the stillness as a gleaming black Jeep Cherokee turned in the gates behind them.

"Damn," said Eliot softly, her heartbeat quickening in fright. She stepped back from Julia's enclosing arm as the vehicle approached. A smoke-tinted window hummed and an older, tighter but blurred version of Eliot's face peered out at them, pale blue eyes darting curiously to and fro between Julia and Eliot.

"Hello, Daphne," said Eliot calmly. "What are you doing here?"

"Just on my way to the farm, darling." Daphne Bancroft Holmes's eyes were busily taking an inventory of the scene. "Jack said your sick visitor was still around, so I thought I'd drop by and see if I could be of any help."

The X-ray gaze took in Julia's leg brace and in the same moment, Eliot saw, as if through her sister's eyes, the spectacular long bronzed limbs and athlete's body revealed by lurid purple and green Lycra shorts and bright yellow singlet. Suppressed amusement mixed with the vaguest jangle of alarm and both sensations clashed in a pulsing thud of her heart to produce an awareness that was both unpleasant and caused her to blush. Momentarily she wondered what Daphne might have seen as she'd swept into the driveway, but her sister seemed more interested in social niceties.

"Aren't you going to introduce us, Eliot?"

Although they were so similar, in Daphne's voice there was no mellow timbre but rather a perceptible crackle of antagonism. Within herself Eliot felt an instant retreat into defensiveness.

Julia limped forward, placing herself between the sisters. "Julia Ross," she said and stuck out her hand.

Daphne's chubby, freckled, discreetly diamonded, puce-clawed paw nervously grasped Julia's. "Daphne Bancroft Holmes. I'm Eliot's eldest sister, of course. *So* pleased to make your acquaintance," she said, all beaming bonhomie even as she continued her inspection. "And you're the famous tennis player, of course?"

Julia agreed and turned to Eliot. "And I'd better be getting back to Kurrunulla. I've got a session with

Greg," she said, her eyebrows semaphoring that Eliot should indicate what she wanted her to do.

Eliot grinned, an unconsciously tender grin. "You better had," she said. "You don't want to be late. Take the car."

Daphne and Eliot watched the elderly Volvo disappear and, as was their ritual, Eliot waved until she could no longer see her daughter's small hand. She was reluctant to go into the house, feeling that if they stayed outdoors at least, she was not quite so trapped by her sister's gimlet eyes and small mind. But Daphne had no hesitation.

"Do you think it's wise, Eliot?" Her voice hissed and sputtered and tranquility was gone.

"Wise?" Eliot was genuinely puzzled but the crackle in Daphne's voice made her uncomfortable.

"Oh, come on. You know what I mean."

Eliot squared her shoulders. "I'm afraid I don't."

"Letting Morgan go off with her like that."

Eliot refused to acknowledge her dawning understanding of what her sister had in mind, but already a sick feeling lodged in the pit of her stomach.

"Are you in a hurry or do I have to offer you coffee?" She turned away from Daphne and marched back toward the house.

"For heaven's sake, Eliot. Everyone is talking about it."

"Everyone? Talking about what?"

"Your lesbian friend."

"I don't like what you're implying." Eliot's heart had begun to beat in what abruptly turned into an angry tattoo.

"We are the laughingstock of all our friends, Eliot." The way Daphne snapped out her name felt like a slap and Eliot knew, without looking, that her sister's expensive face would by now be pinched white at lips and nostrils.

"Don't be silly, Daphne," she heard herself say in a tone designed to appeal to reason. She took a deep breath. "I won't talk about this." She went on firmly, "You're being ridiculous."

"Ridiculous!" Her sister's voice whiplashed the soft morning air to shreds. "My niece is being influenced — for god's sake and I don't know what else — by an unashamed and brazen lesbian. Heavens, Eliot, you might not care about the reputation of our family, but what about Morgan? How often do you let her go off with that pervert?"

The last word was spat so hard it stung Eliot's ears and she drew back in shock.

This can't be happening to me, she told herself as she marched furiously into the house. This can't be my own sister. She found herself behind the kitchen counter and looked up from the coffee pot to find Daphne's eyes, pink-rimmed with animosity, boring into her.

"Well?" Despite expensive renovation, Daphne's jowls still quivered, turkey-like, when she was really upset. Perhaps it was this faintly ridiculous aspect, or perhaps it was her new-found but growing sense of herself, but Eliot knew that, for the first time, she was not about to back away from Daphne's rage.

"Well, what? I can't believe you're saying this. It's disgusting." Eliot's tone was mild, but her words inflamed her sister.

"Disgusting!" Daphne's voice had risen to a discreet shriek. "*I'm* disgusting! Eliot! I am appalled at you. Have you any idea how upsetting this is for Jack? For all of us?"

Eliot almost dropped the canister of coffee beans as her temper flared. "Jack! Upset! What *are* you talking about, Daphne? *I* am upsetting that two-timing bastard?"

"Don't shout, Eliot."

"Oh for chrissakes, Daphne. This is my house and I'll shout until your silicon shrivels."

"Eliot!"

"And what's more," Eliot heard herself say as if in a dream, heard the coffee canister banging down on the counter, "if you say one more stupid, ignorant, embarrassing thing about what might happen to Morgan, you can get out of my house now."

"You're hysterical."

"Damn right, I'm hysterical. How dare you, Daphne." Again the canister hit the counter.

"I am thinking only of my niece." Daphne's chin was up but she had also edged toward the door.

Eliot shook her head, trying desperately to clear the haze of outrage and disbelief from her mind. "You cannot be serious, Daphne," she said in a quieter but, she hoped, equally dangerous tone. "Tell me exactly what kind of danger Morgan is in."

"You know what I mean."

"I'm sorry, I don't. You'll have to spell it out."

"You're being very aggressive, Eliot. I think Jack

has every reason to be concerned. Perhaps it's early menopause."

Eliot restrained herself from hurling the coffee beans at her sister's perfectly coiffed head. "Discuss me with my husband at your peril, Daphne," she said in ice-edged tones. "Now, either you tell me exactly what's on your mind or you leave."

Following the well-trodden patterns of a lifetime, Daphne Bancroft Holmes opened her mouth to tell her younger sister how to behave. But she caught the expression in Eliot's eyes and stopped. As their maternal grandmother's clock ticked benignly on the wall the two women glared at each other. Then habit got the better of Daphne. As she would no doubt tell her husband that evening, she simply could *not* let it rest.

"Have you not heard about lesbians, Eliot?" she asked stiffly.

"Heard what?"

Daphne snorted, clearly beginning to regain the sense of herself that Eliot had momentarily knocked askew.

"Predatory lesbians," she pronounced, slowly, as if to an idiot. Despite her anger, Eliot felt a bubble of laughter well inside her and it burst out in a giggle. "This is no laughing matter, Eliot," Daphne said severely.

Eliot shook her head. "No, it's not. It's hideous, actually. I can't believe that my own sister can come out with such shit."

"Eliot!"

"Are you really suggesting that Julia is going to molest Morgan?"

"How can you use that word?"

"Which word? *Molest?*"

"You know perfectly well what I mean. The 's' word."

"You are completely fucked in the head, Daphne."

Daphne gasped and reeled back as if struck. "Eliot!"

"Eliot, nothing. People like Julia do not molest little girls, Daphne. It's men like Jack and your own dear Henry who do that."

"Eliot!" Daphne's voice had once more risen to a tiny shriek. "I am not going to listen to this filth!" She scrambled with trembling hands for her car keys and little Chanel bag. "I think you ought to see Dr. Marchant, Eliot. Jack's right, you need hormones, or therapy."

Daphne backed away from her sister, but Eliot did not follow. Already elation was turning to sour sadness. Only when the house was once more adrift in birdsong did her shoulder muscles release their iron grip on the tendons of her neck.

But then, as she reviewed the morning, she was forced to acknowledge that unwittingly, Daphne had saved her from making a complete and unaccountable fool of herself. "What on earth was I thinking of?" she said, half-aloud, and covered her face with both hands to shield her embarrassment from the sunny morning as she recalled her impulsive move toward Julia.

"No, no, no, no," she whispered. "Never again."

* * * * *

Julia sat on the bench in Greg Bartlett's gym and tried to concentrate on lifting and lowering the weighted bar with her injured leg. It was harder than usual, mainly, she realized, because there was an even greater weight burdening her thoughts.

"What's on your mind, Julia?" Greg's voice broke in gently. She let the bar drop and exhaled a long and inadvertently tremulous sigh.

"This and that. Nothing much," she lied. "You know how it is."

His expression was sympathetic but quizzical. Over the long days of sweat and pain their relationship had gone from pleasantly professional to warm friendship. After the overnight abandonment by the Denverses, Greg had become trusted by Julia even though her capacity to trust had taken quite a battering. He had exhorted her, cajoled her, bullied her and joked with her and Julia had quickly come to depend on and be fond of him. Not least because the Greek god–handsome face — with which the media had been so in love during his tennis career — was a façade behind which was a man whose gentleness and intuitive skills with a broken body were complemented by a mind that saw through her habitual bullshitting and her carefully cultivated bravado and could offer succor to the frightened brat who lurked within.

On their third session together, Julia broke down weeping with frustration at the pain that she simply couldn't overcome or ignore. It prevented her from completing the most basic regime in her fitness repertoire and as tears ran down her cheeks, his hitherto coolly professional demeanor cracked and he'd taken her in his arms and rocked her like a baby, soothing her as best he could. When a splash on her singlet revealed his own tears, they ended up laughing and crying in each other's arms, sitting on the polished wooden floor of the gym, and Julia gradually learned from him his own story of injury and bewilderment.

When the door to the consulting room squeaked and a dark face peered around it, Greg beckoned. "Ray, just the bloke we need. Bring some tissues, will you, love?" A moment later, Ray Freeman, former U.S. Open finalist and now Kurrunulla Lodge's resident medic, unself-consciously joined them on the floor.

"It's about time you met my better half, Julia," Greg had said. "Ray, meet my good mate and fellow wreck, Julia Ross."

Ray handed over a wad of tissues and planted a kiss on Julia's wet cheek. "Heard a lot about you," he said, giving her free hand a firm squeeze.

In a haze of tears, laughter and nose blowing, Julia took in the mop of loosely curled black hair and the startling bright hazel eyes in a wide, pale brown-skinned face and realized she had met not only her first Aborigine, but her first gay Aboriginal champion athlete and doctor.

"Are you . . . ?" She stopped and blushed, looking from one smiling face to the other.

Greg grinned and helped her out. "We met at Roland Garros," he explained. "I hate clay and didn't get past the opening round and he came unstuck to a nobody in the second, so we probably would never have got together if it wasn't for Paris."

"So how come ..." Julia gestured around at the expensively kitted out gym.

"I broke both my knees in a car accident. And he wanted to finish medicine, you know? So we decided on this."

Julia nodded. "How wonderful — for you both."

It was Ray's turn to grin. "Yeah, and we owe it all to these." He gave one of Greg's horrifically scarred knees an affectionate stroke.

Greg nodded. "I didn't think so at the time, but they're a blessing in disguise." He held up his finger as Julia opened her mouth, where a question was forming. "I'm not saying I'm glad I was hit by a car. But *now* I'm not sorry about the way it changed my life. It needn't be all bad, you know."

"So what's with the blubbing, then, bro?" Ray wiped his finger across Greg's wet cheek. "She upsetting you? Want me to sort her out?"

Greg grinned and kissed the sturdy brown hand. "Reckon we both need sorting out, love. She's feeling a bit sorry for herself and I ended up feeling a bit sorry for myself, too."

Ray shook his head and sighed. "Jeez, I dunno. Can't leave you alone for five minutes and the sky falls in." He laid his hand on Julia's neatly scarred knee. "How's it going then, eh?"

Before Julia could speak, Greg answered for her. "She's doing brilliantly. I've never seen anyone recover so quickly. But I don't think her knee's the only problem. I think there's heart trouble, too."

Ray looked startled, then Greg winked at him and rolled his eyes and Ray nodded. "Okay, so who is it?"

Julia began to splutter a protest, but the encircling brown and bronze arms playfully bore down on her.

"I think it's trouble," Greg said earnestly. "I think she's fallen for Eliot."

"I haven't. I mean, *No,* I have *not!* I . . . This is . . ." She faltered in the gaze of their knowing eyes. "Okay, okay. I think she's pretty fabulous, I admit. And Morgan is just the best kid — and I don't even *like* kids! And Eliot's been wonderful to me. This time has been so . . ." She shook her head, unable to express her pleasure. "And . . ." Again she faltered as the grins on the faces of the two men slowly faded to looks of concern.

"What're you looking at me like that for?" she asked, disconcerted by the obvious change in the atmosphere.

Ray looked at Greg who nodded and Ray took Julia's hand in both his. "I've known Eliot a long time," he began gently. "Greg's known her even longer. He was at school with her brother. And we've known Jack Barron as long as she has." He stopped and sighed, as if trying to pick his words before going on. "Put it this way: Eliot's been a good wife to Jack even though the bastard doesn't deserve her. And she's a Bancroft and she . . . what would you say, Greg?"

"She isn't allowed to forget it. And so far, she hasn't," Greg offered.

Ray nodded. "That's about it, I know she likes you a lot 'cause Greg's told me how she is with you.

But you've gotta know that she's carrying some awful heavy baggage. Know what I mean?"

Julia nodded. "I met her sister this morning."

Greg snorted. "Daphne? That monster."

Ray nodded agreement and went on. "She's more than that, Greg. Remember how she was about Eliot coming with us to Mardi Gras?"

Greg rolled his eyes at the memory. "God, yes." He laughed. "I thought ol' Daphers and Jack were going to call the cops!"

"Yeah, and that's one more thing," Ray said somberly. "Jack hates queers — probably even more than he hates Abos. He doesn't say so out loud, but you can smell it on him. And I know Greg thinks I'm hard on him but I reckon you can smell meanness on him too. Real deep down rotten meanness. Do you get my drift?"

Julia nodded. "I think so. But I don't understand — I mean, he seems happy for them to come to New York with me."

Greg shrugged. "Why not? He's very ambitious for Morgan. Too ambitious, to tell the truth. And you're famous. Jack is very ambitious for Jack, too. If you ever saw him with Eliot's father you'd see that. I bet for him being connected with Julia Ross, Wimbledon champ and most famous player in the world actually cancels out that you're also Julia Ross, dirty lesbian dyke bitch whore — and whatever else he calls you when he's talking to his grubby mates."

Julia shuddered and shook herself, as if to throw off the unpleasant imagery that had suddenly invaded the room. "Jeez," she said softly. "I had no idea. Eliot hasn't said anything."

"She wouldn't," said Greg. "She's loyal to a fault and her way of dealing with him and every other nastiness in that family is to try to keep everybody happy — often at her own cost, I might add."

"Right." Julia took a deep breath and blew her nose one last time. "That's settled all that, then." She grinned brightly at Greg. "Let's finish up. Morgan's music lesson will be over any minute." She got to her feet and flexed her shoulders. "You two are great guys," she said, holding out her hands to them. "You're something else I can be grateful to Eliot for."

Greg and Ray stood, took her hands and drew her into a double cuddle. "Whatever we can do, you know all you gotta do is whistle," said Ray.

Julia nodded, not trusting herself to speak, and hugged each man in turn; then the door burst open and in flew Morgan, all bright eyes, newly gappy smile and pure adoration for Julia.

"Hi Greg! Hi Ray! Hi Julia! Look, my front tooth came out!" She stuck her tongue pinkly in the space.

"How did that happen?" Ray asked, swinging her into his arms.

"I wiggled it with my tongue and then it was bleeding and then it was hanging only on a thread of skin and then —"

"Stop!" Julia and Greg chorused simultaneously. "We'll be sick!"

"Quick!" Greg said. "Somebody call the tooth fairy and give this horrible child her two bucks."

"Two? Mum said I might get one if I'm lucky!" Morgan's eyes sparkled.

"That's inflation for you, kiddo. Now why don't you run along and take this friend of yours with you. Some of us have work to do."

"Okay, come on, Julia. I think we should rescue Mum from Aunt Daphne."

"Great idea, Morgan." Ray kissed the top of her curly head. "See you."

But Eliot didn't need rescuing from her sister, as Julia and Morgan discovered on their return to the empty house. Instead, a note on the kitchen counter simply read, "Back in a while. Don't wait lunch." Whether it was terse or merely simple and to the point, Julia couldn't decide. Then Morgan's suggestion that they walk down to the village for a burger and a swim offered a welcome distraction and she agreed, despite the heat.

A few hours later, it was Eliot's turn to wonder at the two-sentence note written, in Morgan's hand, on the back of her own message: "Gone for lunch. See you." Eliot frowned and momentarily felt at a loss. Instead of a solace, her visit to Rachel Taylor had been disconcerting and, without consciously anticipating it, she'd been looking forward to the boisterous, uncomplicated presence of her daughter and Julia. The house — once her tranquil and comforting retreat and nowadays so full of disheveled and noisy life — felt merely empty. It wasn't until the phone rang with an invitation from Ray to join them all at Kurrunulla Lodge for his special barbecued duck and pork that she was able to settle in the studio to an hour of therapeutically methodical brush-cleaning.

"So, where've you been sweetie?" Rachel Taylor's voice had been even more sardonically plummy English than usual. "No time for your old pals, hmmm?" Nevertheless, she'd swept Eliot into a sweet, flower-scented embrace and then examined her face carefully. "So. Tell all. Are the rumors just rumors or are they *dreadful* rumors?"

Eliot was disconcerted, as ever, by her friend's directness. The actress had been married to Todd Black, Aussie screen hunk, for fifteen years, but she could still play the bossy, demanding English upper-class lady when it came to interrogation.

"What do you mean?" Eliot asked, and knew she sounded unconvincing. "I mean, what's the difference?"

"Rumors, my darling, are delicious but ultimately disappointing because they turn out to be untrue. *Dreadful* rumors are the real thing."

Eliot pursed her lips. "Well, it depends on what you've heard."

Rachel threw back her head and laughed, displaying a mouthful of famous teeth and a healthy pink tongue. She laced her arm through her friend's and gave her a little tug. "Come with me, darling, into my parlor. I think you have *lots* to tell me."

Reluctantly, but with unspoken relief, Eliot allowed herself to be drawn through the glamorous expanses of the Taylor-Black residence. It was, in effect, a beautiful theatrical setting for two beautiful theatrical people. Rachel spent little time in it — unless she and Todd were being photographed for some admiring publication or another. Instead, Rachel moved right on through to the luxuriant jungle of a lovingly cultivated semi-tropical garden and beyond to where the property's original one-room shack still stood — what Rachel chose to call her parlor.

It was where Rachel conducted her "private life" — the discreet affairs with a succession of actors and actresses with whom she might be working at any given time. Many years before, after Rachel and Todd had dazzled the opening night of one of her first solo exhibitions by buying the two main canvases, it had been Eliot's turn to be adored for a couple of months; these days their friendship was light-years beyond that fleeting passion and Eliot could enjoy her friend and their intimacy without the emotional rollercoaster that had made the affair so exhilarating and exhausting.

And she also understood, without pain, how Rachel's affairs and the old shack were, in reality, nothing more than her bulwark against the goldfish-bowl existence that had engulfed the Taylor-Todds. "I don't give a bugger about being famous and this silly great mansion, darling. It's a pain in the neck, to be honest. But it's Todd's antidote to growing up dirt poor and drought-stricken on a farm somewhere out there." And she'd waved her elegant hand in a vaguely westward direction. Nonetheless, as Rachel had once said to Eliot in the middle of a glittering party in the big house, "It's hell, darling, but a very comfortable hell and if it makes that sweet man feel better — then so be it."

On that occasion. she'd popped another Bollinger cork. Today, however, Rachel seemed to sense that something less effervescent was required. While Eliot admired a new and grotesque ancient tribal carving, Rachel rummaged among the bottles in the colossal fridge which dominated the shack's back veranda and returned triumphant, clutching two icy bottles of beer.

The two women settled themselves into the depths of an old, soft leather sofa, drinks in hand, and Rachel waited, an expression of probing expectancy on her face. Finally, Eliot's small attempt at composure melted in the heat of her gaze and she sighed and gazed into the pale gold bubbles and said, "So what are the rumors, Rach?"

"Ah. Well. It depends who you're talking to. Let's see . . ." She counted on her fingers, "I've been told — categorically — that you're having an affair with Julia Ross. That you're *not* having an affair with Julia Ross. That Julia Ross has retired and is coaching Morgan to be the youngest-ever Wimbledon champion. That you have been having an affair with Julia Ross for years. And . . ." She paused and her flippant mien underwent a subtle change. "That you and Jack are getting divorced and he's going to make sure he gets custody of Morgan." As she ticked off the last item on her little finger she turned wide eyes on Eliot. "Now, you know I don't give a bugger what you get up to, darling, but I don't like the sound of the last bit. And I do think you might have at least rung me instead of just disappearing into your love nest."

Eliot gulped on a mouthful of throat-freezing froth and coughed violently. Her stomach had already turned over three times. "Christ, Rach." She coughed again. "What are you talking about. I mean, you don't believe it, do you?"

Rachel's face remained neutral. "Which bit did you have in mind?" she asked, upending her own bottle in a long, smooth gurgle.

"Any of it — I — look, I'm sorry I haven't been 'round..."

"Haven't even rung, darling. You've been here weeks and you haven't rung once. It's odd, you have to admit. And look at it from my point of view. *Everyone* — and I mean everyone — has been ringing me and was I supposed to humiliate myself? *Humiliate* myself — and confess that I didn't have a bloody clue? Of course, I didn't, I simply made up some even juicier items and passed them on instead."

Despite the mix of cold beer, unease and near panic in her stomach, Eliot laughed. "Rachel, you're awful. All you mind about is that your reputation as the CIA of social Sydney is on the line."

Rachel sighed dramatically and rolled her eyes heavenward. "Well, there *is* that side to it, of course, but —" She stopped and took Eliot's hand. There was no trace of humor in her face. "This does sound pretty bloody sticky, darling. I mean, you have got that gorgeous creature living practically under your roof, haven't you?"

"She's at Kurrunulla Lodge ... but she is at the house a fair bit. There's a good reason ..."

Rachel held up her hand and shook her head. "Perception, darling, perception. Who gives a stuff about the reason? Who gives a bugger about the truth. The *perception* is that you have the world's most famous lesbian over for tea and cucumber sandwiches and I'm afraid that makes you just about married to her."

"Rachel! Don't be ridiculous."

Rachel sighed. "I'm not being ridiculous, darling, and you should damn well realize it. You *know* how these things work. God, how long have you known me? I trip in my stupid, bloody silly sandals leaving a bloody silly restaurant and suddenly I'm a roaring drunk. It took me eighteen grand — *eighteen bloody grand* — and a pack of lawyers to sort that one out and I *know* there are still some stupid bastards who look at me and wonder whether I can learn my bloody lines anymore — not that you'd want to learn some of the crap I'm offered these days. Christ, did I tell you about the film script . . ." She caught Eliot's half-smothered grin and slapped her forehead with her hand. "Oh god, I remember, we're supposed to be talking about you. 'Nother beer?"

Eliot shook her head and waggled the half-full bottle. "I'm fine." While Rachel strode off to ransack the fridge Eliot lay back in the sofa's depths and stared at the patterns in the aged pressed-tin ceiling, trying to gather herself from the maelstrom of conflicting emotions and thoughts that Rachel had released. But before she had even begun to order her thinking, her friend was back.

"Darling, sometimes you are so impossibly naïve, it's unbelievable."

Eliot shrugged, her feelings a little ruffled. "Perhaps that's an overly cynical view, Rachel," she said sharply. "The thing is, I am not having an affair — with anybody." She ignored Rachel's muttered, "Pity," and went on firmly, "Julia's become a good friend to

Morgan and me, and Jack and I haven't mentioned divorce."

Again Rachel muttered, "Pity," then frowned and shook her head. "But I don't understand how you came to be harboring this extraordinary creature under your very own roof, Eliot. You *have* to explain."

Eliot shrugged. "It was Morgan, really. Somehow or other, after we first met her, she and Julia sort of hit it off and I think Julia really enjoyed her . . ." She shrugged. "I don't know. Her enthusiasm, maybe, or simply that Morgan just adores her and is not over-awed by her either. I think it was probably quite refreshing." She shook her head. "Somehow or other, when the Denvers — they were her sort of entourage — deserted, it just kind of happened. Greg and Ray have also been part of this, by the way, but really, it's mainly Morgan."

Rachel's eyebrows shot up and she choked theatrically on a swig of beer. "Good heavens. Here I am rejoicing that you seem to have got out from under the thumb of that beastly Jack and now I find you're being bossed around by that seven-year-old tyrant."

"Don't be silly, Rachel. It's not like that."

Rachel patted her hand soothingly. "I'm teasing you horribly, darling. Take no notice. I certainly shan't."

Eliot grinned. "Good. Well I hope you'll just tell any of our so-called friends that these rumors are just that. In any case, Julia has invited us to New York with her and we're going on Friday, which is partly why I came over."

If Eliot had smacked Rachel on the tip of her

perfect nose the actress couldn't have looked more startled. After a long and goggle-eyed minute during which Eliot tried to drain her bottle without having it trickle down her chin, Rachel finally found her voice.

"You're going to New York — *who's* going to New York? Is Jack going?"

Eliot shook her head and said matter-of-factly, "Jack's taking his floozy to Hong Kong."

This time Rachel's face indicated that a blow to the solar plexus couldn't have produced a bigger shock.

"I beg your pardon?" she said faintly.

Eliot smiled. "Don't tell me the rumor mill has missed *that* one?"

Rachel took a long pull at her beer then set it down with exaggerated attention on a small, ornately carved Indian table. She seemed to be carefully considering what to say next and when she finally looked at Eliot, there was no frivolity in her eyes. "This isn't the first time, is it?"

Eliot pursed her lips and shook her head. "No, but he's never done anything like this before — I mean an extended trip — it's just been afternoons in hotels and the odd night in the Blue Mountains. You know — the usual."

Rachel grimaced and her grin was restored. "God save me from ever falling for anybody — man or woman — who wants to take me to the Blue Mountains. It's almost as bad as wearing brown socks and open-toed sandals."

Eliot shuddered. "Don't. What a horrible thought."

Rachel looked grim again. "Yes, but this is even more horrible. Are you sure?"

"As sure as I can without actually catching them at it."

Rachel shuddered. "Ugh. Stop. Who is it?"

"She's twenty-three and a junior in his chambers." Eliot ignored Rachel's violent gagging sounds. "I think she's called Tanya or Tonya." The gagging noises were louder. "And that's about it. The main thing is, it means Morgan and I can go to New York with Julia."

Rachel gasped, as if reminded of the real meat in the deliciously extraordinary sandwich she was being offered by her friend. "You're serious?" she croaked.

Eliot patiently explained to the stubbornly unsporty Rachel the significance of psychological preparation to the well-being of a top tennis player and how Morgan seemed to be a key factor in Julia's immediate recovery. Her friend's face ran the gamut of emotional responses until it finally settled into plainly pole-axed.

"My god," she finally gasped in an uncharacteristically strangled voice. "No wonder you haven't phoned me. But you still haven't told me whether you've done it yet . . ."

It was Eliot's turn to look startled. "Done it?"

Rachel snorted and her dramatic eyebrows emphasized her exasperation. "Eliot! You've obviously got the screaming hots for the girl. So have you been to bed with her yet?"

"Certainly not. I don't . . . I mean . . . You don't understand. We're just good friends."

And through Rachel's raucous laughter, Eliot heard her own words, mocking her and telling her plainly of their hollowness. She got up and moved about the room, unwilling to watch Rachel's unrestrained amusement and unable to respond. She picked up and replaced *objet* after *objet*, refusing to look at her friend and unequipped to find a way out of the predicament in which she seemed to have landed.

Finally, Rachel stopped laughing, a fresh outburst of giggles petered out, and she blew her nose vigorously on a large and beautiful silk paisley handkerchief; then she patted the sofa. "Come. Sit down, darling," she said in a tender voice. "Let's get to the bottom of this. I know you want me to."

Eliot turned to her friend, bewildered. "I don't understand, Rachel," she said softly. "I'm sorry I haven't been over, but I didn't know what to say." Eliot looked down at her feet. "We've been ..." She paused and frowned. "It's been difficult with her injury and Greg's therapy regime and ..."

Rachel smiled and the sardonic twist was back. "And you've been happy in your love nest."

Eliot's eyes were anguished. "We — I — we haven't. I don't know what's going on, Rachel. I mean, I know you and I ... but I've never really thought I was a lesbian."

Rachel frowned. "I suspect I should probably be insulted, but it's such a ridiculous statement, I don't think I can be bothered."

Eliot was on her feet again, pacing the room. "I didn't mean, oh god, you know I love you, I always will but, I mean, it's years and ..." She dragged her hands through her hair in a gesture of furious confusion. "Am I going crazy? Daphne and Jack both think I'm menopausal and ought to have some hormones or something."

"Darling! The last thing you need is more hormones. I think that's your problem — raging lustful teenage-style hormones. And if you're crazy, it's because you're crazy about that gorgeous creature and you should probably be doing something about it. Menopause! Ha! Not all of us turn into shriveled old prunes just because we don't need tampons anymore. Some of us just need something delicious to munch on."

"Rachel!" Eliot's upwelling of laughter was also, she recognized, an upwelling of relief, and her friend looked gratified that the cycle of anxiety seemed to be broken.

"For God's sake come and sit down and stop looking as if doomsday is scheduled for next Tuesday."

Eliot grinned and sat. "Friday, actually. We're supposed to be going on Friday."

Rachel rolled her eyes. "Well, at least you haven't lost your sense of humor. Now, tell me — really tell me — what the hell is going on."

CHAPTER FIVE

Thinking it over later, Julia realized that the frantic forty-eight hours following Daphne's headlong departure from the Bancroft house and Eliot's long and ultimately therapeutic afternoon with Rachel Taylor had made it impossible for her to talk to Eliot about anything other than the practical questions and answers of imminent leaving. And even as they lay snug in reclining seats in the high-pitched hissing quiet of the jumbo jet's nose cabin, they had Morgan, quite literally, between them.

Eliot had returned that afternoon late and unexplained from "just seeing an old friend," to find Julia and Morgan playing air guitar to Deep Purple. She'd laughed and clapped at their efforts. Nevertheless, Julia had felt instantly foolish and the CD was stopped in mid-screaming riff, despite Eliot's protests. Then the phone had rung and when Eliot answered and said, brightly, "Jack!" Julia knew that when she turned back to them, her eyes would be just slightly unnerving.

It was a look Morgan had identified and explained some days earlier. They had been shopping at the local surf gear store and had been sprung by a newspaper photographer. At Julia's instigation, she and Morgan acted up with a couple of boogie boards until Eliot had come into the shop through the rapidly gathered throng and said, "Please stop it," in a quietly modulated but razor-sharp tone. Startled, Julia glanced at her and had seen, for the first time, a glittering chill in the hazel eyes; then Eliot turned on her heel and walked out of the shop and disappeared.

Julia and Morgan quietly replaced the boards. Julia told the photographer she'd had enough and signed the credit card slip for her purchases. On the way back to the car they discussed being bratty — as Morgan put it.

"Mum doesn't like it when I'm bratty," Morgan said and sighed melodramatically. "I think we were being bratty in the shop."

Julia listened attentively to this observation and quizzed Morgan on exactly what this meant. "Did we really tick her off?"

Morgan sighed. "I'm afraid so. She doesn't think you should do silly things in public."

Julia nodded. "She's big on dignity, your mom. It's good. I forget."

Morgan nodded earnestly. "Me too. But I can give you lots of tips on how to avoid Mum's snake eyes."

"Snake eyes?"

"Yes, when she gets really mad her eyes go like this." Morgan demonstrated a glittery, cold-eyed look that was by then eerily familiar. "And her eyes go all sharp and icy and really scary. And she doesn't say much, but boy, is it *fierce!*"

Julia grinned and nodded, understanding perfectly Morgan's description of Eliot's shiver-inducing manner. "Does she ever whack you?"

Morgan looked shocked. "Like, hit me?" Her expression was horrified and she shook her head vehemently. "No! But once when Aunt Verity did Mum made her nose bleed. It was really cool."

They were still laughing as they reached the car, to find Eliot looking, Julia thought, slightly sheepish. "Sorry I was a grouch," she'd said. And the snake eyes were gone.

The dreaded look returned that afternoon when Eliot handed over the phone to Morgan and said, "Your father wants to talk to you." She walked out onto the veranda and sat on the low bench that afforded the best view of the ocean beyond the headland. After a few minutes, Julia left Morgan chirruping happily and followed her.

"You okay?" she asked tentatively, wary of the sudden storms that could blow up and obscure Eliot's usual serenity.

"Jack will be seeing us off at the airport tomorrow," she said in a flat and emotionless voice. "He'll take care of the car for me."

Julia nodded slowly, trying to feel her way into Eliot's dramatically changed mood. "That's nice. So I guess I'll get to meet him."

Eliot's eyebrows rose. "I've no doubt that's why he's taking time from his busy schedule."

Julia hesitated, her stomach in a knot of apprehension, then she took a deep breath and said, "Do you still love him?"

The half sob, half sigh that rocked Eliot's body wrenched at Julia's heart, but she sat helpless and still, even though she would have put her arms around those vulnerable shoulders.

"Love him?" Eliot shook her head. "I don't think I know what that means anymore." She leaned back, her hands clasped about her right knee, and stared into the luminous early evening sky.

"I love what we used to have. At least, what I *think* we used to have." She turned and smiled brightly at Julia. "It's hard to tell. I sometimes wonder whether I was fooling myself all along. I mean, for instance, I know Jack likes to be much more sociable than I do. So maybe he was always bored out of his mind." She half laughed, "And I've never been much good at the social wifely duties. Perhaps I'm being unfair to him."

"How so?" Julia's tone was protective, defiant. "You're good company; you're great to be with — ask Greg, ask Ray." She paused. "Ask me."

Eliot smiled This time it was pure warmth, the diffidence gone, but lurking behind the blue eyes, Julia could see uncertainty. Her desire to touch Eliot, to hold her close and reassure her, to keep her fears at bay, was almost overwhelming. But she sat still, immobilized by the possibility that she might, by precipitate action, lose this precious friendship that she had achieved.

"Speaking of Greg and Ray, we should be thinking about dinner. There's a fish that needs attention." Eliot's voice was firm and light, similar to the squeeze she gave Julia's arm. "You're a great comfort," she said softly. "I do appreciate it." And she was gone, leaving Julia to fantasize about placing her own hand over Eliot's and leaning forward to touch her lips to Eliot's finely etched wide pink mouth.

When Julia finally gave up her fool's quest, Morgan had disappeared to the bathroom and Eliot was busy behind the kitchen counter. Her demeanor was affectionate but distracted by the need to prepare the substantial king fish that Ray had brought straight from his favorite fishing spot earlier in the day. With her long cream-colored linen shorts and pink T-shirt protected by an apron, Eliot frowned as she methodically chunked a sharp cleaver in a see-saw motion through a mound of green leaves whose pungent perfume filled the warm air.

Julia settled herself on a high stool, carefully placing her leg in its newly and increasingly flexible bent position. "That smells great. What is it?"

"Coriander. You'd know it as cilantro, I think."

"Ah. I've heard of it. So what are you going to do with it?"

"Stuff the fish with a mixture of coriander, garlic, shredded ginger and sweet chili sauce, wrap it in paperbark, and Ray's going to cook it in hot coals in the sand. How does that sound?"

Julia grinned, "Fabulous. Like the kind of thing they show you on *Come to Australia* videos."

"I have to admit it's our little party piece. We did it once when Jack had his snotty legal types here and a visiting English high court judge. They were quite staggered by the white honky and her Man Friday cooking on the beach."

Julia frowned. "Mostly you sound sad, but that sounds angry."

"I'm sorry. Sheer self-indulgence. Forgive me."

Julia bit her tongue on the response that she would probably forgive Eliot anything and, instead, offered to open a bottle of wine.

The lightly chilled Ashton Hills pinot noir turned out to be the first of many bottles whose cork was pulled that night and it was an unusually subdued Julia who watched, from behind protective dark glasses, Eliot's car draw up in front of Kurrunulla Lodge next morning. But Morgan's bubbling excitement turned the somewhat head-achey leave-taking into an effervescent and joyous occasion.

Greg and Ray loaded Julia's bags and while Greg quietly gave her last-minute advice and instructions, Ray strolled with Eliot to the carp pool, his arm about her waist, their heads close together. Julia watched them even as she listened intently to Greg. Eliot, a headache admitted and hidden behind huge sunglasses, was still impossibly elegant in a soft, stone-colored linen suit that Julia's increasingly knowledgeable eye guessed as Armani. She was talking urgently to her friend who was grinning and shaking his head as they turned and came back toward the car.

Ray stuck his hand out to Julia and shook it as he enveloped her in a hug. "You go well now, sister-girl," he said to Julia, "and look out for my little sisters, eh?"

"I'll do that Ray, and thanks a million for saving my bacon."

Ray wrinkled his wide brown nose. "No worries. You get on the blower if you need to. Okay?"

Greg put his arm about her shoulders. "That's for certain, Julia. I want a promise. Any problems, ring, anytime. Promise?"

Julia nodded and swallowed the rising lump in her throat. "I promise." And they were on their way.

They drove in a companionable silence broken only by the rhythmic sussurations in the back seat from Morgan's Walkman. They were crawling in the slow traffic that, according to a resigned Eliot, seemed permanently attracted to the road around Botany Bay. When the car phone rang, Eliot hit the remote button and Julia knew instinctively who it was as assertive but well-modulated tones filled the air. Perhaps too, it was the incessant use of endearments that, she thought scornfully, could only be deliberate. From everything she knew of the Bancroft-Barron marriage, it didn't ring true that "darling" should represent almost every other word of the short, one-sided conversation that also told them he was running a little late.

Nevertheless, at the terminal Jack appeared like a knight in pin-striped armor, striding across the concourse wearing his success and handsome masculinity like weapons of war. He was more than striking, Julia saw, and he was powerful in a way that went beyond physical. She recalled Ray's warning about his "deep down dark meanness" and wondered whether it might be more the fanciful description of a jealous and protective male than an entirely accurate and dispassionate summation. Despite her own wariness she found herself warming to Jack's dazzling smile and genial two-handed handshake.

"Great to meet you, at last!" His voice was as empathic as his lingering handclasp, and Julia saw that his eyes were everywhere as he checked her out minutely. "Eliot has told me so much about you, haven't you, darling?" Belatedly he gave his wife a fleeting kiss, leaning from the waist so that his lips and her cheek were their only point of contact. Then he turned his attention to Morgan and hugged her and gave her a smacking kiss on the cheek.

Eliot, Julia noticed, instantly fell into a state of passive, faintly smiling semi-animation as Jack took over the business of checking them in and dealing with the bags. Whatever Eliot's emotions were, they were impossible to gauge, and Julia stood back and allowed Jack to do as he wished, sensing in him a need to show her that he was still in charge of his family and that his wife still relied on him. And at the same time, his friendliness toward his wife's famous friend was in equal parts disarming and suspect.

Julia felt herself to be drawn to him and at once distinctly circumspect as he unconsciously demonstrated his cocksure maleness. It was not a battlefield upon which she had any intention of setting foot; and she merely smiled gratefully at his assurance while trying to recall how many times in the past ten years she had successfully negotiated herself into and out of airports around the world. It was a bit like counting sheep and, when Morgan finally tugged her arm and said hadn't she heard, it was time to go through the barrier to the Customs and Immigration hall, she realized it had had the same effect.

Hours into the flight, after Morgan finally tired of her personal video screen and snuggled down into her blankets, Julia ordered champagne. When the flight attendant completed his serving rites and left them, Julia held up her glass to Eliot. "Thank you for being a terrific friend."

Eliot chinked her glass against Julia's and smiled for the first time in hours.

"Thank you too," she said wearily. "Especially for the airport."

Julia frowned. "What do you mean?"

"Jack. Thank you for not taking him on."

So she had noticed, had known, had sensed the undercurrent. And three hours later, it was still on her mind. Julia smiled wryly. "I suppose there's no point saying, 'I don't know what you mean'?"

Eliot shook her head and almost grinned. "No point at all. He wanted to show you who's boss. You knew that."

"Ah, well. No prisoners taken and no injuries sustained. Actually, I rather liked him."

Eliot nodded and said, in neutral tones, "He's very likable."

In silence they drank champagne. Then Julia took a deep breath and asked, "I'd give a lot to know what you've been thinking, or what you felt about all that."

Eliot smiled and held out her glass. "It won't cost much, just a top-up." Julia filled her glass then watched Eliot stare fixedly at the rising strings of bubbles as she said slowly and clearly, as if — like the bubbles — the thoughts were already formed and ready to appear, "I watched him come marching over to us and I waited for some kind of response in me, but there was none. Believe it or not, in itself that was rather exciting."

Julia said nothing, waiting instead for Eliot to continue her thoughts.

Eliot frowned with the effort of analyzing her feelings. "It registered in my mind" — abstractedly she touched her forehead, then her belly — "rather than viscerally." After a long pause, she came back to Julia from the champagne-bubble reverie. "I think I'm finally unmoved by him, and you have to understand that he's dominated my life for more than fifteen years."

Julia held out her glass. "Perhaps you should drink to that — to the end of domination, I mean."

After a fleeting hesitation Eliot returned the toast. From that point, as the crystal flutes touched, it seemed to Julia that Jack Barron receded as fast as the Australian coastline while the Boeing hummed eastward across the Pacific.

Transferring to the New York flight in Los Angeles, a camera flash was the first and belated indication that Julia had been recognized by an opportunistic papparazzi. Without hesitation and instinctively, Eliot dropped her hand onto Morgan's shoulder and steered her away, but not before the flash had caught the trio in a photograph that made the gossip rags within three days.

Julia spluttered over her coffee cup. "Oh god, listen to this. 'Julia Ross and mystery gal pal en route for New York hideaway.' " Julia read aloud in a breathless TV announcer's voice as they sat at breakfast in the kitchen of her apartment. She passed the magazine to Eliot who, tight-lipped, glanced at the page. Morgan, meanwhile, munched enthusiastically on her newly discovered American cereal.

"The big mystery, gal pal," Julia went on mischievously, "is how in hell you managed to look so good after fourteen hours in a plane. *That* is a mystery worth solving and marketing."

But Eliot was clearly not amused. Indeed, when she looked up from the magazine there was something close to fear in her eyes. In response to Morgan's muffled request through a mouthful of crunchy stuff, "Let's see, Mum, let's see," she passed it to her daughter without a word and got up from the table.

"I'm going for a run. I'll see you later," she said to the room at large, her voice pinched and tense, then she was gone into the chilly morning before Julia could even begin to intervene.

Since their arrival Julia's morning schedules were hectic, split between the phone, business meetings, appointments with medical specialists and business advisors. Morgan's was no less so as she was caught up in the whirl of coaching and lessons that Julia's people had organized for her. Each day, the two moved from session to session and from expert to expert, leaving Eliot to her own devices. She read, walked in Central Park, prowled the museums and once or twice, went to watch either Julia or Morgan. But as she sat in the cafe at the Museum of Modern Art with her second cup of coffee, she knew herself to be restless and uneasy with her own company. It was an alien sensation and served to magnify the specters and gremlins that now seemed to haunt what had previously been easy solitude.

After just two days of this new kind of troubled loneliness, surrounded by the atmosphere of ceaseless activity, and a city whose beauty she could scarcely bear to acknowledge, she became reluctantly infected with the enthusiasm and, almost in defense, began tennis lessons, weights and endless meditative laps of the tropically heated pool in the basement of their building. It had taken just over a week and she was feeling physically almost buoyant enough to leave her ever-present unease behind. Just as often as she walked, she now ran.

This morning, of the "gal pal" snap, despite flutters of unidentifiable panic in the pit of her stomach, she enjoyed the awareness of physical quickening as she pounded the now-familiar winding track through Central Park. And with the tangible ease came also mental clarity, and her thoughts began to coalesce around the flutters of apprehension in her gut. Why had the photo knocked her so badly off balance? she wondered, passing a puffing figure she belatedly recognized as one of her favorite movie stars. What was wrong with the picture, aside from the stupid insinuation of the caption? She ran on, adrenaline fueling the rhythm of her long, easy stride and, despite the internal disquiet, enhancing the glorious feeling of almost flying over the ground. Then, in an unheralded flash, with the growing exhilaration came lucidity and a calm and inexorable interior voice.

It's because I like the photograph, said the voice. *It's because I find it exciting seeing us like that — together, framed, captured — I* like *the expression on Julia's face as she looked at me. I* like *that the camera caught it. That nobody can take it away from me. And it's there, for all time, no matter what. I like it. I like it. I like it.*

She hit the top of a crest and the vivid blue late-winter-almost-spring sky burst above her and tears of sheer energy-enriched euphoria and intense cold pricked her eyes. She paused momentarily, enjoying the dramatic cityscape and the sparkling response bursting like fireworks from her nerve endings. But just as quickly the elation turned, like a roller coaster, dropping her into despair as she ran on, proficiently and automatically loping and swerving down the twists and turns of the track.

What am I doing? What am I going to do? Where will this end? Jack will know. *He'll sense it. He'll see that picture and he'll* know. *Know what? Know what?*

There was no hiding place from the knowledge that flooded from her unconscious to the forefront of her mind. The core reason for her apprehension became clear and the fright of it set wings to her heels. She ran on, her stride lengthening with each acknowledgment of recognition, so that hills and outcrops passed by in a blur of bare tree trunks and undulating parkland. Her breath smoked the wintry air in pulsing gusts and her cheeks burned with the cold as she at last admitted the cause of her discomfiture.

Yet, even as her thoughts turned to Julia, she felt another and more alarming burn start deep inside in places untouched in years. The faster she ran, the more clearly she could feel and reluctantly grasp the origin of the new radiance that had entered her body and her life. And she began to accept that she couldn't out-run it even as her lungs and heart felt as if they might burst from her body with her exertion.

"Whoa!"

Eliot felt rather than heard Julia's laughing command as she stood on the track in front of her. Sheer momentum carried her yards past and then she pulled up, legs trembling, heart pounding, sweat streaming down the small of her back, her breath tearing at the air.

"Hey, you trying to beat the world record or you just seen a bear?"

Eliot could barely speak. "Bears? There are *bears?*"

Julia laughed and shook her head. "I don't think so. But I can't think of anything else that would make you go so fast." She checked the complicated watch on her wrist. "Have you just done the three-mile track?"

Eliot nodded, wiping her sleeve roughly across her forehead and unable to suppress a smug grin as Julia's eyes widened.

"The whole track — the entire three miles?"

Eliot nodded again. "I ran. I didn't walk."

Julia laughed. "I *know*. And I think you've run something like six-minute miles!"

It was Eliot's turn to look surprised, then she shrugged and grinned. "I've been getting fitter."

"Fitter! My god, lady, I can't do six-minute miles —couldn't, I mean — Have you done this kind of thing before?"

"I was a long distance runner in high school." Eliot was pleased to notice through the two fingers placed on the thumping vein at the base of her neck, that her heart rate was already slowing.

"Uh huh. You are full of surprises, Eliot." They began walking away from the track toward Fifth Avenue and the smile left Julia's eyes. "But it doesn't really explain why you just took off like that. You okay?"

Eliot ran her fingers through her spiky, sweat-wet hair, scraped it back and wiped her face on her sleeve again. "Can we talk about this later?" she asked despairingly. "I . . ." Her shoulders lifted in a gesture of perplexity. "I need to think it out myself first."

Julia swallowed hard and her eyes were wide with apprehension and bewilderment, but she nodded and patted Eliot's arm comfortingly. "Sure. I've gotta go practice anyway." She began to turn away but Eliot reached out and stopped her.

"Morgan is going to do an art workshop this afternoon. Maybe we could take off somewhere. I *have* to talk to you."

Julia's eyes clouded with foreboding, but still she calmly nodded and smiled. "Sure. Whatever."

Eliot tightened her grip on Julia's arm. With her index finger she lightly touched the frown creasing the smooth skin between Julia's expressive dark eyebrows. "I'm not asking you to volunteer for the firing squad," she said gently.

Julia grimaced. "Well, in my experience, when somebody says 'I have to talk to you,' it's usually bad news."

Eliot smiled. "I'm sorry. I didn't mean it like that." Obeying an impulse, she leaned forward and lightly kissed Julia on the cheek, then she turned quickly away before she could act upon her second impulse.

For Julia, the rest of the morning was close to torture. She found it difficult to concentrate and her timing was off in everything she undertook. She knew that her progress had been extraordinary. She was aware of the amazed eyes of the therapists at the gym and the sidelong looks that followed her everywhere as she limped — less and less noticeably — about her self-imposed daily regime.

"Don't push yourself too hard," Eliot had begged the day she insisted on turning in her full leg brace for a cut-down version that simply supported the injured knee. And still she persevered, willfully exhilarated by each day's small accomplishment. But today, no matter how hard she focused on forming strokes or completing sets of exercises, Eliot's face and words kept intruding.

"I have to talk to you . . ." What could she mean? What could she want to say? There was something

about Eliot's cool elegance and quiet self-containment
that Julia found simultaneously appealing and for-
bidding. Eliot seemed able to make her feel the most
interesting person in the world one minute and
coltishly, doltishly childish the next. And it wasn't
anything that Eliot did, it was more the way Julia
found herself reacting.

Eliot was so unlike other women of her
acquaintance; the rest of the girls on tour, even the
older, retired players who were now the organizers
and officials, didn't have the qualities that Julia felt
herself both drawn to and intimidated by. It was a
curious situation to be in. The night before, as
Morgan and Eliot curled up in front of the television,
Julia had desperately wanted to explain it to Andrew
Connelli. His management consultancy had taken care
of her business arrangements since the morning she
had woken up, seven years earlier, to find she had
more than $8 million scattered in bank accounts
around the world and a queue of tax collectors with
their hands out from more countries than she could
even remember visiting, let alone playing in.

"What's going *on*, sweetie darling?" Andrew's voice
had drawled down the phone in his best reproduction
of a world-weary English queen, which he was.
"Gorgeous piccy of you in *True Lies*. But who's the
new squeeze? How dare you not tell me? How can I
pretend to know everything when I know absolutely
nothing. You bad, bad girl."

Julia glanced toward the sofa where nothing about
the two gleaming heads gave any indication that they
were interested in her conversation. Even so, she felt
herself blushing as his voice crackled into her ear;
hearing Eliot described as her "new squeeze" was

even more incongruous than the "gal pal" magazine caption. Although the frisson of excitement that fluttered inside gave the lie to what she said next.

"It's not what you think, Andy," she said with a coolness that she didn't feel.

"That's what they all say, darling." The voice crackled with more giggles. "So what am I *supposed* to think?"

"I want you to think about reorganizing my schedule," Julia said crisply, giving up on the idea of any kind of serious or confessional conversation with her business manager while Eliot and Morgan were in the same room. "I need a meeting with you, and not over the phone. Meanwhile, could you find out Billie Jean's commitments in the next couple of months. I'm going to do some work with her. And could you be a doll and get in touch with Martina and sound her out. She rang a few weeks back and offered to help. I need to call in the favor, if she can find the time." Julia smiled and wrinkled her nose at Morgan whose ears had pricked and whose head had swiveled at the mention of the magic names.

"Fine darling, fine. Just making a teeny weeny *aide memoire* for myself. You know how I hate having to remember things in my own head, and my diary is downstairs. Do you want to make a time now, or may I call you back?"

"Now, if you can bear the stairs, I'm not in my apartment at the moment."

There was a dramatic pause, then Andrew's carefully expelled breath hissed in her ear. "I see," he said, and his tone made it clear that whatever he thought he was seeing, the sight was lurid.

"Don't get the wrong end of the stick, Andy."

Julia's tone was quiet but menacing; Andrew Connelli knew only too well that Julia didn't take well to being teased and she knew he was squeezing his lips shut on a smart retort.

"Very well, darling. Why don't we just say ten tomorrow morning and I'll clear away whichever poor soul has legitimate claim to that appointment. Hmmm?"

"I'd be grateful."

"Very well, then. So I suppose I can wait for the gossip until I see you?" Julia did not respond. He sighed dramatically. "So. See you then, darling. *Ciao.*" And in his usual stylishly abrupt fashion, he was gone.

Now, as she returned, almost reluctantly, home from that appointment, she knew that Andrew's disappointment at the circumspect nature of the gossip she'd offered had much to do with Eliot's strange distraction and agitation of the early morning, and her own apprehension as to its possible real meaning.

In the hotel lobby she hesitated, torn between a longing to go to her own penthouse apartment and hide from what seemed likely to be the inevitable — ill — tidings, and an equally strong wish to see Eliot and to find out the worst before trepidation turned her mood to bleak. For the first time, she regretted that she lived in an apartment only ten floors above Eliot's hotel suite. Eventually she decided to get the bad news over first. From the bank of internal phones, she rang the Bancrofts' suite; her spirits leapt and sank simultaneously as Eliot answered, and then Julia was on her way up.

In the open doorway Eliot was waiting, wrapped in an all-enveloping white terrycloth robe, her hair wet and slicked back.

"I thought your meeting would be longer."

Julia shrugged. Business with Andrew was always businesslike, and in the face of Julia's anxious refusal to be forthcoming about her "squeeze" there had been no point staying longer. None of this was she about to tell Eliot.

"You wanted to talk, I thought I'd get back as soon as I could." Her heart quickened with a mixture of fright and anticipation as the angular and handsome face softened into a smile of tangible warmth and obvious pleasure.

"I must do something with my hair."

Julia waited, abruptly leaden with acquiescence as Eliot disappeared into the bedroom. She had not moved from the spot when Eliot returned, clad in sweatshirt and jeans with a towel wrapped turbanfashion around her head. She continued to wait as Eliot poured her a glass of orange juice, then she sipped at it slowly and wandered over to the stereo set-up. She pressed the start button and Mozart filled the jagged atmosphere with healing sound.

Julia finally found her tongue. "What's going on, Eliot?" she asked, her voice gentler than she had anticipated.

Eliot turned to her. This time her face revealed anxiety. After eight exquisitely excruciating bars of music, she finally spoke. "I think Morgan and I should go home early — tomorrow." She could not hold Julia's gaze. "I don't want you to feel deserted. Or that I don't care. But I really think we should go home."

Julia nodded, unable to think of any better response in the face of the numbness that swept through her.

Eliot went on, stumbling over her words. "I hate to do this to you right now, Julia. You've been wonderful to us, and I know Morgan loves it here — and loves you too, but . . ."

Still Julia waited, feeling the inertia of disappointment creeping through her limbs. She could think of nothing to say that would not sound trite. Eliot and Morgan were due to leave on Saturday, so what difference would a day make? It was absurd and dangerous that she should feel this degree of dependence. Better that they should leave now. She nodded but still said nothing, absentmindedly sipping at the orange juice.

"Speak to me," Eliot pleaded. "Say it's okay. It's not going to mess you around."

Somewhere inside, the careful indifference slipped and Julia banged down her glass and snorted. "What do you mean 'mess me around'? What do you mean 'okay'? Sure I'm okay. Sure it won't mess me around. What do you think I am? And who do you think you are, for chrissakes? Mother Teresa?"

Eliot flinched at the snarling retort and Julia saw there were tears in her eyes. She turned away, unaccustomed to the icy clamp that settled around her heart and the pained confusion in her mind.

"I want you to understand why I think we should go," Eliot said quietly, the faintest tremor in her voice revealing her distress. "I can't risk people thinking..." She paused and Julia pounced.

"Thinking what? That you've caught lesbianism from me?"

"Julia! No! It's not that. You don't know Jack. He could take Morgan away from me."

"But why, for chrissakes?" Julia could hear her voice rising but she didn't care. "You haven't *done* anything. I haven't *done* anything..." Angrily she paced away and stared back at Eliot, her eyes as impenetrable and dark as coal and the lines of her face set in planes of sullen and smoldering fury.

"So?"

Eliot shook her head and sighed. "You know how the media works. Look what's happened already — the way people have reacted to that stupid photo. And I'm worried about Jack and my family and..." She paused and then said, "And my friends."

Julia paced to the window and then back to a spot midway across the room. A muscle in her jaw fluttered and she was aware of a surge of rage and frustration churning around inside. Finally she turned back to Eliot and burst out, "So I guess this must have been pretty boring for you, hanging out with a dumb jock, without your smart friends." Her words sounded self-pitying in her own ears and she swung away from the lingering sound of them to the huge window that hitherto had afforded them such pleasurably spectacular vistas of the Central Park skyline. This morning it reflected only her brooding face and bleak, angry eyes, and then, Eliot's arms reaching to hold her.

"Please don't do this," Eliot whispered. "You know

this has been a wonderful time — for all of us." Julia felt Eliot's forehead between her shoulders and she shivered. "Don't do this," Eliot whispered again. "I can't bear it."

Slowly, reluctantly, drawn by the pain in Eliot's voice, Julia's rigid posture relaxed; she slowly turned and found herself pinned by a gaze of peculiar intensity. Eliot seemed to be searching beyond the surface and Julia couldn't look away or move as her sense of rage and outrage dissipated as quickly as it had flared.

Beyond the window, the day seemed to be frozen in the same moment, as if aware that something might be about to occur to take her and Eliot into uncharted territory — along one rocky perilous path, or another. But for the time it took a gull to float by their window toward the reservoir, she had no idea what it might be. Then, as if under a spell, Julia saw Eliot's hand reach up and tentatively caress the tight aching line of her jaw.

"Don't be angry," she heard Eliot say. "Please don't be angry."

There was confusion and longing inside Julia as she attempted a smile. Carefully, warily, she clasped Eliot's hand and held it to her cheek for a long moment. It temporarily assuaged the slow burn with which she'd been living for weeks; then hesitantly but instinctively, she brought the hand to her lips in a gesture that was both courtly and heedful and brimming with desire. Julia heard Eliot's sharp intake of breath as her lips touched the palm and each fingertip in turn.

Eliot made no move but watched hungrily Julia's every movement; then as her lips lightly touched the tip of Eliot's little finger, a low moan escaped her throat, her hand tightened into a fierce grip on Julia's fingers and there were tears in her eyes.

"Julia . . ." Eliot's voice shook and its tone and the unmistakable underlying urgency struck Julia's consciousness like a match to a fuse. The spark took hold of Julia's blood with the speed and ferocity of wildfire and there was no time for doubt or caution anymore. Before her, Eliot's wide blue eyes and parted lips were her only focus and, like a thirsty explorer on a blazing uncharted day, she bent her head and prayed that what she saw was no illusion.

Eliot reached up toward Julia. Deep in places she had forgotten about, a yearning had begun to build as she'd watched, captivated, while the rose-pink and full lips delicately demonstrated more clearly than words Julia's feelings of tenderness; and her dark eyes had expressed the depth of emotion that lay below that tenderness.

"Julia . . ." She heard herself speak again, in a voice she barely recognized as her own. As the dark head bent toward her, Eliot reached up, her mouth hungry for the sensation of Julia's lips, starving and yearning for their full, sweet-tinged softness. Even as her mouth opened to Julia's tongue, she knew herself to be frantic for more. There was no way to go but forward into Julia's ardent embrace and as Eliot clasped the broad shoulders beneath her hands she was rocked to the core by the raw wanting and need to touch that crashed ferociously through her veins. As Julia's mouth explored hers, Eliot absorbed the aching familiarity of Julia's physique with feverishly moving hands and with every nerve in a body that somehow now seemed entirely connected to her searching fingers.

She shivered convulsively as Julia's fingers traced down the line of her neck and spine beneath her sweatshirt. Obeying the honeyed pain of her own craving, she pushed herself higher into Julia's embrace, but there was no relief for her burning breasts in the contact; in the blur and flurry of sensations, all she knew was that she wanted and needed more. Then Julia's strong hands grasped Eliot's hips and instinctively, Eliot's legs parted as their bodies came together in an undulating and electrifying caress. Eliot shuddered at the power of the inner convulsions that had begun readying her body to receive what it hungered for.

"Julia," she murmured, as her body obeyed its own commands, "Julia, please . . ."

Julia's tongue and shallow breathing were hot and cold in Eliot's ear. "What?" she whispered. "Tell me . . ."

Eliot stopped her with searching tongue and lips that spoke eloquently of inner and as yet indescribable craving. Then her courage returned.

"I want you." Eliot's voice was low but clear. "I want you to take me to bed. I want you . . ." Tears had begun to course down her flushed face, as if the power of her desire, once spoken, had released them, had released her body's heat.

Julia kissed her wet face and took her hand. "Hey," she whispered, "it's okay, sweetheart. I got you. You got me. It's okay. Come on. But I think we should go to my place." She slipped her arm around

Eliot's waist and again kissed the tears as they stumbled in each other's arms toward the door.

Behind them and beyond the huge window, the anonymous windows of the buildings beyond their corner of the great park continued to glitter and shimmer so that it was impossible to tell which glitters and shimmers belonged in the mysteries of the city and which did not.

CHAPTER SIX

For most of the passengers and crew aboard the westbound 747, the flight to Sydney from Los Angeles was routinely endless. But for Eliot, it was barely long enough to even begin to make sense of the mental and emotional disarray that seemed to have occupied the place where her mind had previously been in residence. And her physical exhaustion was equally profound, not least because she was unable to express or acknowledge any of it. Unlike her daughter, whose own emotional tumult had been expressed without inhibition and with fatiguing and uncharacteristic gusto. Within an hour of waving Julia good-bye at La Guardia, Morgan's mood had seesawed repeatedly from deepest tearful despair to over-wrought elation as she began to turn her thoughts homeward. On the first leg of the journey, to Los Angeles, she had been at first fractious then imperious and finally close to obnoxious in her exuberance. Now, she lay curled beside Eliot, her nest-like seat at full recline, finally lulled by the unbroken hum of the plane's engines into what looked like dreamless and happy sleep.

Eliot envied her daughter her tranquil expression and peaceful demeanor. Morgan's peach-skinned face was so placidly beautiful and trusting, it made Eliot's heart ache. Yet she looked somehow less like the excited child who had left Australia and more a composed, self-contained young . . . Young what? Still not adolescent, but somehow and definitely no longer a kid. Her aplomb had visibly increased as she'd learned with lightning speed to be at home in New York; and her confidence had been boosted daily in Julia's company and by the intensive attention she had received from the new cronies on the hotel staff and the coaches at the tennis center where she had been treated, rather alarmingly, as if she were Julia's fully-fledged protegée. She was no longer Eliot's little girl.

Eliot sighed and wondered, fleetingly, whether anything was hers anymore. Everything that she had previously known now appeared to be lost in a morass of new thoughts, new knowledge, new feelings and conflicting desires. She closed her eyes, but there seemed to be no way of escape from the confusion and loss that threatened to envelop her. Instantly she became even more acutely aware of Julia's indelible presence, physically and mentally, in her mind and body. As if shutting out her surroundings only served to bring the absence more vividly to life.

"You feeling okay?"

Eliot opened her eyes to the concerned gaze of a glamorous but motherly flight attendant. She nodded. "Fine, thanks. Just rather tired."

The older woman smiled. "And it doesn't get any shorter, this trip."

Eliot stretched and groaned. "How true."

"Would you like a scotch maybe, or some champagne — to pass the time?"

Eliot shook her head. "No, really. But I'll let you know if I think of anything. Thanks."

"Make sure you do."

Eliot was momentarily tempted to say, "Yes, I'd like you to stay and talk to me. I'd like you to sort out my life. I'd like not to have to think about all this." But she didn't. For all the woman's friendliness and concern, it didn't seem likely to be on the menu. Instead she turned and stared out the window, but as far as she could see, hundreds of square miles of unbroken cloud cover offered no resistance to where her mind wanted to be and, in staring into its mesmeric dappled gray-white mass, she found herself helplessly going back in time.

Sex with Julia had been astonishing. The words and images contained in that single thought came to Eliot in a flash as she shifted involuntarily in her seat and heat ignited the aching soreness between

124

her legs and the newly and extremely stretched muscles of her inner thighs and back. Never before had she experienced such raw and all-consuming passion. It had been like ripping away layers and lifetimes of numbness and finding herself alive and crazy with wanting the touch of Julia's hands and lips and long, limber body. Fumbling blindly in the bedroom in Julia's funny apartment, drunk with the sensation of having her close, Eliot had been aware of the scrape and click of the door lock and that Julia had insisted they come up to her apartment and not stay in the Bancroft suite.

For one guiltily dismissed moment, she understood that it was Julia rather than she who was thinking of possible consequences. But consequences seemed a long, long way off as she stood waiting on trembling legs, beside Julia's bed, her heart pounding in the unfamiliar jagged rhythms of apprehension, amazement and exhilaration. And that sense of exhilaration quickly overtook and smothered the shadows of apprehension as Julia's serious eyes and smile bathed her in a glow of rightness and sweetness. Some strange and tangible warmth in Julia's expression made her spirits soar. The rich novelty of the feeling was intoxicating and she closed her eyes to better savor its newness.

"You nervous?" Julia whispered against her neck and damp hair as she dexterously slipped her hands beneath Eliot's sweatshirt.

"A little." Eliot heard her voice as a shaky and breathless undertone and added the obvious truth, "Very, to be honest."

Julia's hands slid around and down her back and pulled her close. "Me too," she said softly, her warm breath an irresistible pleasure against Eliot's throat. "I want this so much I'm terrified."

Her words and their meaning had the effect of tiny explosions deep in Eliot's belly. As Julia's mouth sought her own, once again the passionate craving that began coursing through her veins threatened to collapse her knees and turn her entirely to water. She was abruptly desperate to be horizontal, to feel Julia's weight crushing her into life; and she stepped back to the bed, drawing Julia with her. As she had before, she whispered, "Please . . ." then Julia knelt between her legs and roughly tugged at the fabric of her jeans.

In the three days following that first touch of Julia's tongue on Eliot's craving flesh, it was as if she were abruptly and utterly remade in the image of a woman whose sexual appetite had never before been so richly awakened. Her habitual demeanor of cool restraint was melted and abruptly supplanted by an unquenchable desire to be close to Julia, to touch her. All the while Eliot marveled at the sensuality in which she found herself enfolded and she reveled in the way Julia encouraged her and unabashedly reciprocated her newly kindled passion.

With Morgan safely in the care of her new friends and pro tennis minders, Eliot gave herself up to the unaccustomed sensations of happiness and sexual pleasure. To unexpectedly catch Julia's adoring gaze as they crossed a street or savored the bare-branched landscape of Central Park was, for Eliot, a luxury and joy that could only lend enchantment to their time together. That it was a time borrowed from real life she had no doubt, but that seemed only to concentrate its sweetness and heighten the delight.

Eliot propped herself on one elbow to better take in the beauty of the elongated body that sprawled elegantly beside her own. Unaccustomed to such female richness, she dwelt on each part with conscious intent and, she realized, without shyness. She drank in the form of the chocolate-nippled breasts. Each one was voluptuously full but neatly and symmetrically contained on the broad and finely fleshed ribcage. She savored the vitality of Julia's body and the honey-pale skin of her breasts and buttocks, enjoying its obvious strengths and contrasting richly curved softnesses. She smoothed away a tangle of dark, damp and curly tendrils of hair from Julia's face and placed her lips on the wet skin at the base of her neck in the lightest kiss. Julia's languorous sigh acknowledged the touch and a tiny smile lifted one corner of her mouth, but she lay still, as if consciously basking in the painterly strokes of Eliot's gaze.

Sensing the implicit permission and aware of her own wish that she prolong her frank exploration, Eliot inhaled Julia's sharp, salt perfume and allowed herself to continue. The shoulders beneath her searching fingers had a sculptural quality, the lines of the neck making perfect geometry with the bone structure and clearly defined musculature of back and arms. The smooth arc into the waist was accentuated by unusually narrow hips and the small buttocks that were drawn in two precisely rounded curves which connected the torso with the beginning of the famously long and curvaceous legs — the left knee lividly scarred and still vulnerable.

"You are beautiful," Eliot said quietly into the top of Julia's head. "Do you look like your mother or your father?"

Julia pursed her lips and considered the question then, with one languid hand, made a see-sawing gesture of half-and-half. "My mother and I look more like each other than not and I'm like my dad in temperament, so I'm told."

"You don't know him?"

Julia shook her head. "Not really. He died when I was a kid and I didn't really know him before that."

"That's sad. How did it happen?"

Julia grinned. "You really don't know, do you?" She laughed at Eliot's embarrassed face. "He was murdered. Shot. He was a big-time badass — Frank Rossi. It made the cover of *Newsweek*: huge scandal. Links to politicians, international links, links to big business. You name it, he had links."

Eliot shook her head in obvious amazement, then said, "Is that why you're 'Ross' and not 'Rossi'?"

Julia laughed. "It wasn't fashionable to be part of an ethnic minority then and my mother thought it might be safer for me." She stretched contentedly beneath Eliot's stroking hand. "I kind of regret it because I'm always being asked whether I'm 'ashamed of my roots' and crap like that, but she did what she thought was right." She took Eliot's hand as her fingers sketched the outline of her jaw. She examined the strong fingers with the no-nonsense well-shaped nails still rimmed with remnants of paint and kissed each one. "It works both ways too, you know. You heard me talking to Andrew Connelli? Well, when you meet him you'll probably think he's an upper class Englishman — but he's really Irish." She grinned at Eliot's look of disbelief and went on, "Truly. His mom's name is Siobhan O'Connell. He thought Connelli was funkier — especially around my mother's associates!"

Eliot laughed and leaned forward to kiss Julia's wide, unlined forehead and gasped as warm hands closed over her breasts.

"You do extraordinary things to me," she whispered, allowing herself to be drawn down to lie, full length, along Julia's body.

"Good," Julia said, against her ear. "I want you to feel extraordinary. I want you never to even think about leaving me."

Eliot laughed and shivered as Julia's fingers slid into the wetness that she had previously supposed to be a memory of her long-gone teenage past.

"You're beautiful. In every way," she said, her voice shaky as Julia's fingers sought and found a most sensitive reaction.

Julia wrinkled her nose. "Does that matter to you?" She withdrew the caress and despite her attempt at control, Eliot moaned tremulously. After a moment's indecision she broke with the reticence of a lifetime, took Julia's hand and replaced it. Julia grinned triumphantly and repeated her question as her fingers resumed their slow but insistent penetration of Eliot's defenses.

"Matter? I don't know." Eliot thought for a moment, fighting for clarity against the waves of desire that threatened to engulf her and finally said, "Probably, yes, it does. I like beauty."

Julia sighed contentedly, her tongue tracing the whorls of Eliot's ear. "I'm lucky then."

Eliot shivered with delight and almost forfeited recognizable thought but managed to say, faintly, "Am I supposed to say, 'No, I wouldn't mind what you look like'?"

Julia grunted a negative as her mouth became otherwise engaged in an exquisite investigation of Eliot's left nipple. "I wouldn't have believed you anyway," she muttered and gently bit into the engorged flesh.

Eliot's back arched involuntarily as electric currents burnt through the last of her reserves of propriety. She thrust her fingers through Julia's hair and crushed the soft lips into her breast as sensation after sensation scorched through her. After a moment she was able to speak and, in a shaky voice and between sharp intakes of breath, said, "Just as well I was honest."

Julia pulled away and regarded her quizzically, then smiled and said softly, but with total conviction, "I think you'll always be honest with me. And much more important, I think, no matter what, you'll always care." She laid her hand in an unadorned caress on Eliot's cheek. "I've known that since the night I got drunk." The simplicity of Julia's sureness and the depth of trust in her face were overwhelming and Eliot momentarily closed her eyes on the surge of love that filled her heart.

CHAPTER SEVEN

Morgan stirred in her sleep and Eliot tucked her blanket closer beneath her chin. The tranquility in the child's face was a sharp contrast to the sight that had greeted Eliot on the night Julia had so guilelessly recalled. Eliot's heart and stomach collided as she heard, once again, Ray Freeman's alarmingly quiet voice on the phone.

"Could you get over here, Eliot. We've got a bit of a problem with . . ." He hesitated before going on in a tone that implored her, by its urgency, to understand.

". . . our young friend. We don't want to bring anyone else in if we can help it."

"What can I do?

"Dunno yet, but you do seem to have a way with her."

Eliot had glanced at her watch and grimaced. It was close to eleven and she'd been quietly pottering in the studio, cleaning brushes, as was her pleasantly meditative late-night habit. She'd been looking forward to a long bubbly soak before slipping into the solitary luxury of her bed and its clean sheets.

Ray picked up her unspoken hesitation and his voice was close to pleading as he went on, "I wouldn't be ringing if I didn't think it was an emergency, El. The bloody hired help walked out today and she's hit rock bottom."

"The Denverses?"

"Buggered off. And good riddance, if you ask me. But she's taken it hard and the bloody music is enough to drive anyone to drink; and she won't even open the door to us."

A chill clutched at Eliot's throat as she remembered Julia's dejected description of the consequences of lack of belief, and she tucked the phone into her neck and wiped her hands on her sweatshirt.

"Give me five minutes. I'll walk over and come in by the side gate. Can one of you get over here in case Morgan wakes up?"

Greg and Ray met Eliot at the small gate half-hidden in a rambling hedge that afforded access to both properties. By the light of her torch Eliot could see the fright and deep concern on both faces.

"What's happened?"

Ray scratched his head and sighed. "Big row this afternoon out on court. I'm surprised you didn't hear it. Yelled the bloody place down. It's a bad scene, El, can't talk to her; she just stormed off to her cottage and bang, on goes the bloody heavy metal."

Greg sighed. "Luckily we're having a quiet spell at the moment and the cottages on either side are empty, otherwise . . ." He shrugged. "I'm sorry to do this to you Eliot, but she does seem to listen to you and I'm at my wits' end. Unless we can quiet her down tonight without having to call outside help it's bound to get out."

"I didn't realize it was so bad. She was fine when she came over yesterday."

"It's something to do with you and Morgan," said Ray. "It really cheers her up. But I tell you, I've never seen such a wicked slump. It's more than the knee — and that's bad enough — but we can get her over that and she knows it. There's something else and she's not talking. Today she was more than despondent."

Greg nodded. "I'm pretty sure she's drinking, smoking dope maybe, and if you can't get her to open the door I think Ray ought to go in."

Eliot shivered despite the warmth of the summer night. "I don't know about this, Greg," she said dubiously. "I hardly know her. I barely know what to do when Morgan's sick, let alone somebody who seems determined to have a major nervous breakdown."

Ray laid his hand on her arm and squeezed gently. "I know you can help her, El. Please . . . she needs you, I know it."

Again Eliot shivered, but this time the reason was different. She thought of the unlikely friendship that had bloomed between Morgan and Julia — despite Julia's occasional best efforts to be surly. And she thought of how Morgan's persistent adoration had also drawn Eliot to the player's plight — albeit at first as a reluctant observer — and then, as Julia's deep-down gentle sweetness had gradually been revealed, as a genuine, if cautious, admirer.

She relented. "Okay, but I really haven't a clue."

Greg's sigh was brimming with relief. "In this instance, that makes three of us," he said and, after giving her a hug, disappeared into the night down the leaf-strewn track toward the lights of the Bancroft house.

Ray and Eliot walked side by side, in friendly if apprehensive silence, along the low-lit winding pathways of the resort. Before long the steady boom of a bass line and nerve-wrenching tattoo of over-amplified drums and the endless wail of guitar heroics told Eliot they were close to their destination.

"My God, if I was a neighbor *I'd* be complaining. What a racket."

"So far we've managed to say there's just a bit of a party, but we can't let it go on. Okay, here we are."

Eliot stood back as Ray knocked loudly on the door. It seemed doubtful that anybody inside could hear him over the hubbub within. Eliot took his arm. "This is hopeless, Ray. And I don't like it. It doesn't feel right. I think we should go in."

"I've got the pass key."

"Use it, then. I've got a bad feeling about this."

Ray brought out a bunch of keys from his pocket, chose one and slipped it into the lock. The door swung open and they were assailed by noise and a frighteningly unhealthy stench.

"Jesus!" Ray staggered back and gagged. Eliot pushed past him. In the flickering gloom of an assemblage of large and gloomily multi-colored candles that stood burning on a low coffee table she immediately saw Julia's body, sprawled flat on her back on the couch.

"Lights, Ray," she yelled above the din. "And do something about that bloody racket." As light flooded the room the source of the smell became immediately evident. An upturned and empty rum bottle lay on the polished wooden floor in a puddle of vomit, close to Julia's limp hand; and, for a heart-stopping moment, Eliot thought that she might be dead. Then she saw a bubbling breath disturb the putrid slime that disfigured Julia's waxen lips. Oblivious to the stink and disarray, Eliot knelt beside her, grabbed a handful of sticky, ruined hair and pulled Julia's head back; the action wrenched her mouth open and Eliot hooked her fingers inside and grabbed for her tongue and cleaned out her mouth.

"Snuff those wretched candles so we can get a bit of air in here," she said to the plainly paralyzed Ray. "Then you'll have to help me turn her on her side. And we need cold water and a wet towel, Ray, there's a good fellow."

Between them they struggled with Julia's dead weight until they succeeded in turning her body and drawing her heavy limbs into the semi-fetal and life-preserving position. Then Eliot took the soaked towel from Ray and cleaned Julia's face and neck.

"There's nothing I can put water in." Ray's voice was thin and shaking.

"Ice bucket. Fill it and see if there's any bottled water in the fridge. Then I want you to go find some salt. Lots of salt."

In the sudden acute silence, Eliot could hear herself and had time to be vaguely amazed at her own sharp and decisive tone. Obediently Ray followed her instructions and, while Eliot continued to swab Julia's face and neck with cold, fresh water, he disappeared back to the main building in search of salt.

In his absence, Eliot tried to rouse Julia, but so deep was the level of unconsciousness, she was rewarded only by the faintest groan that barely disturbed the shallow breathing and inert body; and Eliot experienced a wave of deep and true fear. She shook Julia roughly and stung her own palms with a series of sharp slaps to her pale cheeks. Again Julia groaned, somewhere deep and far away, too far away.

"Come on," Eliot whispered in her ear. "Wake up, Julia. Come on! Come back." Julia took one long tremulous breath and her heavy black lashes opened for a moment. She almost smiled at Eliot, then the dark brown eyes blurred and crossed and closed again.

"How is she?" Ray had returned with a box of premium rock salt.

"Not good. If we can't rouse her, I think we'll have to get help."

"Oh jeez. Poor kid."

"Kid nothing," said Eliot tartly, but something in Ray's eyes stopped her going further.

"She's all right, El. She's been through a lot."

Eliot sighed. "I know, I'm sorry, it just seems such a bloody waste."

"We'll get her right. Come on, what next?"

"Well, if this doesn't wake her up. I don't know what will. We'll have to call an ambulance." Eliot bunched her left fist until the knuckles of her first and second fingers formed a sharp point. With the fingers of her right hand she felt her way across Julia's sodden, sticky, filthy T-shirt until she had located the sternum, then she dug her knuckles hard into it and rolled her fist back and forth with most of the weight of her own body behind it. For a moment nothing happened, then as Eliot continued to apply the pressure, Julia erupted out of unconsciousness with a roar of pain and flung away from her torturer's grasp.

"Shi'!" she yelled. "Tha' hur'!" She groaned, coughed, sneezed violently and messily and tried to pull herself upright on the couch. Eliot sat back on the coffee table and watched her dispassionately. Julia moaned and retched a dry, stomach-wrenching retch, touched her chest and put her hands to her face as if checking to see if she was still in existence. Eliot smiled grimly at Ray; she knew that as long as they could keep Julia conscious, she was safe.

It had turned into one of the longest nights of Eliot's life. Following her instructions, Ray painstakingly siphoned a generous handful of salt into a large plastic spring water bottle and shook it vigorously until the salt dissolved; at her insistence he repeated the process until he'd mixed three bottles of salty water.

"Now what?" he'd asked Eliot anxiously, watching Julia's lolling head and listening to her animal-like moans and rough breathing.

"You go to bed, I'll take care of this part."

"You sure?"

"You squeamish? She's going to be sick. A lot."

Ray shuddered. "Right. Well, okay then. I'll give Greg a bell, eh? What time will you be finished?"

"Probably not till the morning."

"Jeez, El, I never realized. I mean, you've done this before, haven't you?"

Eliot smiled wryly. "In a manner of speaking." She picked up one of the bottles of salty water. "I'm going to try to do two things. First, make her so sick she'll get rid of all the garbage she's swallowed and — secondly — *that* should make sure she'll never do it again."

"Christ. You sure you wanna —"

"It's for the best," Eliot said firmly. "Believe me. Now you get on and I'll see you first thing."

He stood up, unable to hide his relief. "Okay." He leaned over and hugged Eliot but was visibly repelled by the sour reek that now also permeated her clothes and hair. "Call me if there's any problem."

"I will, but I think the main thing is to make sure everything is normal out there. And Greg will have to stay with Morgan."

Getting Julia to drink liters of salty water was not the easiest task Eliot had ever set herself, but the extent of Julia's drugged, drunken defenselessness helped and Eliot's tender but implacably firm insistence had done the rest. She perched on the arm of the couch, placed her knee behind Julia's back to force her to stay upright, then slowly but surely persuaded, cajoled, bullied and crooned her into drinking almost all of one large bottle of the water. As soon as it was down she repeated the action of their first meeting and hauled Julia to her feet. It was more difficult as the virtually inanimate frame swayed against her and Julia's legs repeatedly gave way as Eliot frog-marched, half carried her to the bathroom.

"Leave me, leave me alone," Julia wept. "I need to lie down. I need to sleep."

"You need to walk and you're going to be very" — Eliot maneuvered her through the bathroom door —" very sick."

Julia rubbed her hand across her face, moaning piteously and beginning to shiver convulsively. "Let me lie down, Eliot," she whispered. "Please . . . let me lie down."

Eliot sat her on the floor on a thick toweling bath blanket and wrapped a robe around her shaking shoulders. "Julia. Listen to me. You have poisoned yourself. You must stay awake. If we can get rid of it, you're going to be better a whole lot quicker than if it stays down. So you must stay awake. Do you understand me?"

There was a long pause, then Julia breathed a long, tremulous and defeated sigh and nodded. "I'm sorry," she whispered. "I dunno what happened. I'm really, really sorry . . ." Suddenly she began to retch and Eliot placed one hand comfortingly across her heaving stomach and the other to support her forehead. "No, don't," said Julia despairingly, as she tried to brush away Eliot's hands. "Leave me."

"Sweetheart, you need help," Eliot said softly, gently rubbing the spasming abdomen. "It's okay, don't worry. Just do this for me. Come on." And as Julia wept and succumbed to her own helpless needs, so Eliot resigned herself to a long, difficult night.

By three-thirty in the morning, Julia was only too aware of her circumstances as she roused herself from a fitful doze while the explosive and irresistible impulse to vomit once again overtook her. She was simultaneously ashamed and profoundly relieved that with each now uncounted bout of violent gagging Eliot's hands had been there, to soothe and take some of the strain. Not for the first time, she found herself envying Morgan who, she would be prepared to bet, had never had to feel ill without that comforting touch to take away some of the misery.

By five, as the windows facing out toward the beach began to fill with the translucent gray of dawn, Julia became more and more painfully aware of what had befallen her. And even more aware that she needed to explain herself to Eliot who still sat beside her impassively, mopping, stroking, cleaning and even, she recalled in a dazed flashback, softly singing a wordless lullaby when Julia had sobbed. At the same time, she was aware that Eliot wasn't exactly amused by her behavior and she knew she couldn't blame her for that.

Eventually, as the magpies began their early morning chatter, Julia was able to drag herself into the shower and stand, legs trembling and stomach still cramping, under a fine spray of warm water. She allowed it to run into her mouth, nose, eyes and ears, shuddering as its pleasantness contrasted so starkly with the too-recent horror of the night; drinking it down and spitting it out until she began to think that one day, with an enormous amount of luck, she might just feel clean again. And, eyes closed and tear-stung, she silently savored the impersonal but intensely soothing sensation of being soaped and rubbed down from head to toe in a way that she dimly recalled from childhood visits to her grandmother. Finally, without fuss or comment, Eliot had wrapped her in the first of several large soft towels and led her gently to her bed.

As Julia lay back into the clean sheets, her head swathed in a towel turban, she began to shiver. Eliot pulled the sheet and woven cotton blanket up to her neck and tucked her in, then sat on the edge of the bed and mopped at Julia's still damp face with the corner of another towel.

"You might still be sick a few more times," she warned. "But I think you've just about done it by now." She stood the ice bucket on the bedside table. "Use this if you need to and rinse your mouth out with fresh water." She placed a water bottle beside the bucket and turned the shadow of a grin on Julia. "I promise it's not salty."

Julia smiled wearily, remembering her violent but ineffectual protests of the night as Eliot had forced more and more salty water down her thirsty but protesting throat. "I believe you," Julia said in a voice so hoarse it was almost gone. "I know I've behaved like a real jerk but you gotta understand . . ." Tears stood in her eyes and she wiped them away roughly. "You and that kid have been lifelines for me. I couldn't really tell you why, I mean, I like kids but — well, you know, I'm not Michael Jackson —" She shrugged, bewildered. "I could take it that the Denverses didn't want to hang about. I can understand that. It's a professional thing. But —" She flung her arm across her face so Eliot could not see her eyes. "The last straw was finding that Morgan is going off to stay with a friend this weekend." She sighed an exasperated sigh and shifted her arm so that she could peer at Eliot with one eye. "It made me realize how much I've come to rely on a seven-year-old. That she's actually my friend and, you know what? I also realize that I haven't had a friend in a real long while." She shook her head and hid her face once again. "It's pathetic, don't you think?"

Eliot shook her head. "Not really. I realized much the same thing just the other day. When the chips are down I've got one friend. I don't think that would be considered a particularly good score for someone of my age. I'm sure it shows there's something deeply amiss."

"Maybe you're just very discerning."

"Maybe, but I doubt it. Now look, you should sleep. In fact you will sleep, whether you like it or not, because you're exhausted. When you wake up, ring Ray, the private number is on that pad. I'll make sure he brings you some glucose water."

"Yuk. Why?"

"Call me old-fashioned, but it's what my mother always gave us when we were sick. Do me a favor and just drink it. You probably won't feel like anything else anyway."

Julia sighed. "Yes, boss." She grabbed Eliot's hand. "You know I can't even begin to tell you how grateful I am?"

Eliot nodded. "I know. Now I'm going home to bed. If you wouldn't mind me rather than Morgan's evidently more fascinating company, you're welcome to come over on the weekend."

"Thanks. I'll take you up on that." Julia was reluctant to see Eliot go, but she released her hand and her eyes were already closing as she heard the door quietly click. Her dreams were untroubled and she had awoken hours later with abdominal muscles that felt as if she'd gone ten rounds with Evander Holyfield, but her heart sang at the prospect of Saturday.

CHAPTER EIGHT

Eliot stirred stiffly in the aircraft seat, the memory of Julia and the present — which was her absence — suddenly collided and she shivered. She tried in vain to push away a sudden and unmistakable sense of foreboding that enfolded her along with her return to the moment. Even as she struggled to shrug off the unfamiliar weight of dread, her thoughts lurched back and forth between the extraordinary happiness she had experienced so briefly after those strange days at the beach house and the even more extraordinary pessimism and dull pain that were, with each passing mile and minute, slowly over-whelming her. The conflicting wrenches on her emotions would soon, she felt sure, begin to make her physically ill. She pressed the Call button and ordered a large scotch with plenty of ice from the solicitous flight attendant.

"I'll remember this sky." Julia's tone had been neutral as they lay loosely entwined, watching the black silhouettes and the glowing arc that was the New York night sky. Eliot glanced at her, inscrutable in candle-lit profile. She was certain Julia was talking about more than the twinkling universe beyond the plate glass, but could not think of a way to acknow-ledge it. Instead she kissed the corner of Julia's mouth and asked, "What will be your schedule for the next few weeks?"

Julia shuddered at the intrusion of reality and sighed. "Train, coaching, practice. Small tournament in a couple of weeks. Maybe an exhibition match. See how I go, talk to people, see what they reckon. Train, coaching, practice, take it as fast as the knee will go. Aim for a couple of easy ones; if that goes okay, then start to crank it up and go for broke."

"Wimbledon?"

"Might as well. It's the one I want. It's the one I was aiming for anyway. No point dodging around the ridges."

Eliot lifted Julia's hand away from where it lay cupped on her breast and kissed each knuckle. "I think you're brave."

Julia snorted. "Brave! Nah. What else am I going

to do? Bravery is when you've got choices and you make the hard one. For me, to play is the easy route. To make another decision — go another road — that'll be brave. Believe me."

Eliot slid her hand along Julia's thigh to caress the scarred knee with her fingers. "You're very tough on yourself."

Julia grinned. "I have to be if I want to win." And the expression in her eyes told Eliot she was not necessarily thinking of battles on the tennis court.

But Eliot couldn't begin to acknowledge what this wild, ruthless and resourceful creature might really have in mind. Instead she sidestepped her suspicions by lowering her mouth to Julia's quiescent right nipple and teasing it into life with the tip of her tongue. It was, she had already and quickly learned, an extraordinarily gratifying thing to do and, with only vestiges of her earlier nervousness, she began to deliberately and slowly relish the sensations of limitless power that came from pleasuring Julia.

"Have you had many girlfriends before?" Julia's voice was tremulous and her breath short as she watched Eliot's shimmering honey-headed progress from right breast to left breast and then slowly and deliberately down to her navel.

Eliot looked up, her eyes wide with apprehension. "Why? Am I doing something wrong?"

Julia laughed, reached out and caught Eliot's face between her hands and drew her up to kiss her. "Wrong!" she said, between butterfly touches. "Nothing you do is wrong." She traced the outline of

Eliot's mouth with her index finger. "You couldn't be further from wrong if you tried," she said quietly. "I was just..." She grinned a lopsided and embarrassed grin. "I was just wondering. That's all. You've never said. I've never asked and I was suddenly..." She rolled her eyes and groaned. "Jealous."

"Jealous! You jealous of *me*?" Eliot's eyes reflected mystified disbelief. "I don't understand."

Julia shrugged. "It's simple. And totally unreasonable. I want to know who else you've done this to. And I want the answer to be nobody."

Eliot lay back on the bed and laughed. "You are a funny thing. You're one of the most extraordinary young women one could ever hope to meet, and you're jealous of *me*?"

Julia nodded, her expression impenetrably dark. "You don't get it, do you? Or maybe you don't take me seriously."

Eliot's amusement died in her throat. She reached out and cupped the glowering face tenderly in one hand. "If there is one thing I do, it is to take you seriously, Julia," she said gravely. "That's why you're crazy to be jealous. I know this might sound hopelessly old-fashioned for an international jet-setter, but I've had one affair — a long time ago, with someone who is now my best friend — and I've not gone to bed with anybody else but my husband since I married him. That should tell you that I take you very seriously indeed."

Julia stared into Eliot's eyes as if she was seeking the actual thought impulses behind her words. Unflinching, Eliot held her gaze. Finally Julia turned her face into Eliot's shoulder and sighed.

"I'm sorry," she said, her voice muffled against Eliot's skin. "I guess it's because you make me feel like such a kid sometimes — like when you call me a 'young woman' — it sort of puts such a distance between us and I feel like a fool."

Eliot rolled onto her side and gathered Julia in an embrace of arms and legs that held her fast. "You're fourteen years younger than me," she said into Julia's massed curls. "In my book, that makes you a young woman. I suppose I'm amazed that you take *me* seriously. I mean, look at me. I'm embarrassed to consider your achievements beside what little I've done with my life. I'm amazed that we met — although we can thank Morgan for that — I'm amazed that you like me and I'm even more amazed that you like me . . ." She hesitated, suddenly abashed, then pressed on. "That you like me, like . . . this."

Julia slowly lifted her face from Eliot's shoulder until she could look right into her eyes. "My god," she said wonderingly. "And I'm supposed to be the fool."

Eliot sighed wearily and drank deeply from the heavy tumbler. In the cool, dry atmosphere of the aircraft cabin the ice had barely begun to melt and the almost undiluted whiskey burned her throat; she shuddered at the taste and feel of it. As the ache in her heart fought for ascendancy over the soreness of her sexual muscles she wondered whether her present predicament could be classified as foolishness, or

148

maybe bad timing, or perhaps the aberration of a woman on the threshold of midlife crisis — whatever that was supposed to be.

But before she could analyze further Morgan stirred and opened her eyes, frowning for a moment as she took in her surroundings, then she turned to Eliot and her eyes were fully awake. "Mum, when is Julia coming back to Sydney?"

Eliot's stomach knotted into a chilly coagulation of apprehension, guilt, loss, sorrow, yearning and overly cold alcohol. She swallowed on rising nausea and tears and managed to say, lightly, "I don't really know, sweetheart. She's got a lot of catching up to do. She's going to be terribly busy."

Morgan snuggled into her blankets. "I really love Julia, you know."

Eliot reached out and stroked her daughter's forehead. "I know you do, sweetheart. And she loves you too."

Morgan's serious face lit in a hopeful smile. "Does she really, Mum? Has she said so?"

Eliot touched her cheek and smiled, ignoring the confusion of emotions that were threatening her ability to reassure her daughter, to be her mother. "She said so, sweetheart. Promise."

Morgan's sigh was tremulous with delight and relief. "Does she love you too, Mum?" Her eyelids were drooping and Eliot drew her blanket closer under her chin, momentarily unable to speak.

"Does she, Mum?" Morgan's sleepy face was anxious. "I'm sure she does."

Eliot leaned over and kissed the top of Morgan's head and managed only to say, "I'm sure she does, sweetheart — now go back to sleep," before tears threatened. She turned away to her glass and peered with fierce concentration at the ice cubes while taking long, slow and deep breaths, trying to stem the rising tide of loss and pain before these unaccustomed feelings overwhelmed her.

Even now she knew Julia was somewhere in New York. Getting back to her real life as a champion athlete, as a superstar, a celebrity, a multi-millionaire; back to her life as a beautiful, young and attractive woman who had the world — and any number of equally gorgeous, talented and appealing young women — at her feet. And she, Eliot, was returning to her rightful and dutiful place as part-time artist, mother and wife, on the roster of school function helpers, and beside her husband at the dinner tables of Sydney's political and legal glitterati.

Without warning, Eliot found herself bursting with the desire to giggle at the picture of desperate ordinariness she had managed to paint. At the same time, never in her life had she felt so downcast and at a loss to resolve the quandary in which she found herself. It would be some time, she knew, before the shock waves of Julia's precipitate entry into her life subsided. And — she now began to understand — she had no true idea at all of how long it would be before she recovered from Julia's inroads into her heart. Despair settled like damp, gray fog and she closed her eyes against it and, before she knew it, was asleep.

CHAPTER NINE

As Eliot and Morgan gathered their belongings and checked for stray items the friendly flight attendant appeared at Eliot's elbow and spoke in a low voice. "If you'd like to come with me Ms. Bancroft, there are special arrangements for your disembarkation."

Eliot was puzzled. "Special arrangements?"

The flight attendant bent toward her so that her intimate tones traveled no further than Eliot's ears. "I understand there may be press waiting. Photographers."

Eliot's heart sank and met her stomach as it flipped. The combined effect was appalling and she knew her face had gone pale. "For us — me — are you sure?" she asked in a shaky voice, but the memory of the previously innocent photograph of Julia and her "gal pal," now given undeniable credence that was no less frightening for being secret, was burning in her mind even as she asked the question.

"I'm afraid so," said the flight attendant. She grinned conspiratorially. "I must say you take a good photo!"

Eliot stifled the groan before it reached her lips and glanced around at the other passengers. None of the sober-suited travelers seemed remotely interested in a non-power-dressed woman and her little girl. She rummaged in her bag for dark glasses and tried, without success, to still the panic that was threatening to rise up and choke her.

"Ready Morgan? Got everything?" She heard her voice and was surprised at its steady, normal tone.

"Yup." Morgan was refreshed, chirpy and excited.

"If you'll just follow me, we'll get you out of here in a minute." The flight attendant and the other crew members seemed no more or less solicitous and friendly than they had been when Eliot and Morgan first boarded the plane, but she couldn't help scanning their faces as she sought evidence of something else — curiosity, perhaps, or some glimmer of expression that would tell her they knew her secret.

At the door, the flight director nodded and smiled and Eliot shook herself inwardly. *Don't be ridiculous,* she silently scolded. *You're being paranoid. Nobody knows, it's just that stupid picture in that stupid*

152

magazine. She smiled back and waited while Morgan shook hands with the woman, then they were out of the plane into the covered walkway and following the impossibly calm and well-groomed flight attendant.

Halfway along the corridor an immaculately uniformed young man met them and conferred inaudibly with their escort who turned to Eliot with a warm smile. "Justin will take care of you from here, Ms. Bancroft. Hope you had a pleasant flight."

"Very, thank you." Eliot was bemused as the uniform named Justin transformed himself into a smiling, friendly man who took her arm and gently but firmly led her and Morgan through a door and out onto a bare steel landing. For a second they stood, blinking, bathed in the sunshine of a late Sydney afternoon and the full awful roar of jet engines. Carefully he ushered them down the steep bare metal stairs to the tarmac where a white car with darkened windows waited. Consternation joined the other sensations in the pit of her stomach as Eliot realized it was her father's official car and standing beside it was the familiar burly figure of his driver and best mate, Charlie Lacey.

"G'day, Eliot. G'day, Morgan," Charlie said in the circumspect way that Eliot knew would remain unchanged in the middle of either a major political scandal or an earthquake.

"Nice to see you, Charlie," she said, not sure if it was strictly true. "Where's Dad?"

The driver tipped his head in the direction of the back of the car. "Waiting for you. Why don't you both hop in and we'll get moving."

He held open the passenger door and Morgan dived inside to be engulfed in her grandfather's arms.

As Eliot followed, she was aware — not for the first time — that Morgan was an icebreaker of Antarctic capabilities.

"Hi, Gramps! I am *so* pleased to see you. I have *so* much to tell you and I've got you a really good present and would you like to see me practice tomorrow? I've improved like amazingly and you will be *so* impressed . . ."

Senator Harold Bancroft, known to his friends as Harry and to his political foes as "that dangerous old bastard," cuddled his only grandchild and grinned a grin of benign indulgence as she chattered. He was slow in acknowledging the presence of his younger daughter, however, and Eliot realized that she was not the only one using Morgan as a shield and distraction. She drew down one of the fold-away seats opposite her father and perched on it, bewilderment and misgiving warring with her. Finally as the car began to move across the tarmac she knew she had to speak.

"Hello, Dad." Her mouth was dry and her throat constricted and neither were relieved by the cool light she saw in his eyes.

"G'day, Eliot." His voice was gruff, his smile formal. She had seen him greet the Leader of the Opposition with more warmth.

"What's going on, Dad?" She knew she had to plow on. Not only was there no going back, but there seemed to be nowhere else to go anyway.

"I was hoping you'd be able to tell me that, girlie."

Eliot had so rarely heard that cold tone outside the Senate that her heart froze and she knew her face had also gone rigid. She cast about in her mind for a response, but none came. Then, over her shoulder, Charlie Lacey offered her temporary respite.

"Just coming up to the Customs and Immigration office, Mr. B. You want me to take care of it?"

"That'd be grand, Charlie. I'll stay here and catch up with my grand daughter."

As dusk settled over Sydney, Eliot sat in her favorite wing-backed and worn leather armchair in her father's study, watching him mix one monumental and one not so monumental gin and tonic. Between them, on his desk, was the offending magazine open at the page which featured the now-infamous photograph of Eliot and Julia. There, for all the world — and Senator Harry Bancroft and his family — was his daughter Eliot's arm, quite obviously and inarguably around the waist of a tall and famous young woman and, correspondingly, there was Julia's arm. unequivocally lying with seemingly easy familiarity across Eliot's shoulders.

The lucky lens had caught them laughing at each other and their faces were intimately close. That Eliot was carrying a pair of crutches in her free hand and that Julia was holding the hand of Morgan Bancroft Barron was not apparent because the photograph had been cropped until it contained just two women in an apparently special romantic moment.

That Julia had, moments before, said to Eliot and Morgan, "For God's sake, you two, please don't let go of me now, I think I'll take a tumble on my fanny if you do," was — Senator Bancroft had snapped at his crestfallen daughter — hardly the point.

"You are being disingenuous, Eliot," he'd said, his words snapping and hissing dangerously. And Eliot was at a loss to find a response that didn't sound, in her own mind, either like guilty excuses or self-justification — two things she very much wished to avoid. Instead, she took the drink proffered by her father and miserably took a sip while he stood beside his desk and fixedly stared down at the magazine as if the intensity of his gaze might somehow explain the inexplicable.

On the other side of the world, Julia was standing at the kitchen window of her apartment, staring out at the silhouettes of rooftops and occasional lit window shapes. It was four o'clock in the morning. She was munching peanuts and not really seeing very much that was in front of her. Instead, images of Eliot flashed like video clips across her mind. She leaned her forehead against the window pane. It was cold but soothing, seeming to numb the agitation that was making her head ache and sleep an impossibility. And she too was wrestling with explanations of the inexplicable.

Behind her the wall clock ticked. It was a small, comforting sound and it gave her an idea. Quickly she counted off the hours on her fingers, her spirits rising and heart beating faster. At her desk she turned on the reading lamp and sat back, to gather her thoughts and wait for her heart to slow. She looked about the room, and not for the first time since her return from Australia, she felt irritation at its decor. The framed autographed rock band posters on the walls looked as tired and trite as the black vinyl sofa and over-sized chairs and stained Mondrian-style rug. She was suddenly aware that her bookshelves were stacked with molding magazines and newspapers, programs, piles of yellowing faxes — and very few books. On one wall, pinned to an office-size cork-board, were souvenirs of countries and places visited: dolls, flags, a wineskin, masks, a lei made of plastic frangipani; even, she noticed wryly, a fluffy koala and plastic kangaroo. The board was the only feature of the room that did not reek of disinterest and indifference but rather it smelled of dust and chirpy irrelevance.

"This is not a grown-up's apartment," she said aloud. She reached for her organizer to find Eliot's phone number. She dialed, listened to the unfamiliar beeps and clicks, then heard the voice that would probably always cause her heart to lurch in its moorings.

"Thanks for calling. We can't come to the phone at the moment, but please leave a message after the tone and we'll get back to you. Jack Barron can also be reached on ..."

But Julia didn't want to know where she could reach Jack Barron. She replaced the receiver with a snap and sat back in her chair, disconsolate and irrationally aggrieved. Her living room seemed even more uncomfortable and inappropriate than it had thirty seconds before. She got up and began lifting the framed posters from their hooks and stacking them in the lobby. An hour later, she was sneezing, covered in dust, and the souvenir wall was also empty. Its previous decor objects were in two giant green garbage bags awaiting consignment to oblivion beside four more bags containing the musty contents of the bookshelves. Julia stood in the doorway and scrutinized the result of her efforts. Already, despite the once-witty, trattoria-style, brick-with-creeping-ivy wallpaper — which now, for some reason, looked merely silly — the room seemed somehow bigger and easier on the eye. Julia checked her watch. It was still too early to call Andrew Connelli and get him to find someone to paint the place and dispose of the furnishings, but it was not too late to try Eliot again.

This time Julia forced herself to listen to how to get in touch with Jack Barron, then coerced a smile from herself and spoke. "Hi, Eliot. Hi, Morgan. Hope you got home safe. It's Julia. I'm in New York and I'd love to hear from you. You got my number, 'bye."

Julia gently replaced the receiver on its hook and breathed a sigh of relief and profound regret. She had left a successfully cheery and noncommittal message and nothing in it, neither words nor tone of voice, would betray to anyone her true feelings and aching wish to say... What? "Eliot, I'm in love with you. Please abandon your daughter and never mind your shit of a husband and your stuffy family and your life and your friends, come to New York and make me happy." Is that what she wanted to say?

Again, Julia's sigh was the only sound within the apartment to break the silence. She listened to the muted noise of the city slowly coming to life in the predawn beyond her windows and was grateful for it. Her eyes stung and her knee ached. Her head was spinning with weariness but she knew, from the raw-skin, exposed-nerves feeling of her body that she would not be able to sleep without pills and she didn't want to do that.

She considered music, but after flicking through the racks of CDs, she failed to find one that appealed. She wondered three things: when and why she had bought so many duplicates of so many Dire Straits albums, what time Tower Records opened, and finally, whether they actually stocked Mozart and Monteverdi. Maybe there were special record stores for that kind of music, she mused. Briefly she considered whether or not she could call the Met but a call to a bemused operator at Information gleaned the knowledge that, useful though it would certainly be to insomniac and tyro music lovers, they didn't seem to have a twenty-four-hour information line.

Maybe Andrew would be awake by now? She checked her watch and knew that at six on a Saturday morning the only thing that might cause him to be awake would be the outbreak of World War Three, live and exclusively on CNN. She sighed again and wished she could stop herself doing it, because it seemed to be filling the apartment with a miasma of self-pity; then she saw she had paced to the kitchen and back to her desk and her hand was once again on the phone.

Scrolling through her organizer she became increasingly aware, as she flicked through its listings, of how few people she knew well enough to talk to about her dilemma; and as that realization became clearer, she also began to understand just how much she needed to unburden herself. At that moment the phone rang and Julia jumped out of her skin. She snatched up the receiver before the answering machine could cut in.

"So! You're there. I figured you'd be in Osstralia!"

"Angie!" Julia was truly shocked and her reaction was automatic. "Do you know what *time* it is?"

"In London? Sure." The Andreadis laugh was infectious and Julia smiled.

"You're in London?"

"Passing through, spending a coupla days with the new squeeze. What's this I hear about you getting mixed up with a married woman?"

"Who do you hear that from?"

"Is that a yes or a no or a maybe?"

"Angie . . ." Julia stopped and soberly considered her reply. If she had felt even a fleeting temptation to blurt out her feelings to her ex-partner she was brought up short by the recollection of her nickname on the circuit: C.I.Andreadis. To tell Angie anything could imperil Eliot's situation, and to do that would, without doubt, destroy any hopes Julia might want to have for the future. "Angie," she began again, trying to feel her way into a response that would satisfy but not feed the relentless curiosity that was crackling right across the Atlantic. "I don't know what you've been told but it's all crap."

"Seen the picture, seen the picture." Angie's tone was gleeful.

Julia sighed — this time she didn't mind the sound, it was exasperated rather than despairing. "Oh for God's sake, Angie. She's a friend and her seven-year-old daughter is the owner of the hand I'm holding, if you look closely, but they cropped her out of the photo." Julia crossed her fingers and went on, "My 'gal pal' is a happily married wife and mother."

"Yeah, and so was Judy Nelson. Now come on. What you up to, girlfriend?"

Julia's heart was clutched by a spasm of fright. Angie, she knew from exhausting experience, was relentless in pursuit of gossip. She took a deep breath and steadied her voice into a tone of bored exasperation that she absolutely did not feel. "Angie, there is nothing to tell you, because there is nothing to tell you. What can I say?"

"You can say what you think about the rumor that there are some pretty hot snaps around of you and your happily married wife and mother."

Julia laughed and it sounded genuine for one good reason. "Now I know you're crazy." She sat back in her chair and relaxed, feeling that the last hurdle was behind her. "You're pulling my leg, admit it."

A moment's silence was followed by Angie's deflated, "Oh. So you really mean it then? Damn, it seemed like such a good story." It was her turn to sigh before she brightened with a new thought. "Talking of pulling your leg, how is it? Is it true you're thinking of playing Wimbledon?"

"That's one story you can pay your sources for. My knee is pretty good and I have every intention of playing Wimbledon."

"Shit."

"Thanks. Good to have your support and encouragement."

"Aw, don't get all duchessy. You know we all want you back on the tour. But just for once I'd love a crack at it without having to run into you, that's all."

161

"Well, bad luck. Unless I actually lose my leg, I'll be there."

Angie's giggle was ominously wicked. "With or without your gal pal?" And she hung up.

It was a long few minutes before Julia replaced the receiver, while she waited for the waves of alarm to subside. Then she considered trying Eliot's number once more but decided against it. Behaving like a love-sick fifteen-year-old was not the way to go, she instinctively felt sure. But what else was there to do? She stifled a sigh and looked at her watch. Six-thirty was too early to do anything and too late to go to bed. This time her sigh was heart-felt.

"Eliot!" she said aloud. "Damn you."

CHAPTER TEN

In Sydney, Julia's words were almost echoed by Senator Harold Bancroft as he angrily regarded his youngest daughter. "Damn it, Eliot. I don't understand. How can you sit there and tell me there's nothing to worry about?"

"Dad, I've already explained how the picture happened. You know — of all people — how these things get twisted." Eliot's heart was numbed but pounding. So far she had been able to answer her father without lying, because his barrage of questions had fallen wide of the mark. But she dreaded a direct challenge; she had never lied to him before and didn't know how she could begin to do it now. Behind his desk he sat back in his chair and stared out the long window at the twilit garden. The silence between them was not comfortable; indeed, it fairly thrummed with tension. Finally he turned back to Eliot and his expression was that of a man unconvinced.

"If there's nothing in all this, I don't understand why Jack rings me from Hong Kong asking if I'd seen that damn picture and I don't understand why he wants an appointment — an appointment, mind you — at my office in Canberra. What is he playing at and what the hell is going on between you two?"

Eliot took a deep breath. The idea of her husband, who had never had more than a polite relationship with her father, wanting to see him at Parliament House, was inexplicably ominous. "Dad, I've barely spoken to Jack since he went to Hong Kong and Morgan and I went to New York. I haven't a clue what this is about. And until we get home, I still won't."

Her father shot back his white shirt cuff and consulted his watch. "Well, I don't know where the bugger is. He said he'd be here an hour ago."

Eliot opened her mouth and closed it again before a comment slipped out on Jack's inability to know when to stop being a lawyer and start being a husband and father. Instead she said, in as reasonable a tone as she could dredge up from her weariness and anxiety, "Dad, we've been flying forever. Morgan is exhausted. Why don't we get Charlie to drop us home and we'll sort this out in the morning?"

She watched her father wrestle with the good

164

sense of this suggestion and finally give in to it. He pressed a button on his phone and within minutes the room was full of Morgan's fractious high spirits and the impervious presence of Charlie Lacey. As they left Harry Bancroft hugged his granddaughter warmly and gave Eliot a passing kiss on the cheek. From the front doorstep he lifted his hand to wave but his face was unreadable. Eliot's heart sank; she had never felt at such a distance from her father, except for the day she told him she wanted to marry Jack Barron. Which was, she mused, ironic.

"Your house or Jack's house?" Charlie Lacey's voice cut into her thoughts and she jumped.

"Oh, Jack's house, I suppose, Charlie. My car's there, I hope."

Charlie glanced over his shoulder to where Morgan was already more than half asleep on the back seat. "You've got my mobile number if you need anything. Like if you want to go down to your place tonight and you don't feel up to the drive. Know what I mean?"

Eliot squeezed his arm gratefully. "Thanks, Charlie." She stared determinedly out of the window as tears pricked her eyes. "I don't quite know what's going on. It's all a bit of a mystery."

"I think your dad was quite upset by all the fuss over that picture in the magazine. You wouldn't believe the bloody nonsense they've been digging up. All that stuff from when Jack got burned in the land deal; and every flaming thing your dad's done in parliament, including the business with Carol Bishop."

Eliot gasped. "Oh god, no wonder he's so mad. But that's twenty years ago!"

"When it comes to a good bit of gossip, it doesn't matter how old it is. You know that."

"True. Still, I thought the Carol Bishop business was well and truly dead."

"It would have been, except for the photograph — I mean the one of you and Carol and your dad. I think they must have thought it was Christmas, to have almost a duplicate."

"Poor Carol. I wonder how she is?"

"Last I heard, she's doing very nicely with her country cottages in Tasmania. Don't worry about Carol. It's you I'm concerned about. I mean, you should have seen the mob at the airport. You'd have thought you were Mick Jagger or something."

Eliot groaned. "God, Charlie, you know that picture's virtually a fake, don't you? I mean Morgan has been cut out of it, it wasn't a picture of the two of us. And I was carrying a pair of crutches!"

Charlie grinned, taking his eyes off the road for a moment to wink at Eliot. "We know all about that sort of nonsense, Eliot." Then his expression resumed its previous dourness. "Trouble is, we also know what can be done with nonsense. These so-called news and current affairs hyenas will have a bite at anything that moves. That's what's got your dad so rattled."

Eliot shivered and settled back into her seat as the truth of his words sank in. "Have you seen anything of Jack since we've been away?" she asked tentatively.

She saw that Charlie glanced in the mirror at the already-snoozing Morgan before answering. When he did his voice was muted. "I know he's been in touch with your dad. They had . . ." He cleared his throat before going on. "Words. Bit of a barney, I think you could say. And he hasn't said a word about it. Got him in strife with your ma because he wouldn't say." He chuckled. "They didn't speak for three days."

Eliot also laughed softly. "God, that must have been peaceful for a change."

Charlie nodded and grinned. "Nobody complained."

"So is that why my mother's stayed in Canberra?"

"Reckon."

"Charlie, I appreciate this, you know."

His gruff mutter was inaudible, but the clasp of their hands in a wordless show of faith and affection was all Eliot needed. Again tears pricked her eyes. "God, I'm so tired."

Charlie sighed. "You sure you want to stay in town? Wouldn't you be better off at your place?"

Eliot was silent for a moment then she spoke, slowly, reluctantly, as she voiced her thoughts as they formed. "I think Jack is expecting us. And, I'm really too tired to go a step further tonight. I think I'll try and get down on Monday."

Charlie nodded, then picked up the car phone receiver. "Maybe it'd be a good idea to check your messages if you're not going home till then."

Eliot registered two things: that he didn't call her marital home her "home" and that he was pointedly advising her to do something in the privacy of the car that she could just as easily do at 28 Westwater Road, the heavily mortgaged hillside mansion overlooking the harbor that was Jack's pride and joy. For a moment she hesitated.

"Go on, get it over with now," Charlie urged, his tone so bland that his underlying meaning drowned out the well-mannered thrum of the car's engine.

Eliot punched in the pick-up code for her little house and was immediately glad that she had. Rachel Taylor's inimitable and unmistakable tones purred a laughing "Welcome home" into her ear, followed by a requirement for instant communication. Greg and Ray followed, demanding — in unison — practically the same thing; then Eliot's heart lurched as Julia's voice emerged from a chatter of international beeps and static. Her message was bright, breezy and non-committal and Eliot now knew her well enough to hear the underlying anxiety and to picture the bright smile that was making her nonchalant words possible.

Three or four other messages passed in an unheeded blur as Eliot heard and heard again in her mind the short, friendly message that also conveyed to her an unnerving but sensually stirring depth of longing that was answered by her own heart and heat. She clicked the receiver back in its rest and sat back, glad of the deepening darkness. Ahead, as the aged sandstone retaining walls of the high side of Westwater Road loomed, she experienced a moment of pure screaming anguish, then Charlie laid his hand on her arm and gently said, "Eliot, we're here."

The nightmare that materialized when Eliot and Morgan entered the house was one that no party to it would ever afterward forget. To his wife, Jack Barron's solicitude was more unnerving than his famous temper. He hurried down from the porch to greet them and snatch his sleeping daughter from Charlie's arms. "I'll take care of her," he said brusquely to the older man. "You can get along."

Eliot reached up and kissed Charlie's cheek as he deposited her bags on the front step. "Thanks a million, Charlie," she said quietly. "May I call you tomorrow?"

Charlie's expression was austere. "Think you better. G'night, love." And then, to Eliot's considerable dismay, he was gone into the night. She watched the red taillights of the white car disappear down the street and felt that she was watching a lifeboat vanish over the horizon. She shivered despite the balmy evening.

"You planning to stay out here all night?" Jack's voice was light, affable. Eliot jumped out of her skin but somehow mustered a smile.

"Just seeing Charlie off." She picked up two bags but quickly relinquished her hold as Jack leapt down the steps and grabbed them from her. Before she could move he had all the luggage inside and had returned to slip his arm about her and escort her into the house.

"Darling, it's so good to see you. I missed you both. Did you have a wonderful time?" He squeezed her shoulder and placed a kiss on top of her head.

Eliot was perplexed as she followed him from room to room. In passing she noticed the elegantly coiffed native flower arrangements on the hall table and on the coffee table and the general gleaming state of cleanliness and well-being that permeated the rooms in the form of a scent of lavender and beeswax.

"The house is looking wonderful, Jack."

"I got Greta to come in for the whole day. We wanted it to look extra specially good for the prodigals." He was pouring two whiskies and Eliot could not see his face, but his tone was still light and affectionate. Her unease continued to grow along with her guilt. Perhaps her suspicions were unfounded. Perhaps she was misjudging him. Perhaps it was her imagination — even wishful thinking — that he was having an affair. She took the proffered glass and swirled the mixture of ice, water and whiskey for a moment until it inadvertently mirrored her inner confusion.

She knew, from what her father had said, that Jack had seen the magazine and she knew, instinctively, that Jack Barron — of all men — would not take kindly to being portrayed, even by salacious implication and cheap innuendo, as a cuckold, and his wife as a lesbian. His affability made no sense. She began to find it unnerving as he bustled about, making her a cheese sandwich despite her assurance that she wasn't hungry, and then he was gone, scampering upstairs to check on Morgan.

In the sudden vacuum left by his departure Eliot sat, awkwardly, on the sofa in her own living room, feeling like a guest in a strange house as she took an obliging nibble out of the sandwich. She tried to pin down the source of her disquiet, feeling more and more uncomfortable as she did so. But the sandwich stuck in her dry mouth and the prospect of swallowing was unbearable; she took it and the plate to the kitchen. She tipped it into the garbage bin and with one finger began to poke it beneath a half-eaten croissant and a sodden, grounds-stuffed paper coffee filter. Then she stopped, her finger pointing incongruously at the object which was now the key to the conundrum that was Jack.

In all the years they had been married, Jack Barron had never once voluntarily eaten a croissant. His objection, he'd told her long ago, was that not only, in his view, was there nothing wrong with "good Aussie toast," but also that the butter-rich French pastry was just "too poofy for my liking." Not that either opinion had stopped him gnawing zealously on many croissants and — even more effete — brioches at any number of Veronica Levy's renowned Sunday brunches, but — he'd told her sharply when she'd teased him about his enthusiastic munching — that was not the point.

Now, as she frowned down at the torn croissant, she felt two and two finally coming together to make whatever it was Jack's life had now become. She allowed the bin lid to snap shut and turned to the counter under which sat the dishwasher. As she pulled open the door the equation begun by the pastry fragment was completed by the sight of two sets of plates, two glasses, two coffee mugs and two sets of cutlery stacked neatly and sparkling clean in the machine's innards.

"Oh, Greta," Eliot said softly. "Everyone should have a cleaning lady like you." And she thought about how often she'd begged the human cyclone that was Greta Main not to do the dishes when she came to clean the house. But the thin face puckered into a disapproving scowl and her thin arms snapped into a sinewy knot across the two sensibly corseted fried eggs that were her breasts.

"When Greta Main cleans, Greta Main cleans," Greta had said, each word snapped off neatly like sewing thread between an expert seamstress's teeth.

"But, Greta, if I leave a few dishes, I really don't want you to have to do them," Eliot begged. "And if I think you're going to do them, then *I* will and I don't necessarily want to, right at that moment."

Greta had considered this for a moment then shook her head vigorously. "Them's is as them does," she said firmly. And — Eliot smiled at the memory — to this day, she had absolutely no idea what the old woman had meant by this sage observation, but it had effectively ended the argument on the spot. She allowed the dishwasher door to swing gently closed and straightened up as she heard Jack's footsteps on the stairs. Then he was in the room, filling it with his handsome bulk and dynamic presence and offering to run her a hot bath.

She ignored the question and asked, "How was Hong Kong?"

He paused and frowned. "Hong Kong? Oh, you know, pretty routine."

"Who went with you?"

"Oh well, the usual crew."

"Tanya — Tonya — did she go?"

"Tanya Carides? My junior? Yes, of course."

Eliot nodded, sipping her drink as she leaned against the counter in front of the dishwasher. "Did she stay here last night?"

Jack's eyes momentarily widened before he regained control and his expression became an impassive mask. "What do you mean?"

"Which part of the question is puzzling? Did she — Tanya — stay here — that is, in this house — last night — which is approximately twenty-four hours ago."

For one infinitesimal speck of time Eliot thought Jack was about to tell her the truth, but then his eyes stared straight into hers and he said, in the same easy reasonable tone that he'd adopted since her return, "Of course not, darling. Don't be silly."

CHAPTER ELEVEN

Eliot was at a loss for words. The impulse to hurl her glass at his attractive head and scream, "Don't lie to me! Just tell me the truth!" was hideously compromised and twisted by her own guilt. In effect, she was gagged by self-knowledge. In her own mind at least, her brief, sweet sojourn with Julia had canceled out Jack's affairs, past and present. And when she looked up and saw his speculative, glittering gaze fixing her like a pinned butterfly, she understood intuitively that this suspicion was not hers alone. And at that point, as she began to shake with weariness and apprehension, she knew she could take no more.

"I really have to go to bed, Jack. Can we talk in the morning?" She set down her empty glass and made for the kitchen door but Jack was there before her and, with his arm about her waist, began to accompany her to the stairs.

"I'll be up in a moment, darling. Just got to make a couple of calls." He kissed her neck, his stubbly chin grazing her skin. Unwittingly, Eliot recoiled from the roughness and saw a flash of familiar anger flare in his eyes. But it was instantly gone as he grinned again and scraped his fingers across the stubble. "Sorry, darling, bit rougher than you're used to?"

Eliot's stomach twisted into a knot. There it was, the first clue, the first strike. It was an oblique but unmistakable beginning. Eliot knew that the night would be long and dreadful.

"What *do* you mean, Jack?" Her tone was genuinely fatigued and plausibly puzzled.

"Just a little joke, darling. There've been lots of little jokes about you and your pal this past week. Thought you might like to be in on them." There was no humor in Jack's voice and his expression was blank. Eliot examined his face for indications, for emotion, for recognition, but there were none. She shrugged off the arm that lay heavily across her shoulders and headed toward the stairs with renewed determination.

"Jack, if you're going to be boring about that stupid photograph, then I've got nothing to say. I surely don't have to explain to you, of all people, how that happened."

"Of course not, darling, but I'd love you to explain to my colleagues in chambers and every sniggering cleaner and clerk down at the courts."

Eliot stopped halfway up the stairs and sat down on the step. "Jack, I can't believe I'm having this conversation with you. You've *used* photographs like that in evidence, for God's sake. You know they're crap."

"But what about the others?" His voice was soft; it was the most ominous tone he could adopt. Eliot was glad she was already seated.

"Others? There are no others."

"That's not what I've heard."

It was a fishing expedition. Eliot stood and continued to climb the stairs. "I'm not going on with this, Jack," she said over her shoulder. "It's ridiculous."

"I'm sleeping with you tonight!" His voice was so sharp it felt almost like a slap. Again Eliot stopped and turned; this time she really was surprised. And, despite her thudding heart and coagulated stomach, her response surprised her too.

"Really? I'm amazed you remember that you ever did."

His eyes were narrowed and the lines of his mouth hard as he snarled up at her, "I'm sleeping with you."

Eliot returned his stare even as her stomach threatened to rebel. For the first time, she saw hate in her husband's eyes, but the effect of it was curious: she felt detached from herself and the situation. Aware only that he might hurt her and if he did, that she could endure it. Her voice was maddeningly neutral when she responded. "Is that a threat? I have to say I'm not keen on it."

"I'm still your husband." His face was ugly with the exertion of his rage.

Eliot shook her head in disbelief. "And this is the very late twentieth century, Jack. I believe even you have heard that marital rape is a crime."

"You bitch." His tone had turned molten with anger. "You think you can make a bloody fool of me. Well, I've had you up to here." He drew his finger in a savage slicing motion across his own throat. "I want a divorce."

Eliot's grip on the polished mahogany banister rail tightened as she saw the truth of his demand in his eyes. For the first time since she re-entered the house, he was at last speaking to her honestly and, despite her own detachment and cauterized emotions, it was shocking.

"I don't think you can have both, Jack. You can't fuck me *and* divorce me. It wouldn't look too good in court." Eliot heard her voice as if it belonged to somebody else. It was a crazily provocative thing to say — and Jack was provoked. He bounded up the stairs, taking them in threes. His face was suffused with rage and Eliot wondered fleetingly whether he was going to hit her. But he stopped, one step below, so that his face was level with hers. His contemptuous study was enough to make her involuntarily flinch.

"You think you're smart, bitch," he hissed, flecks of spittle striking Eliot's face. "You think you're so bloody smart. But I'm going to take you for everything you've got." His grin was vicious. "Everything."

With muscles and senses screaming at her to retreat, Eliot stood her ground even as her heart froze. "I know you've been having an affair, Jack." In her own ears her words sounded hollow and frightened and Jack laughed, a great bray of whiskey and stale garlic.

"Don't make me laugh." He jeered. "Prove it. You want to go to court on an allegation like that?"

Still Eliot stood her ground. "Not without a lawyer." Her lips were rigid with tension, but her voice had somehow resumed its normal tone. "Now, I want you to stop bullying me, Jack. And I do want to go to bed." The look between them was glacial, silent and long. "I'll sleep in the studio."

He nodded, slowly, twice, and there was everything but humor in his smile.

"You do that, Eliot." He turned away and began to descend the stairs, then stopped and looked up at her. This time his smile was more a sour smirk. "By the way, where's your lezzie pal?"

For a moment Eliot considered not responding, but her weariness with her husband and his always tiresome and now unacceptable attitudes manifested itself in a resigned shake of her head and disdainful snort. "You let yourself down, Jack. Will you never realize that?"

His chin rose belligerently. "Oh really. *I* let myself down, hey? That's a good one. *My* wife leaves *my* child with a bloody notorious queer and I'm the one who's doing the letting down."

Again Eliot's heart was seized by an icy hand, but her voice remained calm. "You've been chatting to

Daphne again. I'm amazed you two have so much in common."

Jack took one step back up the stairs and his face and tone were a portrait of menace. "I"m warning you, Eliot. Don't push me. Just don't push me."

Eliot swallowed on a dry throat and her deep-seated feelings of fear began to turn to anger. "Don't threaten me, Jack. And that's a warning." She again climbed the stairs but as she turned away, she heard his bounding footsteps behind her. She spun around but too late to save herself or avoid him as he crash-tackled her and they fell up and onto the wide, thickly carpeted landing. Eliot's face struck the banister railing and she felt her lip and eyebrow split and, a second later, begin to bleed and hurt with fierce intensity. Involuntarily she struck out with a fist clenched in exasperation and fury and her knuckles cracked and stung as she connected hard with the bridge of his nose.

"Shit! You bitch!"

Eliot scrambled to her feet, her right eye blinking through a pink haze of slowly trickling blood, and began to back away, but she was winded and sore from the crash landing and was too slow to evade his flailing arms. Again she fell and this time, as she caught sight of his rage-contorted face, with blood coursing down his top lip from his nose, her anger curdled to terror.

"Let me go, Jack!" she whispered frantically. They were outside Morgan's bedroom door and Eliot was still backing away from the enraged man, on her hands and knees, as it opened and her daughter's terrified face turned from one parent to the other. Wide, frightened eyes blinked as Morgan took in the scene in what, Eliot knew with mortified certainty, would be a lifetime's unerasable snapshots.

"Get back to bed!" Jack's voice cracked across the stunned silence and snapped Eliot back to life. She leapt to her feet and placed herself between her husband and child.

"Leave her alone, Jack. Just leave her out of it."

But, sobbing convulsively, Morgan dashed across the landing to the bathroom and slammed the door.

"For chrissakes, now look what you've done." Jack was on his feet, furiously scrubbing at his gory nose with the back of one hand. Eliot remained standing in the doorway to Morgan's room, her head reeling, her lip and eyebrow throbbing and her heart heavy and sick to the core. "You're a bloody disgrace," Jack snarled. But, she noticed, he made no move to advance on her again. Then the bathroom door opened and Morgan marched out. She was carrying a towel and a small, dripping wet hand towel; she strode toward her transfixed parents, her face pale and grimly set.

"Come with me, Mummy." Morgan was staring fixedly and coldly at her father as she spoke and Eliot found herself following the small girl into her room whose door was then closed, firmly but quietly, behind them. "Sit down on my bed." The tone of Morgan's voice was one Eliot had not heard before. She sat, mesmerized as her daughter took the wet towel and began dabbing warily at her mother's cut and bloody face. "I don't think you need stitches, Mummy," she said as she peered painstakingly at Eliot's eyebrow. "It doesn't look as bad as my knee was." She let out a deep and unfeigned sigh that grabbed at Eliot's heart. "And it's not anywhere near as bad as Julia's knee."

"I'm sure it isn't, darling." Cautiously Eliot placed her hands on the child's waist. "Morgan, I'm terribly sorry," she began, then was silenced as the girl wiped at her mouth and bloody chin.

"Don't talk, Mummy." Morgan's tone suggested that she had rather more in mind than cleaning her mother's lip and chin. A moment later there was a tap at the door and Jack's face appeared. Morgan turned to him and took some steps away from Eliot. "I don't want you to come in, Daddy." Her voice was startlingly firm and unlike anything Eliot had heard before. Jack stopped dead in the doorway, obviously at a loss. Morgan remained unmoving in the center of the room and Eliot was transfixed and dazed.

"Don't be silly, darling." Jack's voice was uncertain, cajoling.

Morgan shook her head vehemently. "No, Daddy, I don't want you to come in. I shall phone Grandpa if you do."

Jack's face flushed angrily, but he held up his hands. "Okay. Okay. That's it. I've had it with you two." He pointed his finger, gun-barrel-like but shaking, at Eliot. "And as for you" — his finger wagged furiously — "you're turning my daughter against me. You'll be sorry. I promise you." And he was gone.

Eliot could barely comprehend what was suddenly happening to her life. Her head swam crazily and numbness enveloped her. She listened to her husband's thumping footsteps retreat down the stairs and, after a minute or two, the front door opened

181

and slammed shut; another minute later his car's engine roared into life and a squeal of fast reversing rubber preceded an even wilder engine roar before silence settled back over the house in a cloud of exhaust fumes.

Almost fearfully, and certainly with distinct feelings of shame and sheepishness, Eliot raised her eyes to her daughter's face as the girl returned to her task of cleaning her mother's face.

"I am truly sorry, darling," Eliot said quietly.

Morgan nodded. "I know, Mummy. I'm sorry too. I wish we'd stayed in New York with Julia."

Eliot silently and sadly agreed, but out loud she said, "Daddy didn't mean to hurt me, darling. It was an accident."

Eliot was shocked by the expression on Morgan's face. It was a cool mixture of speculation and skepticism and was distinctly unchildlike.

"Jane-Anne's parents have fights like that all the time," she said eventually. "She says her daddy is always sorry after he's hurt Veronica. Once he even cried because she accidentally got a black eye." She examined Eliot's face as she finished swabbing her cheek, then stared straight into her mother's eyes and asked, "Are you and Daddy going to start doing that sort of thing?"

For several reasons, Eliot gasped, then she shook her head vehemently. "No darling, of course not. Absolutely not."

Morgan pursed her lips and considered her mother's face for a moment, as if assessing the truth of her words. Then she nodded. "Okay. If you promise. But I won't want to live with you if you fight." Eliot nodded, too taken aback to speak.

"Would you like to sleep in here with me tonight?" Morgan's tone was matter-of-fact, businesslike.

Eliot nodded meekly. "Yes please, darling, I would."

"Very well, I think we should go to bed now. It's awfully late." And so ended one of the longest days in the lives of Morgan and Eliot Bancroft.

CHAPTER TWELVE

When Eliot awoke the sun was up and glowing beyond the vivid Mambo fabric blind that Morgan had insisted upon despite her grandmother's outrage at the unsuitability, for a small girl, of the famous "bong" design. For a moment, as she stared with squinting, sore eyes at the vivid colors, Eliot struggled to make sense of her surroundings and the heavy, aching discomfort of her face, then memories of the previous night flooded in and she reached out to where Morgan had lain during their long night of fitful dozes and surreal nightmares. Her side of the bed was empty and Eliot experienced momentary panic, but then the door hinges creaked and she was there, a laden breakfast tray clutched firmly in her hands and an expression of concentrated determination on her face.

Eliot saw the dark shadows beneath her daughter's eyes and her heart contracted and became one with the lump in her throat. She watched the methodical progress of the bare brown feet across the rug. She smiled at the intense focus with which Morgan kept her eyes on the level of the orange juice in its glass. And she knew in a flash of utter certainty and profundity that she would fight Jack to the death to keep her daughter, and also that she would do nothing which could possibly jeopardize her status as Morgan's legal guardian. Even, she realized, if that meant never seeing Julia again.

"I'm going down to the courts for a bit to see if I can get a game with somebody." Morgan had laid the tray down in the empty space on the bed beside Eliot and now stood, hands nonchalantly thrust into the pockets of her bright pink shorts. Eliot divined in an instant, from the angle of her chin and the cool appraisal of her big brown eyes, that she was not invited to be the "somebody"; indeed, that Morgan was telling her that she was having some time-out on her own.

"That sounds good, sweetheart," she said carefully. "And this is a wonderful treat. Thank you." Morgan shrugged calmly but a give-away wriggle told Eliot that she was not as indifferent to her mother's appreciation as she might like her to think.

"I hope the egg is okay, mine was a bit hard."

Eliot tapped the boiled egg with the back of a

teaspoon, it sounded resolutely solid. "Sounds good to me," she said, equally resolutely. "Have you been up long?"

Morgan shrugged again. This time her wriggle suggested to Eliot that she was not being as straightforward as her casual reply: "A while. I wasn't sleepy and I didn't want to wake you."

Eliot decided not to probe, but instead turned her attention to the slightly burnt toast and very milky coffee. "Well, I'll see you later then, darling. Will you ring me if you think you're going to be longer than an hour?"

"Sure." And with a light kiss on her mother's cheek, she was gone.

Eliot tapped the boiled egg smartly and began systematically picking away the cracked fragments of shell with her fingers. Instantly she recalled Julia's remark on another sunny morning that now seemed lifetimes ago.

"Funny, isn't it," she'd begun, peering quizzically at Eliot over the top of her Ray-Bans as they sat at either end of the table on Eliot's veranda. "There are so many different categories of human being, but in the end it comes down to something really simple: the world is really divided into tappers and whackers." And with a cheeky grin she sliced off the top of her boiled egg with one neat swipe of her knife blade.

Eliot smiled back and tranquilly continued to peel shell fragments from her tapped egg. "And what do you suppose it means?"

"Ah. You got me there. Maybe there isn't a meaning." Julia dug into the egg and removed a heaped spoonful. "Does everything always have to have meaning?"

Eliot considered the question for a moment then nodded. "I believe so."

Julia nodded and pursed her lips while she munched on egg and toast. Finally she wiped her mouth with the back of her hand and asked, "So what was the meaning of my performance the other night?"

Eliot regarded her steadily for a long time, then shook her head. "That's for you to know. I can't begin to tell you."

"Were you shocked?"

Eliot thought for a moment and nodded. "A little. Not by what you'd done, so much as the depth of your unhappiness — the fact that you felt bad enough to do that and none of us had realized."

They continued to eat while Julia mulled over Eliot's observation, then she again peeked at her companion over the top of her dark glasses. "How did you know what to do? Ray said you saved my life."

Eliot snorted and shook her head. "That's a bit dramatic."

Julia shook her head. "I don't think so. He sat me down yesterday and told me exactly what happened. I was disgusting. I know I was. And you fixed me up *and* you cleared up for me too. How come?"

Eliot smiled. "I'm a mother. Mothers know about clearing up those kinds of messes."

"But I'm not your kid."

"You needed help."

Julia sat back and sighed a long sigh that was

more pleasure than self-pity. "Nobody has ever helped me like you've helped me. Not ever."

"Well, that's sad."

Julia shrugged. "Maybe. I've never thought about it before. One good thing is you don't miss what you've never had."

Eliot opened her mouth to ask about her upbringing and parents, but then decided she could not and sipped her coffee instead. A moment later Julia answered her unasked question.

"My folks divorced when I was seven. My mom lives in Las Vegas; I lived with her for a couple of years, then I went to live with my grandparents — his parents — until I started for real on the circuit."

"Your grandparents got custody?"

"Mom and I didn't get on. She walked out on us first, then she didn't go for custody. But it wasn't exactly that simple." Julia's voice was as blank as the black lenses of her Ray-Bans. Eliot could see nothing behind them, but Julia's flat delivery of that tiny bombshell of information spoke volumes about her true feelings. Eliot reached across the table, took her hand and squeezed it gently.

"I'm sorry," she said quietly. "That explains a lot, I think."

Julia snorted. "Oh yeah? You think maybe I have a problem with people walking out on me, huh?" Her tone was a mix of derisive and defensive, but she made no move to shake off Eliot's hand.

Eliot stroked the back of the strong brown hand soothingly with her thumb, feeling the sudden tension in the air. "Yes," she said quietly. "I think you probably do. I know I do." She looked straight at Julia who was once again peering at her over the top of the black glasses. "You asked me how I knew what to do for you. How to revive you. Did you notice I didn't answer?"

Julia frowned. "Huh, you didn't, did you. So?"

Eliot moved to sit back in her chair, but Julia placed her free hand over Eliot's and prevented the slight withdrawal. "So?"

For a moment Eliot hesitated, then she took a deep breath and began to speak in a low, slow voice. "After Morgan was born I wasn't too well for months. There were complications and I was in hospital for a while. Afterward I was quite sick and depressed. Jack was always very," she paused and frowned, "very sexually active and I couldn't, at first, then I just didn't want to." She looked up and saw that Julia had removed her RayBans and the dark eyes were even darker as she concentrated on Eliot's words and on delicately stroking her hand. "He began an affair — which I didn't know about and, quite frankly, given the shape I was in, I don't think I would have minded — but Daphne, my sister, somehow found out and she and my mother came round one morning to give me a hard time about being a bad wife."

"No! Oh man! Did you pop her one?"

Eliot laughed. "Nowadays I think I would, back then I was very meek and mild."

"Aaagh!" Julia buried her face in her hands and her groan was also a bellow of rage. "So what happened?"

Eliot sighed and sat back in her chair, her expression somber. "Well, it wasn't so good. I was . . . desperately angry, I think — looking back — but I had no idea how to cope, with any of it. And I didn't feel that I had anyone to turn to. Rachel was away in America. My other sister — that's Verity, by the way — has always been at one remove from the family, very sensibly I suppose, and I just disappeared into this terrible depression. One evening when Morgan was asleep and Jack hadn't come home, I took a couple of sleeping pills and then, when I still couldn't sleep, I took some more. And I think I just lost track of what I was doing." Eliot grimaced and looked slightly sheepish. "I'm afraid an overdose is an overdose — accidental or otherwise — and the treatment is exactly the same."

Julia dropped her forehead onto Eliot's hand and held tight to her fingers for a long minute, then she sat up and her eyes were deep with sadness and empathy. "I'm so sorry," she said softly. "It makes me feel such a . . ." She cast about for the right word, then spat it out. "Brat. A real self-pitying shitty little brat."

Eliot shook her head vehemently. "No, no, no. Hurt is hurt. Sad is sad. You can't put them on the scales and say 'mine is worse than yours.' "

And what would Julia make of her predicament now, Eliot wondered, as she sat back in her daughter's bed nursing what she was fairly sure was a considerable black eye and what she was absolutely certain, as she tried to chew on a corner of toast, was a painful and probably unattractively purple and yellow split lip. She sipped at her coffee, trying to keep the rim of the mug and the hot liquid from her stinging mouth, and attempted to come to grips with the day. That she wanted to get out of a house that no longer felt safe and no longer like home, and down to her own beloved bolt-hole was a conviction so strong it made her skin itch. That she now feared her husband's intentions more than ever before and that she would give much to be able to talk to Julia were equally uncomfortable and powerful certainties.

"Christ, what a mess," she whispered aloud, the sound echoing back from her cupped hands. "What a mess. What have I done?"

And her words also echoed the same question, asked in anguished tones by Julia when she finally realized how close she had come to real harm during her long dark night of despair. It was a question that Eliot had attempted to answer in a dozen different ways during the days that followed by simply being a calm and gentle presence in a life turned upside down by fate and a vulnerable heart.

The evening after Eliot's night-long vigil Julia had appeared at sundown, a large bottle of mineral water and a bunch of pale pink sweet-scented roses in her hands. Her face had been unnaturally waxen and beneath her eyes were dark smudges and she knew Eliot saw that her hands shook; otherwise, her physical recovery seemed remarkably quick and complete — even though she felt unable to meet her rescuer's eyes.

After a moment during which Julia appeared to be memorizing the roses, petal by petal, she finally cleared her throat and said, "I want to say thank you." Then she stared fixedly at the toes of her snowy white Nikes before she swallowed and went on: "And, I want to apologize." She peered with fierce concentration at the evening sky, took a deep breath and said, "And I want to thank you again."

She saw a glimmer of a grin flicker across Eliot's face and this time Julia looked Eliot straight in the eye as she held out the bottle and the flowers. "And most of all, I want to ask you for your company." And with the last rush of words came a tentative and hopeful grin that drew a warm smile from her hostess.

Eliot held out her hands to take the flowers and then reached up to place an affectionate and reassuring kiss on Julia's cheek. "Come on in," she said amiably. "I just hope you're not intending to drink all of that yourself."

CHAPTER THIRTEEN

Julia glanced, unseeing, at the television screen where a *Seinfeld* re-run played in silence. A paperback edition of *The Tenant of Wildfell Hall*, whose cover celebrated a BBC TV adaptation of it, lay in her hands, on her chest, open at page eighty-seven. Her state of mind was strange and new and, in between unprompted thoughts of Eliot, she carefully examined it.

Since their departure Julia was aware that something had changed in her life and it was not merely that she longed inordinately and uncharacteristically

193

for her lover. Where before she would have simply flipped her Rolodex and set in motion a roaring night out, now the very idea filled her with lassitude. Instead, she read, voraciously, obsessively and with growing and intense pleasure. As the days slowly passed, and in Eliot's absence and the continuing absence of a response to her phone messages, Julia wanted only to be alone in her state of melancholy with her newly acquired books and her newly acquired understanding of the love which had lodged deeply and inescapably in her heart.

Each day she spoke to Greg Bartlett. He charted her progress and she noted his advice and instructions, but despite the barrage of questions that went back and forth around half the world, she avoided asking the only question she longed to put to him. In his turn, Greg, the consummate professional and — she sensed — caring friend, never once allowed Eliot's name to pass between them.

"You're doing fine," he urged her, his voice as reassuring as his words. "Go out and have a bit of fun. It won't do you any harm." But every evening, after eating more stir-fried vegetables and noodles than she had previously imagined existed in all of mainland China, Julia would settle on her new sofa, which was as much like the one in Eliot's studio as Andrew Connelli's assistant had been able to track down, and read and daydreamed about the brief and accidental idyll which, with each passing day, took on more and more of the qualities of the mythical romantic tragedies on which she was now hooked.

* * * * *

"Am I being a nuisance?" Julia's question had been peremptory, defensive and antsy, which was how she felt. She was lying on the old sofa in Eliot's studio and had just dropped a heavy glossy magazine on the floor with an unintentionally loud *thwack* which had caused Eliot's shoulders to not quite imperceptibly stiffen.

It was after ten. As she had each evening for almost a week from that first tentative visit, she had arrived on the doorstep after a long day of working out and physical therapy with Greg Bartlett and his staff. It had seemed natural enough that she should become part of the small household and it was difficult to judge whether Morgan or Eliot seemed the more pleased to see her. This evening had been slightly different. Julia was preoccupied and restless. She knew Eliot believed that the novelty of their quiet evenings was wearing thin for somebody she perceived to be a high-living, jet-setting superstar, and Julia felt at a loss as how best to convince her of her easy delight in this new and comforting way of life. At the same time, she couldn't identify the source of her prickling disquiet.

Dinner was long past and Morgan tucked up in bed and asleep. For the past hour, Julia had idly watched Eliot at work on turning that morning's oil sketch into a semi-abstract study of a stand of gnarled banksias caught in the silver-gray sunlight of a break in a rain squall. During that time Julia had flicked idly through a stack of magazines and fidgeted around the studio, changing the music, picking up and replacing objects, occasionally tossing an inconsequential and irritated question or observation at Eliot and, in general, being — as she herself silently put it — a pain in the ass. Then she had said, "Am I being a nuisance?"

Eliot pursed her lips and considered the question for a moment, then raised her eyebrows and shoulders in an eloquent expression that said maybe, maybe not. "You're not bothering me," she said slowly as she carefully wiped her brush on a soft, oily rag. "But I think you're bothering yourself. You're bored."

Julia threw aside yet another glossy magazine and let out a sigh of great exasperation. "That means I'm boring, then," she said grouchily. "If you're bored, you must be boring."

Eliot shrugged again. "That's a pretty harsh conclusion."

"But you're not saying I'm wrong." Julia's chin rose belligerently.

"I think you may have a point, but I'm not sure you're correct in this instance."

"So I'm fascinating?"

Eliot laughed. "And I didn't say that either."

Julia's scowl lifted several degrees and she almost grinned. "You sure you're not a lawyer? You're damn slippery."

Eliot wrinkled her nose. "I *think* I'll take that as a compliment. Meanwhile, let's sort out your being bored. Maybe what you're doing is boring. Maybe you need to find something more interesting. What do you really like to read?"

Julia lifted her shoulders and grimaced. "Don't

really know. Fat trashy books. Throwaway stuff. I spend a lot of time hanging about in change rooms and on planes, so the trashier the better, really."

Eliot nodded and glanced at Julia but made no immediate response; instead she chose a fresh brush — plump sleek sable — and began to roll it methodically between the gleaming blobs of pigment set in heaped whorls around the edge of her thick glass palette. From her vantage point on the arm of the sofa Julia watched, fascinated. As the brush rolled it caught up tiny amounts of each color and Eliot painstakingly repeated the routine until she was eventually satisfied with the rich aquamarine that resulted from the blending process. Then she set down the palette, stuck the brush shaft-first into an empty bottle, wiped her hands on the rear of her ancient, paint-streaked shorts and walked across the room to a set of battered, once white-painted wooden bookshelves.

"Trash is all very well," she said deliberately, head cocked to one side as she searched along the rows of spines. "But," she grinned sheepishly, "pardon me if I sound like Methuselah's mother, but it's like junk food: you feel stuffed as a turkey but really you're still hungry." She began pulling books half out of their places in the packed shelves. "Have you had much chance to read things like Dickens or Jane Austen or the Brontës? Did you do them at school?"

Julia shook her head as she scrambled to her feet, awkwardly maneuvering the cumbersome braced leg. "Nah. I didn't try real hard at school. I was always too good at sports to have to worry. I knew I'd get

197

to college on a jock scholarship — if I wanted." She lowered herself to the rug beside Eliot and began peering at the prominently displayed titles.

"Hey, some of these are movies!"

Eliot smiled. "They were books first, believe me."

Julia drew *Pride and Prejudice* from its slot. "I saw some of this on TV. I *loved* it."

"Well, you might enjoy the original, then."

For the first time that evening, Julia's eyes were sparkling. She flipped open the book and immediately came to the faded citation stuck on the flyleaf and touched it with a careful and almost reverential finger. "Would you look to this! 'Presented to Eliot Jo Bancroft. The Miller Prize for Achievement.' " She chuckled softly at Eliot's abashed grin. "How old were you?"

Eliot squinted with the effort of recall. "Twelve, I think."

"Wow. And you still have it. That's amazing." Julia carefully turned the pages. "And you'll let me *borrow* it?"

Eliot nodded. "I'll let you borrow it."

Drawn in by the first sentence of the novel and her own vivid memory of the television images, Julia began reading and was more or less unaware of Eliot quietly getting to her feet, dropping two squashy cushions beside her and returning to her painting. Time passed in serene silence, broken only by the shush and scrape of brushes on canvas; then the vague question that had been lurking in the back of Julia's mind cut through her absorption.

"Jo's an unusual name. Is it short for something?"

"Usually, but not this time. It was my grandmother's name."

"Is she the one who left you this place?"

"That's right."

And once again there was only a rich and companionable silence between them.

"Mum!" Morgan's excited voice broke into Eliot's reverie. She looked at her watch and was aghast to see it was after ten. She set aside her book and was half out of bed when Morgan burst into the room, still carrying her racquet bag, her face alight with excitement. "Mum! I almost beat Greg. I had two set points! We went to a tie-break!" She dropped her racquets and flung herself on the balding Persian rug at Eliot's feet, her eyes shining and her cheeks gleaming pink spots of exertion.

"Greg Bartlett? Our Greg?" Morgan nodded so vigorously Eliot briefly feared for her neck. "That's marvelous, darling. Julia would be so proud of you. You'll have to write and tell her." She ignored the band that momentarily tightened about her heart; and the cloud that passed across Morgan's face as she nodded again.

"I know she would." She leapt up, dashed out of Eliot's room and returned moments later with her oversize Mambo T-shirt and a towel. "Has anybody rung?"

Eliot frowned and shook her head. "No. Why?"

"Oh, nothing. Just wondered. I'm going to shower, okay?"

"Sure." Eliot watched her daughter's normally guileless face attempting to convey, "Oh, nothing, just wondered," and wondered herself what was going on behind the wide brown eyes. But Morgan vanished out of the door and down the hall before Eliot could even begin to formulate a question. Instead she stared blankly at the open and empty doorway, listening to the sounds of energetic showering and pondered whether this might be the beginning of adolescence and the end of easy intimacy.

Since their return — or escape, as she privately acknowledged it — to the beach house five days before, Morgan had spent more time with Greg at Kurrunulla than she had at home. Eliot knew instinctively there was more to Morgan's absence than simply her desire to maintain her progress at tennis, but the opportunity to sit and quietly talk — as had been their comfort and pleasure all her short life — seemed not to present itself. At that moment, however, the phone rang and the nuances of mother-daughter relationships were temporarily set aside as Eliot steeled herself to answer it, knowing that it was most likely to be Jack, or a member of her immediate but currently hostile family.

In the event, it was worse than any of those possibilities.

"Eliot Barron, please?"

Eliot frowned and said, "Eliot Bancroft. Who's speaking?"

"Oh great! Great. Eliot, it's Dasha Kurosawa, from *In Town Tonight*. How *are* you?"

So ingrained was Eliot's polite upbringing that she said, "Fine, thanks. And you?" before she was able to stop and kick herself.

"Marvelous, really fabulous." Dasha plowed head on, making the most of her easy inroad. "Now, you'll remember *60 Minutes* did a story on your friend, Julia Ross, not long ago? Well, we thought it would be lovely to profile *you* — you know, your career as an artist, how you cope with being a wife and mother too; your friendship with Julia Ross, your daughter's relationship with Julia — all that kind of thing. Sort of warm and personal and very up —"

Eliot managed to shake off the state of dumb-struck coma into which she had fallen and cut in sharply. "Wait a minute. What *are* you talking about? And how did you get this number?"

Dasha was unfazed. "Oh, don't worry, Eliot. Your husband's office was very helpful. We didn't have to approach anyone else —"

"What are you talking about? You have no right to approach anyone and there's absolutely no point. I don't want to talk to you. I have nothing to say to you and if you want to do a story about my career, which I doubt, why don't you come to my next show?"

Dasha barely missed a beat. "Sure, when is it?"

Eliot leapt to her feet, watching helplessly as the breakfast tray upended itself all over her precious old rug. "I am going to hang up now," she said slowly, her voice shaking with fear and rage. "Please do not call me again."

But even as she replaced the receiver she could hear Dasha's still optimistic voice tinnily squeaking: "Which gallery, Eliot? Which gallery?"

CHAPTER FOURTEEN

Dasha, it turned out, was not the only member of Sydney's media community to suddenly decide that Eliot Bancroft — a painter whose library file numbered two small reviews and a note remarking that she was "daughter of Senator Harry Bancroft, see own file; married to Jack Barron, lawyer, see own file" — was a subject sufficiently fascinating to profile. Eliot had only just finished clearing up the mess of her wrecked breakfast and her heart had almost returned to its normal steady beat when the phone rang again. This time she was doubly wary as she answered.

"Eliot Bancroft? Hi, it's Susan Rota from the *Sydney Morning Herald,* I wonder if I could talk to you for a moment?"

"How did you get this number? Have you been on to my husband's office?" Eliot made no pretense of politeness.

"Actually, yes, is there a problem?"

Susan Rota sounded pleasant and concerned. Eliot was marginally disconcerted.

"Ms. Rota. I've just had a call from *In Town Tonight.* They wanted to interview me about my career. Now, I very much doubt that they could identify one of my pictures if it had my name over it in flashing neon lights. Do *you* want to talk to me about my career?"

There was a prolonged silence, then Susan Rota's hearty laughter burbled into Eliot's ear. "Ouch!" she finally said. "I've caught you at a bad time!" And she laughed again.

Eliot smiled, despite her anger. "You could say that."

"Well, what if I told you I have one of your pictures. It's called *Seagrass 2* and I bought it at your last show at the Mainwaring Gallery."

Eliot was totally taken aback. After a few moments during which her mind remained devoid of useful thoughts she finally said, "Well, I'm terribly glad to hear that, but is that why you're calling me?"

Susan Rota sighed gustily. "Hell, no. I've drawn the short straw and get to ask you to answer some questions about your friendship with Julia Ross."

Eliot ran her fingers angrily through her hair and shook her head. "I don't believe this," she said frantically, her frustration boiling over. "There *is* no story. But I know how this works. If I say I won't talk to you, you'll write that and it'll look like there *is* a story. Right?"

After another long pause, Susan Rota coughed, and when she spoke her voice was quieter than before, close to conspiratorial. "Yes and no. Look, I really do admire your work. Hell, why else would I buy it! And I honestly don't want to do a stitch-up job. Okay? And I don't know why I'm telling you this, or why you should believe me, but I'd like you to. Okay?"

"Okay," Eliot said cautiously, wondering whether their conversation was being taped but, having just agreed to some degree of trust, not liking to ask.

"Okay. Well, how about this. Let's say — for argument's sake — that there *could* be a story, of some kind, at some point in the near-ish future. You with me?" Susan Rota didn't wait to find out whether Eliot was or not, but rapidly went on. "And let's say that a reporter who was sympathetic and had an interest in the subject being well handled had left her phone numbers. Okay?"

"Okay," Eliot said even more cautiously.

"Good. So then, when the time is right, we do a wonderful story. You're happy. I'm happy. Even more important, the editor's happy. And even more important than that, *In Town Tonight* is seriously pissed off. What do you reckon? Do we have a deal?"

Eliot couldn't help herself, she laughed. "Look, Ms. Rota..."

"Oh, for God's sake, *please* call me Susan."

"Susan . . . You have to understand, there is *no* story. At least, not the kind your editor wants."

"Sure. I know. But some time down the track you might want to have things told from your point of view. I mean, this divorce thing could get really nasty, don't you think?"

Eliot froze and the phone almost slipped from her hand. "What divorce thing?" Her words stuck in her throat.

"Well, I hear your husband will go for custody of your kid. Is that not so?"

Eliot began to shake so violently she had to grasp the phone with both hands and her voice was hoarse as her throat constricted on her words. "I beg your pardon? What did you say?"

"Is it true?"

Eliot took a deep breath and sat down on her bed but her voice still trembled as she spoke. "Ms. Rota . . ."

"Susan."

"Susan, I have to know two things before I answer any more questions."

After a short pause it was Susan Rota's turn to sound cautious. "Okay . . . shoot."

"First of all, my number here is unlisted. Where did you get it? And the second question is, where did you get the information about a divorce and my husband's intentions?"

Susan Rota let out a long, whistling breath. "I really can't divulge —"

"Oh, come on!" Eliot interjected. "A minute ago you asked me to trust you. Do a deal with you. Now I'm asking the same."

Again the pause was brief. "Okay." Susan Rota's voice dropped so low Eliot had to press the receiver close to her ear to hear her next words. "I can't exactly *tell* you, but let's say you could guess pretty close to home and I'd say yes or no, okay?"

Eliot took a deep breath. "Okay."

"Well, you better have a guess, then."

Eliot did guess and when, at her second conjecture, Susan Rota almost inaudibly said yes, Eliot found herself sitting on the floor beside her bed as her knees gave way to shock and disbelief. Half an hour later, Ray Freeman entered the house in response to her dumbfounded phone call and Eliot was still sitting on the old rug, the phone in her hand.

In response to Ray's "Coo-ee!" she struggled to her feet and met him in the hallway. He took one look at her dazed expression and grabbed her into an all-enveloping embrace and kissed her forehead. "Tell all, sistah girl."

Eliot shook her head and her mouth opened and closed on her incredulity.

"It's Jack, right?" Ray's dark eyes narrowed and became even darker. He and Jack made no secret of their mutual antipathy and Eliot knew Ray tolerated him only for her sake.

"It's unbelievable, Ray." Her throat was arid. "I really really can't believe it." Her breath came almost as a sob but her eyes were equally as drought-stricken. "Jack is going to force a divorce on me and he's going to take Morgan."

Ray's unbelief was instant and overwhelming. "You're kidding me! Since when has he ever taken an interest in Morgan?" He held her close as she shuddered with fright at his words and her own graphic image of the future now opening up in front of her. Arm in arm they let themselves out of the house and walked over to Eliot's studio.

"Oh god, Ray." She dragged her fingers through her hair in a gesture that expressed total helplessness. "It's really simple. And I've been such a fool. The plain answer is he's wanted Morgan ever since he realized she's worth about ten million to him."

It was Ray's turn to wordlessly open and close his mouth. Then, as they slumped together into the welcoming depths of the old sofa, he croaked, "I don't understand."

Slowly, floundering on her own apprehension, Eliot described her conversation with Susan Rota. With each fresh bit of information related, Ray's attitude swung wildly back and forth between dumb bewilderment and seething outrage. Eventually he asked, "Does Julia know what's going on?"

Eliot shook her head vehemently. "Of course not."

He frowned. "Don't you think you should tell her."

Eliot's agitation increased. "No! It's nothing to do with her. It's not her fault. And — please understand, Ray — I don't dare. If Jack found out we were in contact, it'd confirm everything. It's just what he wants. I'm sure of it."

Ray scrambled to his feet and began to pace the length of the studio, to and fro, his face a study of wrath, his fists contorting and releasing as if he was practicing a stranglehold. He stopped at the long windows and stared for a minute at the incongruously peaceful scene. Then he shook his head fiercely and turned to Eliot. "I gotta do something, El. I can't let that bastard just walk all over you."

Eliot placed her hands together in supplication. "Please, Ray. Please don't. He'd want that, you know what Jack can be like."

Ray snorted, the contempt twisting his normally sunny, handsome face into a bitter mask. "Yeah," he grunted. "I know what that bastard is like, all right." He sighed and scrubbed his fingers into his eyes in an action of utter frustration. "But I won't do anything drastic, El, I promise. Nothing until we talk to Greg, okay?"

Eliot breathed a sigh of some relief and her shoulders discernibly relaxed; she joined him at the window where they stood, linked arm in arm, watching a white cockatoo playing trapeze artist on a trailing gum branch until it got bored with its own cleverness and flew away.

"Well," he said finally, gingerly flexing his taut neck muscles, "I guess I better get back to work, see what that daughter of yours is up to now."

Eliot touched his dark cheek tenderly. "Send her home if she's being a nuisance."

Ray shook his head. "Nah. She's great for business. Naturally we're taking all the credit for her development. Makes us look shit-hot!"

Eliot grinned and punched his arm affectionately, then a thought occurred and the question was out before she could suppress it. "Are you in contact with Julia?"

Ray looked startled. "Sure. And Greg talks to her every day."

"Oh! I didn't realize."

"Sure. He's doing a bit of long-distance counseling and coaching."

Eliot couldn't help herself. "How is she?"

"Okay. Physically she's going great guns."

"But . . . ?"

"But you really got to her, El. It's not a medical diagnosis, but personally I'd say she's pining for you."

Eliot swung away from his wide brown eyes, unable to bear the honest affection and concern that shone there. "Don't, Ray. Don't. I can't get involved — not now, not ever — I can't lose Morgan. I can't take that risk."

He sniffed dismissively. "Seems like you're risking a fair bit sticking around ol' Mike Tyson Jack Barron, if you ask me."

Eliot froze. "What do you mean?"

With the tip of one gentle finger he touched her left eyebrow where a thin, half-inch black-blood scab and the yellowing remains of bruising were not quite hidden by her hair. "You been back here nearly a week and we haven't seen hide nor hair of you. What you been hiding? Hit your head on a door? Slip on a wet patch? Isn't that the way these things happen?"

Eliot shook her head. "It wasn't like that, Ray."

He nodded and his own left eyebrow lifted in a skeptical kink. "Yeah, they all say that too. Come on El, it's me you're talking to."

"It was an accident, Ray, truly."

He nodded again but his eyebrow remained unconvinced. "Sure, sure. And if that was an accident, what happens when it's deliberate?"

"I don't think that would happen, Ray. We

weren't fighting. We were arguing. He tried to catch me as I was going up the stairs and I fell."

"Oh great! That's terrific. And what was he going to do when he caught you? Kiss and make up? Eh?"

And Eliot was at a loss for a reply because it had not occurred to her, until that moment, to wonder what *would* have happened — and what would have happened if Morgan had not unwittingly intervened.

CHAPTER FIFTEEN

Morgan's intervention was more than unwitting, however. In New York, Julia returned to her apartment after a long session at the gym to find her answering machine winking. She dropped her gear bag in the laundry and returned to her desk to activate the machine. Andrew Connelli's voice crackled around the room, demanding her instant attention and response; Greg Bartlett's mellow tones followed as a soothing antidote to Andrew's acidity. The final message was from Morgan, and the small trembling voice stopped Julia in mid-step toward the refrigerator.

"Julia, it's Morgan. You said I should ring you if I was in trouble? Well, I'm not but Mum is and I'm scared. I think Daddy might hurt her again and I don't know what to do. Will you help us please, Julia? Will you talk to Greg or Ray or something? And please don't tell Mum I've called you. I think that will make more trouble. And I hope your knee is okay and everything. Do you miss us a bit?" At that, Morgan's voice broke into a half-swallowed sob and tears pricked Julia's eyes. "I don't want to be a nuisance, Julia, but I don't know what else to do." Julia heard the deep intake of breath and could picture Morgan's determined smile as she finished. "And it would be really good to talk to you sometime. I'm practicing every day, like you said. Greg is very pleased with me. So I hope to hear from you soon. 'Bye. Um, I love you lots." And the message ended with a clatter of clumsily replaced receiver.

Even as her heart froze and her mind began to turn over at top speed, Julia checked her watch. It was just the right time to catch Greg and she did. What Greg told her caused her tightly confined emotions to thaw and begin to smolder with rage.

"So what's his price, Greg?" she asked, her calm tone belying the murder boiling in her heart.

Greg's sigh was filled with gall and frustration. "For not going ahead with the custody plan, he wants an immediate and uncontested divorce and title to Eliot's house. And a cash payout too."

"Is that house worth so much? It's just a shack."

"Turns out Jack and her sister are in cahoots

213

with this fellow named Clarrie Summers. You won't know him but he's notorious here. He's been busy stuffing up the most beautiful bits of the Australian coast for about twenty bloody years and he wants to do the same with Eliot's patch. Jack and Daphne have secretly been buying the rest of the land behind Eliot's place which none of us even knew was for sale. If they can add hers to it, they get prime waterfront and a total parcel of about twelve acres."

Julia's eyes were wide as she stared at the rooftops of Manhattan. "My god," she said quietly. "It must be worth millions."

"You got it."

"I can't believe he'd go this far — and what about the sister, that's Daphne, isn't it? It's unbelievable." Julia placed her palm on her forehead as her mind reeled at the realization of the bizarre partnership aligned against Eliot.

On the other end of the line, Greg sighed. "It's big money, Julia. Really big money. People get pretty peculiar when you wave millions of dollars under their noses."

Julia shook her head, aghast. "I'm sorry, Greg, it's still unbelievable. It's . . ." She considered for a moment and shook her head again. "I don't know, it's surreal. And what's this about Eliot being hurt? Morgan's message said she's been hurt. Does she mean physically?"

Greg's hesitation told Julia everything she needed to know; even his caution that "we don't really know what happened, she insists he didn't actually hit her," was insufficient to stop the plan that had begun formulating in her mind.

"Greg, I'll be flying out to Las Vegas tonight. I've

got some business to attend to there first. Then I'll come on to Sydney and I'll let you know flight details later. Would one of you pick me up at the airport?"

"Do you think it's wise? You're just getting back into your stride . . ."

Julia's impatience cut him off, "Greg, I'm coming and that's it. I feel responsible for this. I . . ." She hesitated. "I love her. And more to the point, I can help."

Her coach and mentor still sounded dubious. "You can? Jack Barron is a pretty powerful and nasty fellow, Julia, you *must* be careful."

Julia snorted and she knew her tone of icy scorn was one that Greg had not heard before. "I don't mean to be rude, Greg, but you don't know the meaning of powerful. By the time I'm finished with that creep he'll be wearing his balls for cufflinks."

At the other end of the transglobal phone link she couldn't make out whether Greg's reaction was a gasp or a chuckle.

When Julia put down the phone from her conversation with Greg, she sat for some time in a trance-like state, gazing out of her windows as she settled finally on her choice of action. It was a method that, for ten years, had stood her in good stead for the times of great pressure that heralded her big matches, and she felt its calming and concentrating effects coursing through her veins. Then she quick-dialed Andrew Connelli's number and within an hour was striding restlessly around his penthouse office-apartment, half-listening to his protests and to the murmuring efficiency of Leoluca, his foxy personal assistant, as he organized Julia's flights and rearranged her instantly disrupted schedule.

"Crazy, darling, crazy. All you need right now is more delay in your rehab. And this insane adventure could be downright dangerous. I mean, what if it gets into the press?"

"It won't, Andrew. You, Leoluca and Greg Bartlett are the only ones who know."

"Oh yes, and half the ground staff at Kennedy, never mind anybody else who happens to see you get on a plane for Sydney."

"You're even more paranoid than your mother, Andrew."

Her manager snorted and fluttered his fingers, but the corner of his pink mouth lifted in an irrepressible grin. "I don't think you should malign my dearest mama, Julia, especially as your own dear mama is her very best friend and you want them *both* to help you with this crazy scheme."

Julia patted his cheek fondly. "I wouldn't dream of maligning your mama, Andy, wouldn't dream of it. I just hope you've talked to her and she knows what I need."

Andrew Connelli rolled his eyes theatrically. "Not only does she *know* but she *loves* the idea." He shuddered. "You women really are too too ghastly for words. Frankly I think Shakespeare was being far too kind when he invented Lady Macbeth."

"Was that Glenn Close?"

"The very same."

"She did Cruella De Vil real well too, but she

seemed pretty nice when I met her. I guess that's acting," Julia mused.

Eliot was aghast and numb with disbelief and no attempt at acting could disguise it. She had returned from a morning's sketching out along the cliffs high above the Pacific to find her husband in the kitchen of her house, making himself a cup of coffee. Sitting in one of her grandmother's cane chairs on the veranda was a man whom she recognized from news photos as Clarrie Summers. Jack effected an introduction and the older man struggled to his startlingly small feet and leaned over his equally startling and pendulous belly to kiss her hand.

"Charmed, dear lady," he said, and his lips plopped softly as they attached, remora-like, to her skin.

Eliot suppressed an entirely instinctive shudder and tried to close her mind to the thought that he was as unctuous as an unsavory character from a B-movie and drew her hand back from his clasp. She could think of nothing but getting the two men out of her house and she failed the basic politeness test.

"What *are* you doing here, Jack?" In her own ears her voice was strained. Her husband grinned easily. "We were in the neighborhood and thought we'd drop by. The door was unlocked."

"But it wasn't open." Eliot's slow simmering anger startled her. "I'm busy, Jack. I'm afraid I don't have time to entertain you and your . . . friend is it? Or partner?"

"Dear lady." Clarrie Summers smiled and Eliot suddenly realized the meaning of the word *reptilian*. She could barely bring herself to look at him, but his musty-sweaty-sweet smell was heavy in her nostrils and she could be nothing but aware of his presence on her veranda.

"Clarrie wants to talk to you about the development plans, darling." Jack's tone was somewhere between brusque and silky.

Eliot took a deep breath and a step backward at the same time. "There are no plans, Jack." She swallowed, her throat dry. "This was my grandmother's house and I like it just the way it is." She held up her hand as Clarrie Summers opened his pink lips. "I know you won't agree with me, Mr. Summers, but actually I don't want it to be turned into luxury homes. It probably looks like a seriously under-capitalized old shack to you, but that's all there is to it."

Jack's eyes glittered as he smiled at her over Clarrie Summers's sweat-beaded skull. "Darling, I don't think you quite understand. Why don't we take a little walk on the beach?"

Eliot's heart sank. It seemed, from her present point of disadvantage, that her friendship — and the few sweet secret nights — with Julia were about to turn her life into an unending nightmare. She held up her paint-smeared hands, half in surrender, half to buy herself a few minutes respite from what she suspected was about to happen.

Closing the bathroom door behind her she ran hot water in the basin and scrubbed her hands in baby oil before rinsing away the scum of dirt and paint. She still couldn't bring herself to believe that Jack

218

really meant to go through with his scheme. But she had seen in the strange fire in his eyes that his ambition and determination to have what he wanted would render her own pleas useless.

And as she brushed her hair back off her face, she was also faced with the miserable awareness that her inability to argue with him was compounded by her own guilt and frustration. But even as she splashed her face with cold running water and sniffed at the comforting scent of linseed and soap on her fingers, she found herself remembering Julia.

Eliot was awash in total languor, gazing intently out of the big window of Julia's bedroom at the calligraphy of black tree branches silhouetted against the skyline, and still thinking — idly — about getting out of bed when the phone rang. She rolled over to reach the receiver and felt the protests in her abdominal muscles as well as an overwhelming low-burning glow of fullness and content that somehow seemed to anchor her into her own body. She lifted the receiver and immediately Julia's laughter was in her ear.

"Sweetheart? Eliot?"

"It's me." Even as she spoke, a smile and burst of elation transformed Eliot's sleepy lethargy.

"What're you doing?" Julia's tone was playful.

"Thinking about getting up."

Julia's sigh whispered in her ear. "You still like I left you?" she asked softly.

Eliot pulled a sheet across herself and propped on one elbow. "I'm afraid so."

"I wish I was there."

Eliot smiled. "I wish you were too."

"Really? Do you mean that?"

"I do."

Julia's sharply indrawn breath was slowly exhaled. "You remember this morning?"

Eliot shivered and heat reignited in the wetness between her legs. "Of course I remember."

"You know what I'm doing now?"

"Having lunch with Andrew Connelli?'"

"And I'm eating salad and I'm eating it with my fingers and they're quite salty and" — Julia's tone dropped even further — "I just remembered I didn't wash my hands after I left you."

"Julia!" Eliot began to giggle. "Does he know what you're talking about."

"Nah. He's on his phone. But, anyway, I don't care." Julia's voice dropped to a whisper. "You taste beautiful."

Eliot gasped and laughed. "Julia! You're outrageous."

"And you're delicious."

Miserably, Eliot dragged herself back to the present and the reality of her husband and his friend, drinking her coffee on her grandmother's veranda. She splashed her face with cold water, then stared at herself in the tarnished silver freckles of her elderly bathroom mirror. She could detect no change in her face, but she knew that profound anomaly was hidden there somewhere. No longer was she Jack Barron's rather eccentric but also rather interesting wife; no longer was she the person she had been before boarding the plane for New York. No longer could she pretend she didn't understand the heights and depths of great and tender passion. Despite knowing, with complete certainty, that the press reports were fabricated and the photographs that had been published of her and Julia were meaningless, she also knew, in her heart of hearts, what they and Jack did not: that the truth was not an absolute and that reality was also a concept which could be shifted. Gone were previous certainties — black and white opinions, easy judgments, facile presumptions. In their place was a wiser and warier woman.

More than that, however, she now recognized that as the days had rolled by, and her isolation became intensified by the hostility and righteous anger of her family, she had become increasingly aware that the only person she wanted to see, the person she longed for and dreamed about, was Julia. She pressed her chilled wet hands against her forehead before acknowledging to her reflection and to herself the one fact that turned her heart to stone: Julia was gone.

CHAPTER SIXTEEN

"Hi, Mom." Julia kissed the air beside Antonella Rossi's perfectly blushed cheeks. Her mother's distinctive scent — of choice unguents and Patou's Joy — which had filled her nostrils from the moment she walked into the office, was greatly intensified.

"Darling." Antonella Rossi stepped back from her only child and a tiny quizzical smile almost disturbed the luster of her flawless makeup. "You're not on crutches."

Julia shrugged. "I've made good progress."

"That's marvelous, darling." Antonella smoothed

the lines of her perfectly tailored cream silk jacket and stepped away from the glittering glass-topped desk. "Let me look at you." Her handsome aquiline nose — a shared feature that quite unequivocally marked Julia as her daughter — developed a fleeting wrinkle as she took in Julia's Springsteenesque slack-assed jeans and leather jacket. "You do it to annoy me, don't you, darling?"

Julia surprised herself by not rising to the taunt. Instead she smiled at her mother and apologized, then stuck her fists into her jacket pockets and opened it wide so the sumptuous scarlet silk lining was revealed. "But this is a one-off — Versace — specially for me."

Antonella's eyes lit up and she reached out to finger the alluring heavy black leather; her immaculate scarlet-tipped fingers delicately scraping its surface, causing Julia to shiver.

"Well," Antonella said, her voice almost a purr, "I suppose that's rather interesting, really." But her eyes continued their appraisal of her daughter and remained carefully remote. "But you didn't come here to show me your wardrobe, did you, darling?"

Julia shook her head and turned away from her mother to the dizzying view of Chicago, set out like a relief map, far below. "No, Mom. I need your help." She glanced back at Antonella in time to see her faultless eyebrows shoot an inch or so skyward. Julia grinned. "Thought that would surprise you."

"Surprise? I'm astonished. *You* want *my* help?"

Julia nodded. "Yes, Mom, I do."

Antonella Rossi sat down hard. The peach-colored suede of one of the room's two enormous but comfortingly low sofas emitted a sharp sigh, as if equally

223

shocked. She waved one unmarred hand at the other sofa. "Sit down, darling, for heaven's sake."

Obediently Julia sat and, for a moment, peered at her mother through a small thicket of tuberoses, then she shifted to one side and they were separated only by the heady perfume of the tall white flowers.

"How much do you know about what's been happening to me lately?"

Antonella shrugged. "Not much. You've been in New York with a Mrs. Eliot Barron and her daughter Morgan since you got back with them from Australia. You spent a lot of time at some kind of shack belonging to Mrs. Barron next to a rather nice place run by those two tennis players where you were *supposed* to be staying. Brad Denvers walked out a while back and one of the Australians has been looking after you. What's his name? Greg, I think. Um —" She frowned and leaned forward to consult a pale pink folder which lay on the low table between them. "What else — you've been terrifically brave about that awful injury and we were all very proud of you. And now you're on your way back to Australia because your lady friend is in some kind of trouble with her husband." Her expression, as she glanced at Julia, was blandly disingenuous. "Is that about right, darling?"

But Julia was giggling and flopped back on the sofa, regarding her mother with a mixture of exasperated awe and something approaching an alien emotion, which she recognized as affection. "D'you know what color underwear I'm wearing, Mom?"

Antonella's nose twitched. "Don't be vulgar, darling. And don't be silly. You know how important it is that I protect you."

224

Julia's grin disappeared in an instant and was replaced by an expression that was both sad and sober. "I understand your concern, Mom. Really I do."

Antonella shook her head and emitted something almost as unladylike as a snort. "It is nothing to do with concern, Julia," she said sharply. "You of all people should know that."

Julia slumped back on the sofa, closing her eyes as she pinched the bridge of her nose between finger and thumb. "Okay, Mom, okay. I'm sorry. But really, all that was a long time ago."

Again Antonella's exasperation was denoted by a snort. "Your uncle has just completed his twelfth year in prison and your father has been dead fourteen years," she said quietly. "It might seem a long time ago to you but these things don't die with one generation, my darling, believe me."

Julia nodded and this time her response was as quietly serious as her mother's had been. "I know, Mom. I really do. I'm sorry. If I didn't understand I wouldn't be here asking for your help."

Antonella considered this for a moment then nodded. "Very well, Julia. Now come and sit beside me and tell me exactly what's been going on." She reached for the intercom button on the ivory telephone console that was placed, perfectly symmetrically, beside the vase of tuberoses on the glass-topped low table. "Claudia, darling, would you hold all calls for half an hour, please."

Eliot hesitated and checked her watch before she

225

pressed the button to quick-dial Rachel Taylor. It was
a little after nine, and the morning had a crispness
to it that was rare in the ocean-side microclimate of
Kurrunulla and its environs and suggested that
summer was about to give way to the mild chill and
occasional cold that passed for winter in Sydney. Eliot
shivered and wondered about a thicker sweatshirt,
but by then the phone was ringing and, after four,
the sleepy voice of Rachel Taylor was in her ear.

"It's Eliot, did I wake you?"

"Sweetheart, no of course not." Eliot heard her
friend stretch and in that instant, her warm tones
changed. "Where are you?"

Eliot frowned. "At home, why?"

"Just wondered. What're you up to?" Rachel's
tone was as crisp as the morning air.

"Not much, yet. I was wondering whether you'd
like to have lunch later."

Rachel's silence continued for so long that Eliot
began to wonder whether they had been cut off, then
Rachel said, with palpable caution, "Maybe, where?"

"I don't know, I hadn't got that far. Would you
like to meet at the cafe?"

"No!" Eliot jumped, startled by the sharp tone.
Then Rachel's voice climbed down an octave as she
continued, "Why don't you come here? Or, no, why
don't I come over to you? Except . . . " Eliot heard
her friend sigh. "Are there any photographers
around? Any press?"

"Of course, not! Rachel, what *is* wrong with you?"
Eliot was half-amused, half-fearful of the strange
reaction.

"There's nothing wrong with *me,* darling."

Rachel's tone was sharp. "But I could ask you the same question."

Dismay settled in Eliot's stomach in a cold lump. "Rachel, I don't understand; it's me — Eliot — you're talking to. What do you mean?"

"Darling, you're in every bloody gossip column I pick up. I mean, I know I encouraged you to have your little fling, but I thought you'd be discreet."

"Rachel!" But even as she began to protest, the realization was simultaneously beginning to seep into Eliot's consciousness of just how far out on a limb she was.

Numbly she listened to a voice that sounded like Rachel's telling her coolly that she was up for a part in a major Hollywood movie and was appalled at the publicity now surrounding her friend. As if to keep the refrigerated sound from penetrating her mind Eliot held the receiver away from her ear, but still she could hear Rachel saying, "Frankly, darling, I'm sorry to say this, but I've talked it over with Todd and my agent and they're both very reluctant to let me see you right now and certainly not in public."

"Rachel" — Eliot's throat constricted as tears threatened her composure — "I don't believe I'm hearing this."

"Darling, don't make it any harder, please. I hate this as much as you do, believe me. But you must understand my position."

Eliot's mind was reeling and sudden claustrophobia assailed her. She slid back the door to the veranda and stepped out into the keen morning air, the chill somehow neutralizing the ice which was settling about her heart. "Rachel, we have been friends — best friends — for longer than I can remember."

"Darling, don't . . ."

Eliot shook her head as ice began to turn to anger. "Don't 'don't' me, Rachel. We were lovers once" — she heard Rachel's strangled gasp and plowed right on, her anger fueling a determination to be heard that was yet another new sensation — "remember that, Rachel? Remember that we were in love for a while?"

"Stop it, darling. Stop it. What are you saying? You're not going to talk to the press are you?" The fear in Rachel's voice was unmistakable.

"Oh for heaven's sake, Rachel." Eliot was now too hurt to feel pain. "We're best friends. Or at least, I thought we were. I — me, Eliot Bancroft — love you. Do you honestly think I'd do anything to harm you?"

"Oh darling, I'm sorry." Eliot heard the tears in Rachel's voice. "I'm so sorry. But I can't. I just can't. You must understand. This is a really big chance for me."

Eliot only just prevented herself from throwing away the phone, so deep was her distress and disbelief. "My god, Rach," she half laughed, but it sounded more like a sob. "So all this time you weren't interested in Hollywood because Hollywood wasn't interested in you."

"Now you're being unkind. And cynical."

"Ha! *I'm* being cynical. Oh, Rachel Taylor. Listen to yourself."

"Darling, please understand." Rachel's tone was full of pleading and sadness. "Please don't be angry with me." Her voice dropped to a whisper that Eliot

228

could barely catch. "You know I love you, darling. I do."

"Actually, I don't, Rachel. Not now." Eliot straightened her shoulders which, suddenly, were aching unbearably. "I don't think I know anything about you anymore."

"That's cruel." Rachel's voice was sharper once more. "I warned you. And I warned you to be careful of Jack. Didn't I? And now he's threatening me too. I just can't risk it."

Eliot's heart seemed to stop for a moment and although her mouth opened, she was unable to speak. Then she heard herself say, in an unrecognizable tone, "What do you mean, Rachel? Jack's threatening *you*?"

"Oh darling, I didn't want you to know, but he's got the letters I sent you from India." Rachel suddenly sounded sadder than Eliot had ever heard her and she sighed and half chuckled. "He sent me copies. They were really lovely letters. No wonder you kept them." This time her laugh was sardonic. "But I wish to god you hadn't."

For a split second that seemed to last an eternity, Eliot was frozen as she pictured Jack rifling through her possessions in her studio — the one place which she had always believed to be sacrosanct. And she remembered exactly where she had kept, with other unlikely treasures, the three letters Rachel had once sent her from location. Finally, she spoke. "It's my turn to be sorry, Rachel. I really am. And what a fool. My god, I should know better. But I never . . ."

"Never mind, darling. In a funny way, I'm awfully glad you kept them. And I was glad to read them too

—it reminded me that I could really feel something, once upon a time. Pretty cruel though, don't you think? Jack, I mean."

Eliot's sigh was heartfelt. "I don't think I want to talk to you about cruelty, Rachel. Good luck in Hollywood. I really mean that, darling."

"Oh Eliot, I'm so sorry." Rachel's voice cracked.

" 'Bye, Rachel. I'm hanging up now." Eliot pressed the disconnect button and felt sick. Down on the beach she spied the unmistakable figure of Ray Freeman, waving as he loped along the tide line. She waved back and was unsure whether or not to feel relieved when he turned from his previous course and came jogging toward her.

By the time Ray had extracted from Eliot the reason for her pale and shaken demeanor, he was angrier than she had ever seen him. His hazel eyes glittered behind thick black, narrowed lashes and his wide, full mouth was clamped tight by jaw muscles that stood out in cords beneath his dark skin.

"I don't know what to say, El." He shook his head and seemed almost dazed. "You know I don't like the bastard, but this —" He shook his head again and expelled a breath in a hiss of disgust. "This is unbelievable, even for Jack." He flexed his strong fingers. "I could —" Eliot took his hands but he flung away from her. "No, El, this is really too much." He took a step away from her back toward the beach. "I gotta go, El. Sorry. I gotta work this out for myself."

"Ray, please don't do anything silly. Please."

Ray shook his head, but his eyes were no longer seeing her and she stopped in her tracks, realizing it was hopeless to try to stop him. A few hours later

230

she bitterly regretted that decision when the phone rang and she found an agitated Greg on the line.

"Eliot, I need your help. Ray's been arrested."

"My god! What's happened? What's he done?" But before Greg spoke, Eliot's imagination had already painted an unfortunately accurate picture and Greg merely confirmed it.

"He got into a fight with Jack at his chambers. Christ knows what he was doing there. The cops were called and he's been locked up. Tim Race phoned me five minutes ago, I think you know him, he's our lawyer. We've got to bail him out and I'd really appreciate you coming with me."

"Of course." Eliot's mind was reeling but what she had to do was clear. "It's my fault, Greg. He was here this morning and I told him what Jack's latest trick is. I should have stopped him. I'm terribly sorry."

Greg's tone was rueful and he chuckled before he responded, "Eliot, don't beat yourself up; you couldn't have stopped him. Trust me. Anyway, I'll pick you up in ten minutes, okay?"

"Have you had lunch? I was just making a sandwich."

By the time Greg, Eliot and Ray returned to Eliot's house, it was almost time for the evening news on television. "We'd better check it out," Greg said dolefully as he aimed the remote at the set. "Best to see what they make of it and work out the damage."

Ray had barely spoken a word during the drive back to Kurrunulla and now flung himself onto the sofa and folded his arms across his face. His knuckles were split and bruised; a swelling beneath his left eye was already purple. Eliot followed him and perched on the edge of the sofa, placing one hand gently on his thigh. "Let me get you something, Ray," she said softly.

After a moment, one arm shifted slightly and a hazel eye peered at her. "You gonna forgive me, El?"

"Oh, Ray! Me forgive you?" Eliot shook her head. "It's all my fault, Ray. I got you into this."

"Crap, El. I did what I wanted to do." He sat up and raised his chin defiantly as he looked toward his partner. "I'm sorry I made such a muck-up, Greg. But I'm not sorry I hit the bastard. And I'm not sorry I went down there."

Greg grinned at him as he continued to flick across the channels, looking for news. "I'm not sorry you decked him either, sweetheart. Actually, I'm sorry I wasn't there to get a swing in too. But I think we could have done without TV cameras."

Ray grimaced. "Yep. I wonder who called the bastards?"

Greg shook his head. "Could have been anyone after a coupla bucks. There's no point even thinking about —" On the television a reporter's voice mentioned the name Ray Freeman and Greg stopped in mid-flick. "Here we go," he said and sat down on the sofa and gripped Ray's ankle for support.

CHAPTER SEVENTEEN

In the opulent creamy sheets of Antonella Rossi's guest room, Julia tossed and turned, unable to sleep and infinitely restless. For a while she read, but eventually she gave up trying to concentrate and instead, turned on the TV to see the familiar face of a furiously angry Ray Freeman clamped between two police officers. Instantly she sat up, scrabbling frantically for the volume button and hit it in time to hear the CNN reporter say, " . . . there was a fight and it quickly escalated out of control. Police were called and Aussie tennis legend Ray Freeman was hustled away in handcuffs."

Mesmerized and open-mouthed, Julia stared at the screen as Ray's muttered "No comment" was repeated amid popping flashguns and wild questions from what sounded like a horde of unseen reporters. As the report continued, with many jocular references to Ray's "backhand" and "demon serve," Julia watched in mounting horror .and began mentally counting the PR cost to Kurrunulla's business. But, as the newscaster wound up the segment and went to a commercial break with a broad grin and a joking reference to Ray's medical qualifications and boxing skills, her heart began to return to normal and her spirits to lift.

Without even glancing at her watch she picked up the phone and dialed the Kurrunulla number.

"Good evening, this is Kurrunulla Sports Resort and the home of Ray Freeman, world —" There was much whispering and then Morgan's giggling voice resumed its piping announcement, "World feather weighing champion. How may I help you?"

Julia's mood lifted even higher. "Howdy-doody, Morgan. How're you doing?"

After a split second during which her intake of breath was audible halfway around the world, Morgan's squeak of delight was close to deafening. "Julia! Julia! Mum, Greg, Ray, it's Julia!"

A muffled clatter told Julia that Morgan had dropped the receiver and she was able to take several deep breaths and still her suddenly racing heart at the realization that Eliot was, if not close by, at least close to the phone. Then Greg's deep, soft tones filled her ear and she found herself fighting back tears.

"You okay, Julia?" he asked her and she nodded, scrubbing at her eyes and swallowing hard before being able to speak.

"Fine. Really fine. But I just saw Ray on CNN. What's going on? How is he?"

"He's fine. Hang on a minute, let him tell you."

Julia had another thirty seconds to get a grip on her roller-coaster emotions and then she heard Ray's light, sweet tones. "Sistah girl, how're you going?"

"Good, Ray. What about you? Who've you been beating up this week?"

Ray's laugh gurgled across the satellite links at her. "Aw shit, Jools. Where are you? How come you know already?"

"Chicago, I was watching CNN."

"Chicago! What're you doing?"

"Seeing my mom. What's going on there?" Julia's anxiety was stoked by her wish to ask the question burning a hole in her heart. But Ray chuckled and continued at his own pace.

"Your mum? I didn't know you had a mum! That's great. Give her our regards, hey?"

"Sure, sure. But tell me what's been going on, please." And as she listened to his rueful account of his visit to Jack Barron's sumptuous if now substantially rearranged offices — an account punctuated by prompts, laughter, whistles and ever more colorful descriptions from background voices that she didn't recognize — Julia's amusement and fidgets multiplied until she finally climbed out of bed and began pacing the carpet, laughing and feeling angry simultaneously as the story unfolded. As she turned at one end of the room, she caught sight of herself in the mirrored expanse of the opposite wall and realized, with shocked pleasure, that she was barely limping as she walked toward her naked reflection.

Finally, as she observed the form of her own hand as it cupped her breast, she interrupted and said simply, "Ray, how is Eliot?"

After an almost imperceptible pause she knew he was grinning as he said, "You want to talk to her?"

Julia's heart stopped. "I don't know. I don't think so. I —" But it was too late. She heard his muffled voice tell Eliot to "take it in the study," then a door closed and in the sudden silence, her heart started and stopped all over again as Eliot's soft voice melted in her ear. Although she thought for an instant that she would be tongue-tied for the rest of her life, Julia heard her own markedly normal tones saying, "Hi, how lovely to hear your voice."

"You too, Julia. You saw Ray on TV?"

"CNN sports news. Are you okay?"

Eliot's sigh sounded both weary and wary. "Sure, I'm fine. I'm just really sorry to be the cause of all this trouble."

Julia snorted, "*Jack* is the cause, surely?"

"Let's not talk about that." Eliot's tone suggested that although she was speaking to Julia, she had retreated to some far-off place. "How's your knee?"

"Absolutely fine. According to anybody who's anybody in the knee business, the recovery is phenomenal."

"That's wonderful. So, what now?"

Julia hesitated, watching her leg muscles dispassionately as she slowly lowered and raised herself, holding the brass rail of the bedstead like a barre. "I'm not sure," she said deliberately. "I'm not in that much of a hurry right now."

"But I thought you wanted to get back to playing as quickly as possible?"

Julia shrugged and wrinkled her nose. "I've had time to think about things a bit more." She slipped back into bed and pulled the quilt up to her chin as the full effect of Eliot's voice and virtual proximity began to course through her veins. "The circuit doesn't seem to be where I want to be right now."

"Oh."

The minimal nature of Eliot's response told Julia that Eliot had understood her unspoken meaning. It was confirmed a moment later when she said, in a tone of undisguised panic, "You won't do anything silly, will you?"

Julia's heart sank. "You mean, like punch out your husband?" Her own voice sounded cold in her ears.

"Julia, please —"

"Eliot, just tell me one thing. Did the time we spent in New York mean nothing to you?"

The silence crackled between them, then Eliot's voice dissolved Julia's coolness and turned her heart in a somersault as she said quietly, "It meant everything."

The shock coursed through Julia's body from her brain to her heart and on down to where it exploded in a hot wave of longing. "I'm going to help you, Eliot," she said softly. "Do you understand what I'm saying."

"My darling, please! Julia, I beg you, don't do anything crazy. Jack will take Morgan. I know he will . . ." Eliot's fear was tangible, but Julia only registered the endearment which had accidentally escaped her lips.

"It's okay. I promise, it's okay," Julia soothed. "Jack will *not* take Morgan. Do you hear me? And he won't get your house, either. Believe me."

Eliot's sigh was close to a sob. "Julia, I don't know how else to say this, but I *beg* you not to interfere. Jack says he has photographs" — Julia heard a deep intake of breath — "of us. Not the one at the airport, but some taken in New York. He'll use them, I'm sure of it. And he'll prove I'm an unfit mother and take her."

This time the sob was undisguised and unrestrained. Julia sat bolt upright in bed, wishing with all her heart that she could take Eliot in her arms and comfort her. "Sweetheart," she said gently, "please don't cry. And don't be afraid. I'll be there soon and I'll take care of it. I promise. You must believe me."

"No! Oh god, please don't come, Julia. That's what he's waiting for! Please. Oh god, no. I'm going to hang up now. I don't want — I can't talk to you — please understand. Please —" And before Julia could utter another word, Eliot was gone and the only sound left was the flat hiss of a broken connection.

After a moment Julia slipped the receiver back onto its cradle and lay back, drawing the sheet and quilt up high as loneliness chilled her skin. Beyond the heavily curtained window a dog barked. It was a ferocious sound, as Antonella intended. At night the gardens of the Rossi mansion were not suitable for an impulsive stroll, but, as Antonella had once pointed out to her restless daughter, the untimely and violent deaths of Frank Rossi and his father had all but ruled out that kind of freedom for their successors. And, she further observed to a sulky

238

thirteen-year-old Julia, such precautions meant they were both alive and Antonella was — even then — well on her way to a dominance of the shadowy Rossi empire that many underlings, even in their wildest nightmares, had never considered possible.

Momentarily Julia grinned at that particular memory, but even more quickly, the present shoved its way into her consciousness, She shivered, wondering what Eliot was doing at that very moment, whether she would return to the party and join in again or whether the fear provoked by Julia would get the better of her. Suddenly the plan hatched with her mother seemed less like the logical and heroic scheme she had envisioned and more likely to even further alienate Eliot. Fretful again, Julia climbed out of the high brass bed of her childhood and slipped her arms into her kimono robe. "I want my mama," she said aloud, and the grin that reflected back to her from the mirrored wall was close to a grimace.

"Where's Mum?" Morgan's voice cut through the catatonic trance of dread enveloping Eliot.

"Here, darling," she called and took three deep, slow breaths as the study door burst open and the exuberance of the party erupted around her. Beyond Morgan's excited face, however, Eliot saw the concern in Greg's eyes and Ray's watchful demeanor and, in response, she smiled as widely as she could.

"Is Julia coming, Mum? Is she?"

Morgan's exhilaration touched Eliot's heart and she found herself wishing, deeply, that she could reply in the affirmative. But she shrugged and grinned and said, "I'm not sure, darling. I think she's terribly busy."

Morgan frowned and the light went out in her eyes. "Did she say that? Did she say she's too busy?"

Eliot opened her mouth to lie and then stopped. The flicker of bewilderment and hurt in Morgan's face had set an alarm bell ringing and instead she reached out for her daughter and said, as she gathered her into a cuddle, "No darling, she didn't. But I know she *is* very, very busy."

Morgan was not placated and not willing to stay within her mother's embrace. There was an edge of petulance in her voice as she drew away and flung herself at Ray and said, "So when's she coming? She *said* she would." Then her eyes saucered as she realized her slip and as the attention of the three adults was suddenly fixed upon her.

"What do you mean, darling?" Eliot's voice was quiet and calm even though that was not how she felt.

Morgan stuck out her lower lip and said nothing.

"Morgan —"

Morgan wiggled her nose and stared at the tips of her Nikes for a second, then she looked up at Eliot and her wide eyes were full of resolve as she said, "I phoned her and asked her to help." And before Eliot could remonstrate she rushed on, "She said I was to ring her if we needed help and we *do* Mummy, we *do*."

Eliot looked to Ray, who merely raised his eyebrows, and to Greg, who shrugged his shoulders, then his companion took him by the arm. "I think you two should have a little talk, El," Ray said softly and they were gone, leaving Eliot and Morgan regarding each other suspiciously from either side of a mahogany campaign table whose surface was invisible beneath a tightly packed array of apt if variously unattractive tennis trophies. Finally Eliot's serious countenance was cracked by a grin as she watched her daughter struggling to remain nonchalant.

"Okay, Morgan," she said with as much gravity as she could muster. "Out with it. What *have* you been up to." And Morgan almost succeeded in tying her skinny brown legs in a knot before she could bring herself to confess.

Eliot listened, her daughter's alienated and frightened words of explanation leaching away the residue of bonhomie left by the wine she'd drunk until she felt drained to shaken sobriety. Eventually she gathered the lean little body into her arms and hugged Morgan with unusual ferocity.

"Sweetheart, I'm so sorry," she said into the sweet-smelling tumble of curls into which she'd sunk her nose. "You're not to be frightened."

"I'm not," Morgan said stoutly and pushed herself upright, out of the circle of her mother's embrace. "I know Julia will come. She said she will. And everything will be fine."

Eliot opened her mouth and then closed it again. That Morgan knew about custody battles and the ugliness of divorce, Eliot had no doubt. Whether she could understand and accept that she herself was about to become the object in such a battle, she hadn't yet found the fortitude to ask or formulated the words to explain. But before she could even begin to wrestle with such a quandary, Morgan reached up and kissed her cheek and spoke an uncanny and unnerving echo of Julia's own words.

"Don't worry, Mummy. Everything will be fine. Julia will take care of it, I promise. Believe me."

CHAPTER EIGHTEEN

Some hours later, one-third of the way eastward around the globe, Antonella Rossi reluctantly conceded to her daughter that her black leather jacket was perhaps a tolerably sexy garment. They were standing in the portico of the mansion, their breath, as they spoke, white puffs in the chill spring air. Acceptance of the garment was, Julia realized, symbolic of something more: tacit acknowledgment of an autonomy and respect that Antonella had never before acceded to her daughter.

"Everything will be fine," Antonella said softly,

her hand resting lightly on Julia's sleeve. "The di Francescos will take care of everything. You need not concern yourself, nor take any part."

The two women, so alike and yet, in the tangible energy of the younger and the studied languid stance of the elder, so different stood in a silence that was as close to companionable as was ever likely. The Chicago morning was chilly and gray and seemed to absorb sound and warmth. Julia shivered and thought of the warmth of Australia.

"I may stay in Sydney awhile, Mom," she said quietly. "I'm not sure I want to get back on the circuit as quick as I thought."

Antonella Rossi smiled. "Perhaps you're growing up, Julia." She squeezed her daughter's arm and the fondness in her eyes canceled any possibility of criticism in the remark. "You know we're very proud of you. Whatever you do now can only be more of the same. I'm sure it's time to move on. Victoria said that very thing to me when you had your accident."

Julia grinned and kissed her mother's cheek. "Which reminds me, give her my love."

Antonella tossed her head and the silver streak which began at her temple shimmered. "That old dyke!" She snorted. "She doesn't deserve your love. She left me here — in Chicago, in the middle of winter — to go swishing off to some history conference in Mexico City!"

"So why didn't you go with her?"

Again Antonella snorted. "And do you think the business runs itself?"

"For two weeks? Probably, yes — especially any

business with you in charge of it. Anyway, you'll have to arrange something if you come to Australia."

Antonella's eyes narrowed as she examined her daughter's face. "I see. So this married lady is that important?"

Julia wrinkled her nose and at the thought of what lay ahead, her heart sank. "I don't know, Mom. Right now she doesn't even want to see me."

"Don't be foolish," Antonella said impatiently. "She is a mother. She is afraid for her child." She stamped her foot in its handmade beige suede boot. "You must take care, she is very vulnerable. Don't do anything foolish."

Julia grimaced. "That's what Eliot said."

"And she's right." Antonella's hand closed firmly on Julia's forearm, "I know how she feels, Julia, trust me. I know you and I have our problems but if *anybody* threatened you —" She blinked rapidly as tears that had nothing to do with the cold air threatened her mascara, then went on in a tone that caused Julia to shiver, "I would kill them."

Even as Julia searched her imagination for a suitable response, Antonella's pale gray Mercedes, bullet-proofed to head-of-state specification, drew up at the foot of the shallow sweep of peach-colored marble steps leading to the Rossi front door. She turned to her daughter and smiled. "No long good-byes, darling."

"Okay, Mom." But as Julia swallowed the sudden lump in her throat and saw the tear that had escaped Antonella's guard coursing down her perfect cheek, the years of strict training fell away. She crushed her mother in an embrace into which she tried to distill the unspoken affection which had survived the years of difficulty, misunderstanding and intermittent estrangement. "I think you're an amazing and wonderful woman, Mom," she said, with difficulty. "And I want you to know that I love and respect you more than I've ever told you."

Antonella sniffed and frantically searched her pockets for the lacy handkerchief that was always there. "Victoria said that too." Her voice was muffled by the snowy scrap of fabric. "Maybe I should pay attention to her."

Julia released her struggling mother and giggled. "Maybe you should; after all, she's a crazy old dyke like you. Who better?"

Antonella slapped her leather-clad sleeve. "So where's this respect?"

Julia shrugged. "It comes and goes."

"And now you better go." Antonella completed a complex dabbing of her eyes that miraculously avoided her mascara. "You got a plane to catch." And for the first time in a decade, Julia left her mother with regret and with the icy air suddenly as warm as a summer's day.

In Sydney, despite the balm of an unusually benign spring day, the atmosphere at the table on Eliot's veranda was anything but warm. Lounging at one end was Jack Barron, flanked by two young lawyers whose darkly stark city suits were as seriously out of place as obviously, by their restless fingering of collars and skirts, were they. Beside Eliot, still fiery with barely contained outrage, sat Ray and in the buffer zone between the two parties sat Greg and their barrister, the costly and famously able Vernon Peal.

It would have been obvious to a Martian, Eliot mused, as she watched the group, that the attempted mediation was not working. Moreover, as Jack's shoulder lifted as he turned away and lit an ostentatious cigar, it was even more obvious that there was no chance that it ever would. In despair, she stood up but her husband's voice struck her like a whiplash before she moved a step away from the gathering.

"I haven't finished yet, Eliot. Sit down."

Beside her, Ray began to rise and a growl of hatred rose in his throat. Both Greg and Eliot put out hands to curb him, but he shook them off and stood, glaring at Jack with undisguised and unmodulated hostility.

"Don't speak to her like that, you creep." His voice was low and calm. "If I start on you again, I won't be pulled off by your goons and, let me tell you, I don't care how long I spend inside, it'll be worth it."

Jack's smile was almost disdainful but as the minutes ticked by and he tried and failed to stare down the menacing Ray, it collapsed into something more like a smirk and he shifted uneasily in his seat. "Call him off, Eliot, for heaven's sake," he said, but his tone was uncertain, the braggadocio gone. He cleared his throat. "If I thought he'd behave like a savage I wouldn't have come."

This time it was Eliot's turn to feel her temper on the rise. "If you're being deliberately offensive, don't, Jack. You were invited here to try to put an end to an embarrassing and shameful bit of nonsense and —"

But she got no further. Jack's previously indolent pose vanished in an instant and he sat forward, his mouth an ugly snarl, flecks of spittle hitting the rough-hewn table between them as he virtually spat his words. "Embarrassing! Shameful! You bitch! Don't you talk to me about embarrassing and shameful." He turned to one of his now alarmed young associates. "Jessica, the photographs."

Poor Jessica hesitated — it seemed this was not part of the plan — and she dutifully shook her head, but her reluctance didn't last beyond Jack's roared, "The photographs!" With shaking hands she fumbled in her rather daring, non-black Louis Vuitton brief-case and eventually was able to hand the fuming Jack a large yellow envelope.

Its dog-eared and worn-to-fuzziness appearance immediately suggested to Eliot that it was always to hand, and an ice block formed in the pit of her stomach as Jack's other motive for so readily agreeing to come to her house sprang to mind. And she silently thanked Greg and whichever guardian angel had prompted him to insist that her daughter be taken care of in the comparative safety of Kurrunulla.

"At the very least, this is likely to be an un-pleasant encounter," he'd said to her, with charac-teristic understatement.

That he had been right became apparent a moment later as the contents of the well-worn envelope cascaded across the table for all to see.

Unable to stop herself, Eliot gasped. There, thirty times over, in slightly fuzzy but glossy black and white large format prints, was her unmistakable and undeniable love for Julia.

"You're scum, Barron." Again Greg's soft voice understated his feelings.

Jack sniggered, his composure almost instantly restored by his wife's evident distress. "Nice pix, eh?"

Without even a glance at Jack, Ray gathered up a sheaf of photographs and began to examine them closely. Eliot watched him, mesmerized by his concentration. One by one he handed them on to her and she too, seemingly obediently, started to inspect the pictures. The sussurating shuffle of the photographs was punctuated by the faint but insistent tapping of an expensive loafer on wooden floor boards as one of Jack's associates experienced the beginning of nerve failure. The deceptive tranquility was further impaired by Jack's drumming fingers, but after looking at two or three photographs, Eliot's dread began to give way to a disconcertingly mixed emotion: sadness and joy.

There, indisputable in black and white, was the clearest possible evidence of something she had — without even consciously considering it — given up hope of experiencing. With tears glittering in her eyes, she was arrested by one particular image. It was, she remembered, somewhere in a breezy Central Park and depicted the beatific expression on her own face, upturned to the even more openly adoring face of a windblown, beautiful, laughing Julia Ross, left arm about her lover's waist and right hand tenderly brushing a strand of hair from her eyes.

Eliot turned the photograph toward her husband

with a wry smile. "I don't think you'd recognize it, Jack," she said softly, "but this is a photograph of me being happy."

For an instant, Jack Barron's handsome face became ugly, then he recovered himself and smiled. "Better make the most of it," he said with blood-curdling mildness. "Better remember it. You won't feel like that again for a very long time." And before Ray Freeman could bunch his fists and leap to his feet, his companion and lover, the lifetime pacifist Greg Bartlett, had risen, taken two steps to the end of the table, grabbed Jack by his Windsor-knotted old school tie and dragged him to his feet.

"I was wrong," he snarled. "You're worse than scum, Barron. I don't think I've ever met anything like you. D'you want to put your fists up? I'm going to hit you."

Jack's amazement was equaled by that of the others collected in a frozen tableau around the table. He gaped like a goldfish suddenly spilled from the safety of his familiar tank, then the slow slippage of his tie began to impede his comfort and he scrabbled at Greg's hands.

"I'll sue you, Bartlett," he gargled. He looked around frantically at his two immobilized associates. "You're witnesses!" he screeched, but as the two spontaneously began to back away from the table shaking their heads, his attention turned frenziedly back to Greg. "Let me go you crazy poof! If you lay a finger on me I'll get you. I'm warning you."

Greg released his grip on the ruined tie and Jack stumbled backward, falling in a tangle of legs and cushions over the chair in which he had been so insouciantly lounging. But before Ray or Eliot could begin to intervene, Greg took another step toward Jack and stood over him, his usually calm and handsome face suffused with rage.

"Get up," he hissed. "Get up, you prick."

Limply Jack's legs kicked out at Greg. "Get away from me," he protested, at the same time making no move to rise. He wagged his finger at Ray and Eliot. "You saw what happened. *You* are witnesses."

Ray's snort was expressive enough for them both, but nevertheless Eliot turned away from the scene in dismay and disgust. She did so in time to see Jack's associates slinking away through the shrubbery toward the back of the house. Within minutes, she realized, the sound of a pair of BMW ignitions firing up would be audible. Despite her distress laughter bubbled up in her throat and she glanced over her shoulder to see both her friends roughly pulling her husband to his feet.

"Do what you like, you two," she said. "I think I've got something in my eye."

CHAPTER NINETEEN

When Ray and Greg stepped forward from the excited multi-colored throng to greet Julia as she came through the international gates she felt an ease and elation she had not experienced in a long time. She lifted her dark glasses and kissed each man on his sweet-smelling cheek and said, happily, "Hi guys. Great to see you."

"You too, Julia," said Ray warmly. "We've *all* missed you."

She grinned at him, a quizzical lift to her eyebrows asking the question of who the "all" might be.

He shrugged, understanding her unspoken quandary. "It's tricky, Jools. We've had a spot of bother. Greg will tell you."

Until that moment his partner had been standing back from them, his coolly neutral gaze taking in Julia's recovered range of movement and the restored ease of her physicality. He caught her inquiring glance and beamed. "Phenomenal, Julia," he said proudly. "Never seen anything like it. We're talking — what? — four months?" Julia nodded and executed a couple of on-the-spot dance steps. Greg's enjoyment was tangible. The usually undemonstrative man grabbed her in a bear hug and almost lifted her off the ground. "You're a miracle. And a bloody gutsy one, too," he said and his voice was hoarse with emotion.

There was more emotion on the drive to Kurrunulla as, in turn and sometimes simultaneously, Greg and Ray filled in the missing pieces in Julia's picture of what had been happening to her friends. By the time they reached the lodge she was not only aware of the smoke-tinted windows of the otherwise nondescript di Francesco car that discreetly followed them, but also, she had fixed upon exactly what she intended to do. Back once more in the familiar comfort of "her" cottage she dragged off her jeans, jacket and heavy sweatshirt, sluiced herself in the shower in what she knew would be a vain attempt to ward off jet-lag, and pulled on a pair of shorts and a skimpy T-shirt.

One phone call to Darren di Francesco reassured her that her mother's plan had been conveyed and understood by her Australian partners. Another call, to Jack Barron's chambers, secured the appointment she needed to deliver the content and intention of the plan. Her final call, on the internal system, was to Ray and Greg.

"I'm going over to Eliot's, now," she told them, stilling Ray's immediate concern with soothing agreement that she would call him at the slightest hint of the untoward. "Don't worry, Ray. I promise it'll all be — what is it? — beauty?"

She heard his amusement in his reply, "Nah, either it's 'beaut' or 'bewdy.' "

"Uh huh, maybe I'll just stick to cool. So, see you later." And before either he or Greg could protest further, she hung up, slotted her Ray-Bans on her nose, twisted her distinctive hair up under a Yankees baseball cap and slipped out of the cottage. The side gate into Eliot's grounds was unlatched and, seeing nobody around the nearby tennis courts and with her heart thundering in her ears, she let herself in and quickly made her way through the trees and along the sandy path leading to Eliot's studio.

From within she could hear the surging anguish of massed strings and her heart turned over at its sadness. The door stood open and she peeped in. The sunny expanse of the main work area was empty except for the elderly midi-stack stereo beside which lay a CD case for a remastered and digitized but even more elderly version of Mahler's fifth symphony. The fresh scent of linseed oil told Julia that Eliot wasn't far away and then she heard footsteps and, above her head, a floorboard creaked. She hesitated for some time before taking several deep breaths in a vain attempt to still her pounding heart; with due caution for her knee, she climbed the stairs to the bright white room in the treetops.

Eliot was busy drawing. Three steps from the top of the flight of steps, Julia stopped to watch her, savoring the moment for its tranquility and the unconscious grace and beauty of the woman. As usual, Eliot was dressed in an ancient, shapeless and indeterminately colored T-shirt and a pair of finger-smeared shorts. Her feet were bare and the toenails painted brilliant scarlet. It was that incongruous and out-of-character touch which struck Julia's heart with the knowledge that she loved Eliot as she had never loved any other. She crossed the room in three long, silent strides and placed her lips in the vulnerable spot at the nape of Eliot's neck.

Eliot dropped her charcoal stick and her indrawn breath was a gasp. Beneath Julia's gentle hands, her shoulders stiffened and she sat rigid as Julia tenderly kissed her way to the hollow of her right collarbone, then her whole body seemed to relax and she began to tremble.

"Julia," she whispered and it was not a question nor a statement, more an enjoyment of the banishment of disbelief. She reached up and held Julia's face. "Morgan said you'd come."

"You should pay more attention to that child," Julia muttered into her ear.

Eliot got to her feet and turned into a willing and hungry embrace. Her face told Julia everything she needed and feared to know: Eliot was overjoyed and terrified — and, Julia realized, she felt much the same, if for different reasons.

"How're you doing?"

Eliot shrugged and brushed away a traitorous tear. "Fine."

"Have you missed me?" Julia knew the answer by

the way Eliot's hands tightened on her forearms, but she persisted anyway, lifting Eliot's chin and making her meet her eyes and repeating, "Have you missed me?"

Eliot leaned into the embrace and rested her forehead against Julia's mouth. "I have," she whispered. "I've missed you terribly." She looked up at Julia, an expression both wary and hopeful in her eyes. "How about you?"

In answer, Julia crushed the body she had dreamed about to her, feeling as she did so its extra lightness and thinness. Through tears and a constricted throat she managed to say, "I don't want to be without you again, ever."

"You hardly know me."

"I know everything I need to know. I could know you twenty years and not know you better."

Eliot sighed and snuggled further into the all-enveloping embrace. "Sometimes I think perhaps you're the old head here."

"Yeah, well. I've been doing a lot of reading."

But before Eliot could enquire, the unmistakable high-pitched squeal of a seven-year-old about to achieve nirvana assailed their ears. Within seconds, Morgan's feet were pounding the stairs and in less time even than that, she was scudding across the room to launch herself headlong into Julia's waiting arms.

The reunion was tear-streaked and full of laughter. Julia attempted to reassure Morgan that she would not disappear again, but it seemed uncertain whether the girl would ever release her hand. At last, in despair, Eliot offered her favorite lunch in return for Morgan's cooperation in its preparation, and after some bargaining the three made their way down-stairs and then arm in arm to the house.

As Morgan's current favorite lunch, Julia discovered, was pre-prepared hamburgers and french fries fresh from the freezer, she was able to impart an exhaustive report on her tennis progress as well as closely examine Julia's knee and observe a demonstration of its range of movement while her mother produced food and watched them with, Julia noticed, an expression approaching the beatific.

"I'm taking this child out to the court for five minutes," Julia finally said as Morgan's excited animation began to sap her depleting store of energy. "How long until lunch?"

Eliot squinted at the pan of spitting burgers. "Ten minutes should do it. Are you sure you're feeling up to this?"

But as Morgan was already dragging Julia with all the weight she could muster out of the kitchen, any reply Julia might have made was lost in her chirruping elation.

The silence, after their precipitate departure, was broken only by the spitting and crackling of the burger griddle and the faint hiss from the oven where, in a shallow pan, pre-frenched fries were slowly losing their dead white gleam and turning a reasonably authentic-looking golden brown.

Eliot leaned against the kitchen counter and stood there, her head and heart reeling under the impact of events and emotions. She could see her daughter and — her heart contracted on the thought — her lover, as they made their way through the dappled shade of ancient trees toward the tennis court; the sight filled her with both enchantment and apprehension. Sud-

denly she wished Rachel Taylor could see the joyous
skip in Morgan's step and understand the happiness
contained in this one simple, mundane domestic
scene. On impulse she reached for the phone and
then withdrew her hand. There was enough com-
plication and potential danger on the horizon without
deliberately inviting more, she told herself sternly.
Instead, she pulled open the door of the dishwasher
and began the much more manageable task of setting
the table with plates and cutlery. Still though, flutters
of panic insisted on intruding and she was only too
aware of their source: she could not share Julia's
seemingly easy conviction that she had somehow and
miraculously prevented Jack from destroying her life.

After lunch, with Morgan banished to her
bedroom for half an hour, Eliot said as much to Julia
as they sat in comparative peace over coffee on the
veranda. Julia took her hand and squeezed it, but
Eliot shook her head and withdrew from the comforting touch. "You have to understand what's happening here," she said to Julia with exasperation in
her voice. "I've *seen* the photographs Jack has and I
know he can prove in court that I'm an unfit . . ."
She swallowed before going on, ". . . an unfit lesbian
mother." Her eyes were fear-filled and pleading. "You
must understand."

"I do, I do," Julia soothed. "Hey, look, I know I
was pretty casual about all this — and I'd love to see
the pix by the way. Do we look gorgeous, or what?"
Despite her anxiety Eliot giggled and punched Julia's
hand where it lay open in supplication on the table
between them. "But this is all fixed, darling. I
promise you."

This time there was a flash of anger in Eliot's

expression. "How can you say that, Julia? You don't realize how powerful Jack is. I'm sorry to say he has real influence in this town."

Julia was nodding. "I know, I really do." She glanced at her watch and saw that the appointment she had made with Jack in her name had already been kept by two of her mother's associates and would, by now, be well over. She wrinkled her nose and shifted uncomfortably in her seat. "I have to say Jack is a cream puff against my mom. And while we've been having fun here a couple of her guys have been paying him a visit."

Julia reached out and took Eliot's hand. "I can honestly say Jack will never bother you again," she said solemnly but with obvious embarrassment. "He has done some foolish and bad things in the past few years and my mom's people have a dossier about this thick." She demonstrated. "And it's unlikely he'll do anything bad or foolish again in his whole life. That is," she briefly considered the thought, "unless he's even badder and more foolish than I think."

Eliot's bewilderment was apparent. "Your mother is a businesswoman — right?" Julia nodded. "How can she have that much clout here when she lives in Chicago?"

Julia spread her hands wide. "My mom is everywhere. The difference between her and Jack is that she's bigger and" — she again wriggled in her seat — "much much badder and she's *never* foolish."

The implication of what Julia was saying and not saying was gradually beginning to seep into Eliot's consciousness and the enormity of it caused her body to tingle with the pins and needles of shock. But still she didn't quite dare believe until a motorcycle courier arrived with a package of documents addressed to her — in Jack's unmistakable flamboyant hand — and apparently for her signature.

Julia said nothing as Eliot riffled through the sheets of paper but simply watched, with growing pleasure, the lines of worry and fear begin to almost magically vanish as light dawned: what she held in her hands was Jack's agreement to an immediate and unconditional divorce with no claim for custody of his daughter. The second document relinquished all claim on her grandmother's house, and the third was a signed and witnessed statement in which he withdrew all allegations against one Raymond Watson Freeman.

Minutes passed as Eliot read and reread the documents. At first it was disbelief that made her go back over each page, but finally it was soaring exhilaration and the sheer bliss of feeling months of sickening terror dissipate and disappear. Julia, she ultimately acknowledged to herself, had achieved the impossible. Barely able to breathe and with shaking hands, she carefully set down the creamy-heavy sheets of paper and — even more heedfully — tapped them into a perfect pile, before she felt she could trust herself to look at Julia without exploding with euphoria.

"You've beaten him at his own game," she said at last, and there was awe in her eyes. "I don't believe it. I didn't think anybody could do that."

Julia shrugged and stretched lackadaisically before observing, "Well, I play tennis, don't I?"

Eliot laughed. It was a response she wished she could hang on to forever. Then, as she glanced once again at the sheaf of papers beneath her hand, she realized the accompanying feeling of pure release was not about to go away. She grasped Julia's hand in both her own and shook her head in wonderment. "I don't begin to understand what's happened," she said softly. "And I think I probably shouldn't try. But can you tell me *something*?"

Julia frowned. "Well," she said slowly, kissing the back of Eliot's left hand. "It's the same principle as fighting fire with fire. Kind of a bit too Old Testament for most tastes, but I reckon you do what you gotta do. So, employing a strategy I read about a coupla weeks ago in a biography of Alexander the Great, who — you might like to know — was also a serious badass and not just a cute guy with a big horse. I decided we needed to fight ruthlessness with equal ruthlessness." She grinned disarmingly. "And although that's not an exact quote from the man, it's damn near it." She delicately kissed the inside of Eliot's wrist. "Waddyareckon?

Again, Eliot could only shake her head and Julia looked even more gratified. "I have to tell you, Eliot, it was better than any battle I ever had on a tennis court, even Wimbledon. We — that is, Mom and me — convinced Jack that to fight us would be the worst move of his life; that we would oppose him with even less consideration than he'd shown you. That we would stop at nothing — and we were willing to pay what it took — to beat him. And the sting was that Mom guessed right and bluffed him into revealing deals he's done that would ruin him if they ever became public." Julia held Eliot's hands. "So, one way or another, we got that man by the bits that make his eyes water and he ain't going nowhere."

In that moment Eliot didn't know whether she would laugh or cry. Eventually she decided on the former and gradually, they both dissolved into giggles which only stopped when a stray breeze lifted one precious page of Eliot's release document. Julia slapped her hand down upon it. "Okay," she said, coughing with the exertion of unaccustomed laughter. "Let's get real. You better sign these and get them the hell out of here."

CHAPTER TWENTY

It was a perfect Tuesday morning when Julia awoke. Sunlight, filtering through the shutters which protected the long windows of Eliot's bedroom, glowed cedar red-gold. From beyond the shutters Julia could hear sounds that had already become familiar: the lazy sigh and muffled boom of surf; the shrill grumbling and heated debate from high in the gum trees of whichever tribe of parrots had decided to stop by; and closer to hand, the fluting voice of Morgan Bancroft Barron as she also grumbled and debated — with her imaginary companions — in the room across the hallway beyond the half open door.

"Morgan!" Julia called, her voice smudged with sleep. "Who you got in there this morning?"

There was silence; a moment later Morgan's sprite face peered around the door, her eyes hopeful and her left foot curling in prehensile anticipation around her right calf. "Mrs. Magooley and Old Barnaby Darling," she said.

"Uh huh. And what are they up to now?" Julia extended her hand toward the child who needed no further invitation but took three skipping steps and a flying leap into her arms.

"Well," said Morgan, in her serious lecturing voice, as she snuggled into Julia's shoulder, "the trouble is that Old Barnaby has had a terrible argument with Mr. Jaswant Singh and they're not talking to each other at the moment. And that makes it very difficult for Mrs. Magooley because she has to do their cleaning and she's run out of bath stuff and Old Barnaby won't buy more."

Julia held up one finger. "Okay, who's Mr. Singh? Do I know him?"

"Oh no. He's been away in India for some time and he won't be back until next week."

"Ah. Now I understand. Gee, that could be a problem."

Still sleepy and more than content, Julia listened and made appropriate sounds as Morgan filled her in on the machinations between the tenants in Mrs. Magooley's boardinghouse. Just as she caught herself wondering about the possible location of the establishment, from the doorway came a muffled sound. Julia opened her eyes in time to catch Eliot's quickly suppressed laugh, but her eyes were twinkling with merriment as she said, in sober tones, "Breakfast's ready."

"Yee ha. Let's go, Morgan." Julia swung her up high with both arms extended and dropped her gently on the rug beside the bed. "Get outta here, girl. Let me get myself together." And Morgan was gone in a flurry of pink soled feet and flying curls. Julia stretched with catlike enjoyment as she watched the way Eliot walked across to the windows to push open the shutters. "Didn't hear you get up," she said. "You been working?"

"I have. And I've been thinking, too." Eliot's tone was bright, too bright. Julia's heart contracted.

"And —?"

"I think we should talk."

"That sounds ominous."

Eliot shrugged and didn't look at her. Julia sat up and, suddenly self-conscious and a little nervous, reached for a sarong to cover her nakedness. "Will it wait until after breakfast, or do we have an emergency?"

Eliot turned to face her and her smile was as warm as her eyes were distant. "It can wait."

"Oh great," said Julia sardonically. "A stay of execution." And she could not help but notice, as Eliot left the room, that her lover had not contradicted her.

It was not until close to midday, with Morgan dispatched to Kurrunulla and a swim and inexpert session with the boogy boards in the mercifully small surf that Eliot seemed inclined to talk. And then it seemed, at first, to Julia that the desultory questions and answers that passed between them as they lay on towels on the deserted beach were not really the point. But, in lieu of any real understanding of the source of Eliot's uncharacteristic cloudy mood, she decided to go along with it at least until the sky cleared. By the time Eliot asked her whether she would like some lunch, Julia was close to mystified and, more than that, beginning to feel the riffling breeze of agitation.

But before she could start to remonstrate or even work her way around to a strategic enquiry, a "Haloo!" from the direction of the house, and the realization that the hailer was Daphne Bancroft Holmes, stopped her dead and caused Eliot to utter a rare and eye-popping expletive.

Eliot watched her elder sister's tentative progress across the sand with mounting dismay. In the week or so since she placed her signature in black ink on the documents that severed her ties with Jack and — in a material way, she now reflected — with her sister, neither had crossed her mind in any substantial way. It had partly been an effort of will but partly too, the happy result of being free of them. And now, her chief tormentor for all her life was approaching — a vision afloat in a frock of pink-cabbage-rose-strewn seersucker. Momentarily Eliot considered running away but upon noticing Julia's appalled expression, she decided against this temporarily pleasing course of action.

"Daphne," she said, as her sister's bows cleaved the air between them. "What brings you here?" She was pleased to note that nearly four decades of conditioning had finally failed. If Daphne hoped to elicit a polite response from her younger sister, it was not happening.

Daphne, it quickly became apparent, was quite literally steaming. Her upper lip gleamed with tiny beads of sweat and her breathing was grampus-like. Eliot watched her cabbage-rose-swathed bosom heaving rhythmically and quickly looked away, fearing the onset of seasickness. "I want to talk to you." Daphne's tone was not sisterly.

Eliot did not leap to her feet but instead squinted up at her sister from a position of self-evident relaxation. "I'm awfully busy, Daphne, can't it wait?"

Daphne's snort of outrage and Julia's snort of amusement were inadvertent *a capella* comments on Eliot's question. It was several moments before Daphne recovered the power of speech. When she did, it came in a rush. "You . . . you bitch." She shrieked, then glanced up and down the deserted strand before rushing headlong into an incoherent tirade whose main points she emphasized with wags of her plump, bejeweled forefinger. "Ruined me . . . selfish brat . . . disgraced us all . . . selfish brat . . . millions thrown away . . . granny's pet . . . selfish brat . . . hopeless pervert . . . criminal element . . . selfish brat . . ."

Eventually she paused for breath and Eliot took the opportunity to swiftly interject with four quiet words. "Daphne, please go away."

To her astonishment, Daphne burst into tears and twirled away in a cloud of seersucker, and the sweet musky smell of over-heated, over-plump flesh stomped away up the beach and disappeared.

"My god," Eliot said into the sudden hush, a long few minutes later. "I suppose I have ruined Daphne's life in a way."

"I wouldn't get indigestion over it."

"She *is* my sister."

Julia flopped back, full length, picked up her book and snorted. "Are you sure? I can't see the resemblance at all."

Despite the shocking reverberations of the encounter, Eliot had no choice but to giggle. She laid her hand on Julia's thigh in a gesture that was both appreciative and restraining. "She can't help it," she said, but she hoped the pressure of her fingers conveyed her gratitude for Julia's insouciant reaction to Daphne's extraordinary visit.

Julia was still unwillingly replaying the tape of Daphne's visit in her mind later that afternoon as she lay, in her favorite position, on the old sofa in Eliot's studio. She put her book down. She had read the same paragraph at least eight times and, despite the connection between them that had been forged by Daphne's hostility, she knew she had to confront Eliot's earlier blue mood.

"You read this?" she asked, holding up her paperback edition of *The Bridges of Madison County*.

Eliot turned away from her drawing, peered myopically at the title and shook her head. "No. But I saw the movie."

"Oh yeah? What did you think of it?"

"I liked it. Thought it was really interesting, actually. A lot better than I expected."

"I met Meryl Streep. We were on the same charity thing in New York."

"Really? What's she like?"

"Terrific. Sort of funny and interesting and real intelligent. Not like a Hollywood star — not like you'd think."

"That's refreshing."

Silence floated between them once again and it was not the easy connecting silence Julia had become accustomed to. She determined that this time she would let Eliot break it. To her great relief, she didn't have long to wait.

"Julia." Eliot's voice was suddenly strained. She carefully laid down her charcoal and wiped her hands on her shorts. "I need to talk to you."

"What are we doing?" Julia was deliberately flippant as fear rose in her throat and threatened to choke her.

"I don't mean — you know what I mean."

"No I don't, actually." Julia found a small well of irritation begin to bubble in her gut, it was fed she knew, by the fright she was feeling, but it served nevertheless to galvanize her into something more than the pit of helpless passivity into which she had somehow fallen.

"Darling, don't be awkward." Eliot sounded weary.

The tone only added to Julia's aggravation. "Don't treat me like a kid, Eliot," she said, her tone ominously even. "If there's something wrong here, let's talk about it."

"Okay." Eliot's eyes leveled with Julia's. "Okay. Julia, what do you think is happening here — between us?"

Julia frowned. "I'm loving you. We're having a relationship. I *think* you're loving me — but I don't know, you tell me."

"Julia, I'm a married woman."

Julia's eyebrows rose stratospherically. "And . . . ?"

"This can't go on."

Julia paused, her heart clamped in ice. Then she dug deep as she had so many times before when confronted by an adverse score line, and came out fighting and ready. "Because you're married? Because you're a woman?"

Eliot was caught in indecision. "I'm not sure, I . . ." She caught sight of Julia's book and grabbed it up. "Because this is a romance — like this book. Like that other one you were reading the other day — the horse one . . ."

"*The Horse Whisperer*," Julia offered. Her heart was beating slowly and efficiently, there was no room for error in her reactions.

"That's right, *The Horse Whisperer*." Again Eliot brandished the paperback aloft. "Things always work out in romances — like these," she said, her voice simultaneously sad and fierce. "But it doesn't happen in real life."

Julia's snort of amusement was well short of a laugh, but she knew her game plan was sound, not least — she intuited — because it wasn't a game. "Well, I'd have to dispute that," she said carefully. "Nothing works out in either of them. Well, not for the challenger, anyway."

Eliot frowned. "What do you mean?"

"Okay, I'm not literary. I don't know zip about theory and stuff, you know that. I still look at things like they're a match — know what I mean?" Eliot nodded and sat down on the end of the sofa, drawn in by Julia's approach to analysis. "So, in *Madison County* and *The Horse Whisperer* you've got these two incredibly romantic situations." She snapped her fingers as inspiration struck. "They remind me of this old movie I saw on cable, *Brief Encounter.* You *must* remember it?"

Eliot smiled. "I'm not that old," she said. "But, yes, I've seen it — on TV."

Julia nodded impatiently, her thoughts on a roll. "Okay, so these movies are exactly the same, really. You got a situation where they love each other but they know it's hopeless because if they want to be together they'll fuck up everything for everybody else. I think it's called the status quo?"

"That's right."

"Okay, so in all those three movies — and the books, I guess — these people love each other. They're crazy about each other, but in the end they do the right thing and leave each other; and in *The Horse Whisperer* the guy gets killed!" Julia's voice was tinged with disbelief. "I mean, what is this? Are we being brainwashed here, or what?"

Eliot frowned. "It's an interesting way of looking at it."

"Interesting? Come on!" Julia sat forward and took Eliot's hands in both her own. "Eliot, I love you. I don't know whether I'm supposed to be Meryl Streep or Clint Eastwood. But whichever, I don't think I want to play that game. I don't like those rules. They're not *good* rules — unless you're the goddamn boring husband who gets to keep his woman when she really, truly and desperately loves somebody else."

"Perhaps there's more to life than personal gratification," Eliot said, her tone suggesting she was reading from the handbook of devil's advocacy.

Julia pounced on the loose ball. "Sure, I know

that argument from the nuns. So how come the goddamn boring husband gets to be gratified, then? Why can't Meryl be gratified?"

Eliot laughed and stroked a lock of hair off her cheek. "You tell me — you've got the answers."

Julia shied away from her touch. "Don't play with me, Eliot," she said fiercely. "This is my life — our life — you're messing with. I'm serious. I told you I've been reading. I did a lot when I was in New York. I was alone. I had a lot of time to think. A real lot of time to try to work things out. And I figure if we want to, we can have a life together. *I* want a life with you. But you're not sure you want a life with me. You think you better do the right thing, maybe. Isn't that right?"

Eliot sighed and considered Julia's uncompromising assertion. Finally she nodded. "You may have a point," she conceded. "It's not that I want to do the right thing, it's more than that." She stopped and once again Julia took her hands.

"Eliot, it's not about the right thing. We — women like me and you — we're not supposed to have a happy ending. And I'm not just talking about lesbians. I mean women who don't go home to their damn boring husbands at the end of the movie. How about that video we watched the other night — the opera, the one in the cafe in Paris in the fifties..."

"*La Boheme,*" Eliot offered. She slipped down off the arm of the sofa and entwined her leg — carefully — with Julia's.

"That's the one," Julia affirmed triumphantly. "In *La Boheme* there's this kinda preppy guy who's pretending to be an artist and he's crazy about this girl, Mimi, but she's seriously not Mrs. J.F.K. Junior.

272

So what happens? Do they get to give it a go together and see if they can stick it up the status quo? Do they, hell. Mimi gets this really shitty consumption and that's it: curtains. Goodnight Columbus, so *she* doesn't fuck up society and *he* gets to sing the best song on account of he's feeling heartbroken. And it's the same in another one I saw on cable in New York. *Butterfly* — you know it?" Eliot nodded. "Of course you would. So you know that the whore doesn't get to marry her precious lieutenant, she kills herself — so everybody's happy."

Eliot was laughing but she also reached out for Julia's face and drew her close to kiss her, tenderly, on each eyelid and then deeply and for long on her mouth. "You're wonderful," she said gently. "Maybe if I'm allowed to stay around you a bit I'll learn something."

Julia drew back, suspicious. "Are you pulling my leg?"

Eliot laid her hand on Julia's scarred knee. "Never. Not this one anyway."

"But you're teasing me."

Eliot shook her head. "Not really. I'm laughing because you make such wonderfully good sense and because you're brave and crazy. And," she paused and took a deep breath, "because you actually make me feel a bit brave and crazy."

Julia looked at her speculatively. "What does that mean?"

"It means I love you and I don't think we should uphold the status quo." Eliot kissed Julia between flutters of laughter. "So do you *really* want this secondhand, nearly forty woman with all her baggage?"

Julia sighed. "If there's anybody who's secondhand around here it's me. You *really* want an ex-jock who's only just learning to read?"

Eliot kissed Julia's injured knee. "When I met you I was afraid of the rest of my life. When you met me you told me you had no future. Now" — she took Julia's hand and held it to her breast — "now I'd like you to help me stay fearless and I'd like to help you find a future."

Julia nodded and sealed her agreement with a kiss. "Maybe that's why guys get so pissed off with lesbians these day," she said. "We don't get consumption and die, we don't do the right thing, we really mess things up! I tell you something, girl. Whatever you do, don't *ever* call me Mimi."

A few of the publications of
THE NAIAD PRESS, INC.
P.O. Box 10543 • Tallahassee, Florida 32302
Phone (904) 539-5965
Toll-Free Order Number: 1-800-533-1973
Mail orders welcome. Please include 15% postage.
Write or call for our free catalog which also features an
incredible selection of lesbian videos.

DREAM LOVER by Lyn Denison. 224 pp. A soft, sensuous, romantic fantasy.　　　　ISBN 1-56280-173-1　$11.95

FORTY LOVE by Diana Simmonds. 240 pp. Joyous, heart-warming romance.　　　　ISBN 1-56280-171-6　11.95

IN THE MOOD by Robbi Sommers. 144 pp. The queen of erotic tension!　　　　ISBN 1-56280-172-4　11.95

SWIMMING CAT COVE by Lauren Douglas. 192 pp. 2nd Allison O'Neil Mystery.　　　　ISBN 1-56280-168-6　11.95

THE LOVING LESBIAN by Claire McNab and Sharon Gedan. 240 pp. Explore the experiences that make lesbian love unique.　　　　ISBN 1-56280-169-4　14.95

COURTED by Celia Cohen. 160 pp. Sparkling romantic encounter.　　　　ISBN 1-56280-166-X　11.95

SEASONS OF THE HEART by Jackie Calhoun. 240 pp. Romance through the years.　　　　ISBN 1-56280-167-8　11.95

K. C. BOMBER by Janet McClellan. 208 pp. 1st Tru North mystery.　　　　ISBN 1-56280-157-0　11.95

LAST RITES by Tracey Richardson. 192 pp. 1st Stevie Houston mystery.　　　　ISBN 1-56280-164-3　11.95

EMBRACE IN MOTION by Karin Kallmaker. 256 pp. A whirlwind love affair.　　　　ISBN 1-56280-165-1　11.95

HOT CHECK by Peggy J. Herring. 192 pp. Will workaholic Alice fall for guitarist Ricky?　　　　ISBN 1-56280-163-5　11.95

OLD TIES by Saxon Bennett. 176 pp. Can Cleo surrender to a passionate new love?　　　　ISBN 1-56280-159-7　11.95

LOVE ON THE LINE by Laura DeHart Young. 176 pp. Will Stef win Kay's heart?　　　　ISBN 1-56280-162-7　$11.95

DEVIL'S LEG CROSSING by Kaye Davis. 192 pp. 1st Maris Middleton mystery.　　　　ISBN 1-56280-158-9　11.95

COSTA BRAVA by Marta Balletbo Coll. 144 pp. Read the book,
see the movie!   ISBN 1-56280-153-8   11.95

MEETING MAGDALENE & OTHER STORIES by
Marilyn Freeman. 144 pp. Read the book, see the movie!
                                            ISBN 1-56280-170-8   11.95

SECOND FIDDLE by Kate Calloway. 208 pp. P.I. Cassidy James'
second case.   ISBN 1-56280-169-6   11.95

LAUREL by Isabel Miller. 128 pp. By the author of the beloved
Patience and Sarah.   ISBN 1-56280-146-5   10.95

LOVE OR MONEY by Jackie Calhoun. 240 pp. The romance of
real life.   ISBN 1-56280-147-3   10.95

SMOKE AND MIRRORS by Pat Welch. 224 pp. 5th Helen Black
Mystery.   ISBN 1-56280-143-0   10.95

DANCING IN THE DARK edited by Barbara Grier & Christine
Cassidy. 272 pp. Erotic love stories by Naiad Press authors.
                                            ISBN 1-56280-144-9   14.95

TIME AND TIME AGAIN by Catherine Ennis. 176 pp. Passionate
love affair.   ISBN 1-56280-145-7   10.95

PAXTON COURT by Diane Salvatore. 256 pp. Erotic and wickedly
funny contemporary tale about the business of learning to live
together.   ISBN 1-56280-114-7   10.95

INNER CIRCLE by Claire McNab. 208 pp. 8th Carol Ashton
Mystery.   ISBN 1-56280-135-X   11.95

LESBIAN SEX: AN ORAL HISTORY by Susan Johnson.
240 pp. Need we say more?   ISBN 1-56280-142-2   14.95

BABY, IT'S COLD by Jaye Maiman. 256 pp. 5th Robin Miller
Mystery.   ISBN 1-56280-141-4   19.95

WILD THINGS by Karin Kallmaker. 240 pp. By the undisputed
mistress of lesbian romance.   ISBN 1-56280-139-2   11.95

THE GIRL NEXT DOOR by Mindy Kaplan. 208 pp. Just what
you'd expect.   ISBN 1-56280-140-6   11.95

NOW AND THEN by Penny Hayes. 240 pp. Romance on the
westward journey.   ISBN 1-56280-121-X   11.95

HEART ON FIRE by Diana Simmonds. 176 pp. The romantic and
erotic rival of *Curious Wine*.   ISBN 1-56280-152-X   11.95

DEATH AT LAVENDER BAY by Lauren Wright Douglas. 208 pp.
1st Allison O'Neil Mystery.   ISBN 1-56280-085-X   11.95

YES I SAID YES I WILL by Judith McDaniel. 272 pp. Hot
romance by famous author.   ISBN 1-56280-138-4   11.95

FORBIDDEN FIRES by Margaret C. Anderson. Edited by Mathilda
Hills. 176 pp. Famous author's "unpublished" Lesbian romance.
                                            ISBN 1-56280-123-6   21.95

SIDE TRACKS by Teresa Stores. 160 pp. Gender-bending
Lesbians on the road.   ISBN 1-56280-122-8   10.95

HOODED MURDER by Annette Van Dyke. 176 pp. 1st Jessie
Batelle Mystery.   ISBN 1-56280-134-1   10.95

WILDWOOD FLOWERS by Julia Watts. 208 pp. Hilarious and
heart-warming tale of true love.   ISBN 1-56280-127-9   10.95

NEVER SAY NEVER by Linda Hill. 224 pp. Rule #1: Never get involved
with . . .   ISBN 1-56280-126-0   10.95

THE SEARCH by Melanie McAllester. 240 pp. Exciting top cop
Tenny Mendoza case.   ISBN 1-56280-150-3   10.95

THE WISH LIST by Saxon Bennett. 192 pp. Romance through
the years.   ISBN 1-56280-125-2   10.95

FIRST IMPRESSIONS by Kate Calloway. 208 pp. P.I. Cassidy
James' first case.   ISBN 1-56280-133-3   10.95

OUT OF THE NIGHT by Kris Bruyer. 192 pp. Spine-tingling
thriller.   ISBN 1-56280-120-1   10.95

NORTHERN BLUE by Tracey Richardson. 224 pp. Police recruits
Miki & Miranda — passion in the line of fire. ISBN 1-56280-118-X   10.95

LOVE'S HARVEST by Peggy J. Herring. 176 pp. by the author of
Once More With Feeling.   ISBN 1-56280-117-1   10.95

THE COLOR OF WINTER by Lisa Shapiro. 208 pp. Romantic
love beyond your wildest dreams.   ISBN 1-56280-116-3   10.95

FAMILY SECRETS by Laura DeHart Young. 208 pp. Enthralling
romance and suspense.   ISBN 1-56280-119-8   10.95

INLAND PASSAGE by Jane Rule. 288 pp. Tales exploring conven-
tional & unconventional relationships.   ISBN 0-930044-56-8   10.95

DOUBLE BLUFF by Claire McNab. 208 pp. 7th Carol Ashton
Mystery.   ISBN 1-56280-096-5   10.95

BAR GIRLS by Lauran Hoffman. 176 pp. See the movie, read
the book!   ISBN 1-56280-115-5   10.95

THE FIRST TIME EVER edited by Barbara Grier & Christine
Cassidy. 272 pp. Love stories by Naiad Press authors.
                                               ISBN 1-56280-086-8   14.95

MISS PETTIBONE AND MISS McGRAW by Brenda Weathers.
208 pp. A charming ghostly love story.   ISBN 1-56280-151-1   10.95

CHANGES by Jackie Calhoun. 208 pp. Involved romance and
relationships.   ISBN 1-56280-083-3   10.95

FAIR PLAY by Rose Beecham. 256 pp. 3rd Amanda Valentine
Mystery.   ISBN 1-56280-081-7   10.95

PAYBACK by Celia Cohen. 176 pp. A gripping thriller of romance,
revenge and betrayal.   ISBN 1-56280-084-1   10.95

THE BEACH AFFAIR by Barbara Johnson. 224 pp. Sizzling
summer romance/mystery/intrigue.   ISBN 1-56280-090-6   10.95

GETTING THERE by Robbi Sommers. 192 pp. Nobody does it
like Robbi!   ISBN 1-56280-099-X   10.95

FINAL CUT by Lisa Haddock. 208 pp. 2nd Carmen Ramirez
Mystery.   ISBN 1-56280-088-4   10.95

FLASHPOINT by Katherine V. Forrest. 256 pp. A Lesbian
blockbuster!   ISBN 1-56280-079-5   11.95

CLAIRE OF THE MOON by Nicole Conn. Audio Book —Read
by Marianne Hyatt.   ISBN 1-56280-113-9   16.95

FOR LOVE AND FOR LIFE: INTIMATE PORTRAITS OF
LESBIAN COUPLES by Susan Johnson. 224 pp.
                                          ISBN 1-56280-091-4   14.95

DEVOTION by Mindy Kaplan. 192 pp. See the movie — read
the book!   ISBN 1-56280-093-0   10.95

SOMEONE TO WATCH by Jaye Maiman. 272 pp. 4th Robin
Miller Mystery.   ISBN 1-56280-095-7   10.95

GREENER THAN GRASS by Jennifer Fulton. 208 pp. A young
woman — a stranger in her bed.   ISBN 1-56280-092-2   10.95

TRAVELS WITH DIANA HUNTER by Regine Sands. Erotic
lesbian romp. Audio Book (2 cassettes)   ISBN 1-56280-107-4   16.95

CABIN FEVER by Carol Schmidt. 256 pp. Sizzling suspense
and passion.   ISBN 1-56280-089-1   10.95

THERE WILL BE NO GOODBYES by Laura DeHart Young. 192
pp. Romantic love, strength, and friendship.   ISBN 1-56280-103-1   10.95

FAULTLINE by Sheila Ortiz Taylor. 144 pp. Joyous comic
lesbian novel.   ISBN 1-56280-108-2   9.95

OPEN HOUSE by Pat Welch. 176 pp. 4th Helen Black Mystery.
                                          ISBN 1-56280-102-3   10.95

ONCE MORE WITH FEELING by Peggy J. Herring. 240 pp.
Lighthearted, loving romantic adventure.   ISBN 1-56280-089-2   11.95

FOREVER by Evelyn Kennedy. 224 pp. Passionate romance — love
overcoming all obstacles.   ISBN 1-56280-094-9   10.95

WHISPERS by Kris Bruyer. 176 pp. Romantic ghost story
                                          ISBN 1-56280-082-5   10.95

NIGHT SONGS by Penny Mickelbury. 224 pp. 2nd Gianna Maglione
Mystery.   ISBN 1-56280-097-3   10.95

GETTING TO THE POINT by Teresa Stores. 256 pp. Classic
southern Lesbian novel.   ISBN 1-56280-100-7   10.95

PAINTED MOON by Karin Kallmaker. 224 pp. Delicious
Kallmaker romance.   ISBN 1-56280-075-2   11.95

THE MYSTERIOUS NAIAD edited by Katherine V. Forrest & Barbara Grier. 320 pp. Love stories by Naiad Press authors.
ISBN 1-56280-074-4   14.95

DAUGHTERS OF A CORAL DAWN by Katherine V. Forrest. 240 pp. Tenth Anniversay Edition.   ISBN 1-56280-104-X   11.95

BODY GUARD by Claire McNab. 208 pp. 6th Carol Ashton Mystery.   ISBN 1-56280-073-6   11.95

CACTUS LOVE by Lee Lynch. 192 pp. Stories by the beloved storyteller.   ISBN 1-56280-071-X   9.95

SECOND GUESS by Rose Beecham. 216 pp. 2nd Amanda Valentine Mystery.   ISBN 1-56280-069-8   9.95

A RAGE OF MAIDENS by Lauren Wright Douglas. 240 pp. 6th Caitlin Reece Mystery.   ISBN 1-56280-068-X   10.95

TRIPLE EXPOSURE by Jackie Calhoun. 224 pp. Romantic drama involving many characters.   ISBN 1-56280-067-1   10.95

UP, UP AND AWAY by Catherine Ennis. 192 pp. Delightful romance.   ISBN 1-56280-065-5   11.95

PERSONAL ADS by Robbi Sommers. 176 pp. Sizzling short stories.   ISBN 1-56280-059-0   11.95

CROSSWORDS by Penny Sumner. 256 pp. 2nd Victoria Cross Mystery.   ISBN 1-56280-064-7   9.95

SWEET CHERRY WINE by Carol Schmidt. 224 pp. A novel of suspense.   ISBN 1-56280-063-9   9.95

CERTAIN SMILES by Dorothy Tell. 160 pp. Erotic short stories.   ISBN 1-56280-066-3   9.95

EDITED OUT by Lisa Haddock. 224 pp. 1st Carmen Ramirez Mystery.   ISBN 1-56280-077-9   9.95

WEDNESDAY NIGHTS by Camarin Grae. 288 pp. Sexy adventure.   ISBN 1-56280-060-4   10.95

SMOKEY O by Celia Cohen. 176 pp. Relationships on the playing field.   ISBN 1-56280-057-4   9.95

KATHLEEN O'DONALD by Penny Hayes. 256 pp. Rose and Kathleen find each other and employment in 1909 NYC.
ISBN 1-56280-070-1   9.95

STAYING HOME by Elisabeth Nonas. 256 pp. Molly and Alix want a baby . . . or do they?   ISBN 1-56280-076-0   10.95

TRUE LOVE by Jennifer Fulton. 240 pp. Six lesbians searching for love in all the "right" places.   ISBN 1-56280-035-3   10.95

KEEPING SECRETS by Penny Mickelbury. 208 pp. 1st Gianna Maglione Mystery.   ISBN 1-56280-052-3   9.95

THE ROMANTIC NAIAD edited by Katherine V. Forrest &
Barbara Grier. 336 pp. Love stories by Naiad Press authors.
ISBN 1-56280-054-X 14.95

UNDER MY SKIN by Jaye Maiman. 336 pp. 3rd Robin Miller
Mystery. ISBN 1-56280-049-3. 10.95

CAR POOL by Karin Kallmaker. 272pp. Lesbians on wheels
and then some! ISBN 1-56280-048-5 10.95

NOT TELLING MOTHER: STORIES FROM A LIFE by Diane
Salvatore. 176 pp. Her 3rd novel. ISBN 1-56280-044-2 9.95

GOBLIN MARKET by Lauren Wright Douglas. 240pp. 5th Caitlin
Reece Mystery. ISBN 1-56280-047-7 10.95

LONG GOODBYES by Nikki Baker. 256 pp. 3rd Virginia Kelly
Mystery. ISBN 1-56280-042-6 9.95

FRIENDS AND LOVERS by Jackie Calhoun. 224 pp. Mid-
western Lesbian lives and loves. ISBN 1-56280-041-8 11.95

BEHIND CLOSED DOORS by Robbi Sommers. 192 pp. Hot,
erotic short stories. ISBN 1-56280-039-6 11.95

CLAIRE OF THE MOON by Nicole Conn. 192 pp. See the
movie — read the book! ISBN 1-56280-038-8 10.95

SILENT HEART by Claire McNab. 192 pp. Exotic Lesbian
romance. ISBN 1-56280-036-1 11.95

THE SPY IN QUESTION by Amanda Kyle Williams. 256 pp.
4th Madison McGuire Mystery. ISBN 1-56280-037-X 9.95

SAVING GRACE by Jennifer Fulton. 240 pp. Adventure and
romantic entanglement. ISBN 1-56280-051-5 10.95

CURIOUS WINE by Katherine V. Forrest. 176 pp. Tenth Anniver-
sary Edition. The most popular contemporary Lesbian love story.
ISBN 1-56280-053-1 11.95
Audio Book (2 cassettes) ISBN 1-56280-105-8 16.95

CHAUTAUQUA by Catherine Ennis. 192 pp. Exciting, romantic
adventure. ISBN 1-56280-032-9 9.95

A PROPER BURIAL by Pat Welch. 192 pp. 3rd Helen Black
Mystery. ISBN 1-56280-033-7 9.95

SILVERLAKE HEAT: A Novel of Suspense by Carol Schmidt.
240 pp. Rhonda is as hot as Laney's dreams. ISBN 1-56280-031-0 9.95

These are just a few of the many Naiad Press titles — we are the oldest and largest lesbian/feminist publishing company in the world. We also offer an enormous selection of lesbian video products. Please request a complete catalog. We offer personal service; we encourage and welcome direct mail orders from individuals who have limited access to bookstores carrying our publications.